I0683300

The Boat
Zombie Survivors

Chris Dougherty

Copyright © 2012 by Chris Dougherty
Copyright © 2014 by Severed Press
www.severedpress.com
All rights reserved. No part of this book may be
reproduced or transmitted in any form or by any
electronic or mechanical means, including
photocopying, recording or by any information and
retrieval system, without the written permission of
the publisher and author, except where permitted by
law.
This novel is a work of fiction. Names,
characters, places and incidents are the product of
the author's imagination, or are used fictitiously.
Any resemblance to actual events, locales or persons,
living or dead, is purely coincidental.
ISBN: 978-1-925225-39-6
All rights reserved

Chapter One

August 6, 2011

Randy leaned back and closed his eyes, letting the tip of the fishing pole dip almost to the water. The yellow bobbin bobbed obediently, riding the gentle waves. The sun was warm, and the steady lapping of water against the little rowboat was relaxing. He didn't get much time to relax anymore and wanted to make the most of this small window.

It was very quiet. A steady breeze made the trees on the banks seem to whisper a sweet song of rest. The sunlight off the water dappled strange but soothing shapes across his eyelids. He felt himself sinking into a comfortable abyss. The pole slipped from his loosening hands.

"Randy, *Jesus*, will you *please* pay attention to what you're doing? You've *got* something on the *line!*"

Bonnie. He'd almost forgotten all about her. He glanced back at his wife of forty-some years, taking in the lines of varicose veins, the pudgy way her thighs pushed at the edges of her Bermudas. Her stomach was pooching out under the life vest she wore. Life vest. Jesus jumped up. In the *bay*?

"Bonnie, you don't need a damn vest in the bay. What do you think is going to happen? Whale gonna sink us?"

1

You're the only whale around here, he thought, and then felt bad about it. He was for sure no skinny Minnie himself, and the reality was that they'd both lost quite a bit of weight in the last two months. Not much choice in it.

He felt a tug on the line and started cranking the reel. He cranked slowly, more preoccupied with Bonnie than he was with the line, because chances were better he'd snagged a bunch of debris rather than anything edible.

He turned, straining, to see her better. She was sitting bolt upright in the seat behind his, her hands clutching the sides of the little boat. Her teeth were clenched and thinly veiled panic danced in her tired eyes. The life vest pushed up against the underside of her jaw, doubling her chin, giving her a childlike, vulnerable look. Randy felt the familiar give and take of his feelings: irritation at her constant nagging overtaken by the desire to protect her from anyone or anything. Even if that meant protection from his own unkind thoughts.

"Honey," he said, still absently cranking the reel, "just relax. Isn't it nice out here? Isn't it pretty in the bay?"

Her gaze slid left and right and then back to him. She shook her head, and tears slid into the deep pouches under her eyes. Her chin trembled. She had never gone fishing with him before all this happened. She preferred lunch with the ladies and then a refreshing trip to the mall for more scarves…he would swear she had more than a hundred. So, he'd always fished by himself. Back then, though, it had been mostly freshwater fishing, and he'd done it from the safety of a collapsible chair on the bank.

Everything had changed now, though.

Boy, had it ever.

Randy shook his head, thinking. The line was getting heavier by the second. He hoped it wasn't a tree, all waterlogged with tangled branches.

"What's wrong?" she asked him, her voice edged with panic. "Why are you shaking your head?"

"Bonnie, please. Nothing is wrong. Would you just try and relax? Haven't I told you a million times that attitude is everything? If you would just try—"

He'd turned to face her again as he reeled, straining against the weight on the line–something heavy coming up. Her eyes went past him, and her mouth dropped open in horror. Randy squinted at her and started to ask what was wrong, but before he could say anything, she whooped out a scream loud enough to send birds flying in a panic from the trees along the shoreline.

He turned forward to where her gaze was directed. The line had cleared the water. He'd hooked a man right through the eye socket.

The man's skin was almost entirely eaten away–by fish, by time, or by a combination of the two…it was hard to tell. The one eye he had left was a bleached-out blue, and the retina was floating sleepily off to the side. It looked like he was trying to see back into the water he'd just been hooked from. His tongue was a spongy mass filling the cavity of his mouth, surrounded by white, split lips.

The man on the line groaned. He pulled a waterlogged arm from the water and flailed at the side of the boat. Randy thought it sounded like someone hitting the boat with a baked ham. He felt a little ill and then became aware of Bonnie's scream going on and on behind him. Then he saw why. A small water snake had curled itself into the hole where the man's other eye should have been.

Bonnie hated snakes.

"It's *okay*, honey. It's all *right*. That snake doesn't want you," he said, and turned to try to catch her eye. "He's content where he's at."

The man on the line moaned, and the sound had a choking, burbling quality. A thick rope of mucous and water was draining steadily from a hole in his cheek. His arm flailed again, but this time, his hand banged over the side of the boat. Three of his fingers disengaged from the pulpy hand and splatted onto the floor where they rolled to and fro.

"Gross," Randy said, looking at the fingers at his feet. As he watched, one of the fingers began to scrabble in a half-circle, trying to gain traction, and then it lay still.

Bonnie screamed on and on.

"I don't care, I don't care, Randy, just for God's sake get that thing off the line so I don't have to see that snake anymore, ooooooh I hate snakes!"

She had squeezed her eyes closed, her mouth had squinched up, and she was shaking her head like a little girl who had tasted something awful.

"Okay, okay, hold on, Bonnie, just hang on, honey bunny." Randy dug a knife from his pocket and flipped open the blade. He took one more look at the sinker he'd hooked and regretted the lure he was about to lose, but there was no helping it. He couldn't put his hand that close to the thing's mouth. It would bite him for sure, and then he'd most likely get the sickness, too, and God knows Bonnie would never be able to get the little boat back to the big boat, so then what? Then Bonnie would end up as a sinker, too.

Nope, definitely not worth the lure.

He cut the line.

The sinker did what all the sinkers do: it sank.

Randy sat back and sighed. They still had a few good hours left in the day, but the fun had gone out of it. If only they hadn't come across that snake, but they had, so.

"It's okay, Bonnie, no snake. All gone, see?"

She cracked an eye open and looked. Then she opened her other eye. She smiled shakily at Randy. "Oh, thank you, honey bunny," she said. "Ooh, I really do hate snakes. I just…they scare me half to death. I'm so sorry, Randy."

She smiled, and under the weight of years, he saw the pretty young girl he'd married. He smiled back and then gave her soft knee a squeeze. "No problem, honey, I didn't feel like fishing anymore, anyway. Those idiots on *Flyboy* don't know what they're talking about half the time. I don't know what they were thinking sending us out here. It's a terrible spot to fish."

Because now, the fish had plenty to snack on…it was hard to get them to bite at lures anymore, especially in the bay.

Randy socketed the oars into the oarlocks and began the long pulls that would take them back to *Barbra's Bay Breeze*. Bonnie tickled his ears and neck each time the rowing motion put him back in her reach. She'd got to giggling. Randy laughed and swatted at her darting, tickling fingers. Then he settled more seriously into the job of rowing. Maybe he could think of a good way to round out the afternoon after all.

4

He became contemplative, watching the shoreline as they went past. "Hey, Bonnie, do you think that sinker looked like Al?"

"Al who, honey?" she asked. She was happier now they were headed back. The snake had scared the daylights out of her, but she also didn't like being in the bay in the small boat. The water was too shallow in places. Too full of...

"Al Anders, that sales guy from Mag Industrial? The big, bald guy? Back in...oh, I guess it would have been ninety-seven. Or eight. When we lived down near Baltimore, remember?"

"You mean *Pete* Anders. Pete was the bald man who worked with you at Mag." There was amusement in her voice. She was still holding onto the sides of the boat, but not as tight.

"Oh, that's right! I always did get him mixed up, didn't I, Bonnie?"

"Yes, you always did, honey bunny," she said and laughed.

That guy had been a pretty decent sort, if a bit pushy Randy thought, and smiled a bit sadly. He wondered if old Pete had made it through...not that many had. He scanned the shoreline dreamily, caught up in reminiscence.

The shoreline was thick with shuffling corpses that by all rights, should have laid still. Their combined voices waxed and waned with the breeze. Every few seconds, they surged forward and the ones in the front fell in and became sinkers.

People on the boats called them chum sometimes, too.

Yep, that one he'd brought up had looked like bald Pete. Could have been him, too, for all Randy knew.

Funny world.

Chapter Two

Maggie stood on the deck of *Barbra's Bay Breeze* and watched Randy and Bonnie as they rowed in. She stood by, ready to grab their rope and get the little rowboat tied up. She knew she was supposed to call this part of the boat the prow or the port or something equally nonsensical (to her), but she just didn't feel like it. She was too tired today. Watching Randy and Bonnie was also making her sad, making her miss Joe. How did those two wind up alive as a couple when so many others had not? She and Joe were young; they *deserved* to have survived together. They were only in their thirties, where Randy and Bonnie had to be in their sixties.

She ran a hand through her chestnut hair and consciously put the blocks to her agitation, knowing it was exhaustion and possibly hormones coloring everything in shades of brownish gray.

It was hardly their fault–any of it. It wasn't anyone's fault. Just good luck or bad luck, really. She had to remind herself of that.

Maggie mostly liked everyone aboard the 'ThreeBees', as everyone called it for shorthand. *Barbra's Bay Breeze*, along with being a general mouthful, was also a bit of a tongue-twister. Say it ten times fast, dare ya.

Maggie smiled, but it was faint and brief. Joe used to make up inane tongue twisters and try to get Maggie to say them. Brown bloody brook, or bracket biscuit basket, or laying larger lager. Silly things for silly times. It had even got on her nerves after a while.

What she wouldn't give to have those times back now, though. To have Joe back.

A small, warm hand slipped into hers, and she looked down to see Babygirl standing next to her. Baby clutched a stuffed rabbit in her free hand and gazed up at Maggie with anxious blue eyes. Maggie had noticed that Baby oftentimes seemed to pick up on other people's feelings. Was it because she was a naturally sensitive child, or just scared and watchful? Or was it all those things?

Maggie had found Baby during her trek to the shore. Baby had been thin as a shadow, and when asked her name, had only been able to whisper the generic but somehow fitting 'Babygirl.' She looked maybe six or seven, but she had mentally regressed during her trial on land. Maggie was as amazed as ever that this little one had survived...not many children had. Too vulnerable.

She smiled at Babygirl and squeezed her hand. Baby smiled back. Her hair was angelically white blonde, but thin, and her skin had an almost translucent look to it. She was a beautiful child, but it was a fleeting beauty. When Babygirl reached her late teens or early twenties, her thin hair would only look ragged and her fragile skin would show every bad gene that was just waiting to morph this pretty child into a prematurely aging, white trash stereotype.

Maybe there weren't any more stereotypes, Maggie thought. *Maybe we can at least put those to rest with all the legitimately dead back on land.* Then she shook her head. All the old, bad stuff was probably just as active as those shuffling corpses out there. Just waiting for their time to come around again. Maggie shivered.

"Miss Maggie!" Randy said, and tossed her the rope, making her jump.

Line, she corrected herself, *it's called a line, not a rope*, and she tied it to one of the cleats at the back of the boat (*prow? no...port? Oh, the hell with it*). She reached a hand down to Randy.

"Permission to come aboard?" he said and snapped a salute at her.

Maggie laughed, but she didn't meet his eyes. Couldn't. She was pretty close to tears, she realized, somehow brought on by Randy's good-natured foolishness. Randy continued to stand at rigid attention, grinning and oblivious.

Bonnie noticed Maggie's discomfort

"Randy, *please* just get on the boat so I can get out of this torture device." She shot Maggie a sympathetic glance, and Maggie's smile deepened past polite, warming her face.

Bonnie put her hands out for Maggie and Randy to pull her aboard. She squeaked a little as they heaved her up onto the teak deck. "We saw a snake," Bonnie said in tones you would normally reserve for statements like 'it's malignant' or 'the puppy died.' She shook her head as Maggie tutted and rubbed a comforting circle on her back. "It was huge. A monster! Almost as big as *you*, Babygirl!"

Baby's eyes went wide as she clutched her rabbit tighter under her chin and grimaced with fear–but she was only play-acting, drawn in by Bonnie's theatrical tone.

"Jesus, Bonnie," Randy said, and bent to re-tie the line, huffing a bit over his watermelon of a stomach. "That snake was no bigger than a handful and you know it. Don't scare Babygirl. She'll never come fishing with me if you do that." Randy winked at Baby, and she smiled shyly, tucking herself more firmly behind Maggie.

"There was a sinker on the line, too," Bonnie said, her tone casual. "I didn't think we were close enough to the shoreline to catch one of those nasty things." She shrugged and began to pick at the catches holding her life vest on. Her fingernails were still nicely shaped, if shorter than she'd ever worn them as an adult. *No acrylics on the ThreeBees*, she thought and sighed to herself. At least she had a little bottle of polish tucked away back in her room. Being stuck in this situation was no reason not to look as nice as possible, was it? Although she was starting to get tired of 'Autumn Shimmer' after two months of nothing but. Especially since it wasn't Autumn and wouldn't be for a couple of months.

Maggie had stiffened at Bonnie's words, and she turned to address Randy. "No trouble? With the sinker?"

Randy shook his head and smiled. "No. Not really. It left a few fingers in the rowboat, but other than that…no problems."

"Fingers? In the rowboat?" Baby grabbed Maggie's hand again, even tighter.

Randy leaned over and smiled into Baby's face. "Yes, but don't you worry, Babygirl. Fingers can't hurtcha'!" He wiggled his in her direction in a tickling motion.

She giggled but then looked to Maggie for confirmation.

"Well, we don't really know for sure, though. We should probably get them out of there," Maggie said. She was a lot more cautious than Randy and Bonnie. She'd seen more in the days right after the beginning of the end, been out in it longer as she'd made her way shoreward.

Randy and Bonnie were residents of a town right near here…Cape May? Was that where they said they'd come from? They'd had an easier time of it. When everything had fallen apart, they'd simply taken to the water like anyone else with a boat. People noticed very quickly that, whatever else the walking dead could do, they couldn't swim. It wasn't long before people started referring to them as sinkers or chum.

Maggie and Joe had lived in New Jersey, too, but quite a bit further inland, almost to Philadelphia in a town known for its small, friendly neighborhoods. She and Joe had a Cape Cod on a quarter-acre yard and had lived on their street for thirteen years.

~ ~ ~

The Tuesday that it really broke–June 7th–Joe never made it home from his job in the city. She still couldn't think about it without a heavy knot forming in her stomach.

He called from his cell. Maggie had already been home, standing in the kitchen, still in her scrubs, and she wasn't due back in to the hospital again for the next two days. She was exhausted from her last shift as an ER nurse. There had been so many people who came in with the flu…it had been like some kind of crazy, overnight epidemic…that her original shift had been extended by four hours.

She had the television on the counter turned to a local news station. Joe's voice was broken up because he was on the train. Part of his ride–before the bridge–was underground. He said not to worry and he'd see her soon and to lock up.

He said he loved her.

As Maggie listened to his voice, the television was showing Philadelphia. So many people in the streets. They seemed to be pouring from every building in a human flood. The camera must have been right outside the news station, and it was directed up Broad, a main thoroughfare. There was no word in Maggie's vocabulary for what she was seeing. Chaos, anarchy, pandemonium...none of these words were big enough–bad enough–to describe what was happening. People were being hit by cars, by city busses, by cabs. They were knocking into each other, falling, screaming, crying, and in some cases, fighting.

As she watched, one man–a young man, maybe a student–was hit by a car and knocked to the side of the road. As he struggled to stand, more people ran past, kicking him or running right over his hands, arms, and head as he struggled. Then a car ran over his mid-section, and he stopped struggling. He was tiny and blurry; a blurred mass of denim and blood and books. Maggie stared, horrified, her mouth hanging open as she listened to Joe's chopped-up voice. She nodded as if he could see her and stepped closer to the television. The young man lay still as death. Did she really just watch that kid die? On television? Her mind danced and feinted, trying for a less unsavory explanation...but there was none. "Joe," she said, her voice a shocked rasp. "Joe, I just saw...I just saw a guy, a boy, get..."

The blurry corpse twitched. Maggie stepped back sharply, her heart leaping painfully. Had that kid...? Had he *moved*? "Joe, you won't believe this, but..."

Joe's voice went on and on. He couldn't hear her, she realized. She could hear him, but he couldn't hear her. "Joe?" she said, her voice tiny, a little girl's voice.

The young man moved again, and she felt a shift of hope like warm water in her head, but then that warmth was washed away by icy shock...the young man was dragging himself up onto the sidewalk, but only half of himself. Only his front half. From mid-chest down, he'd been severed. She could just make out the twin lumps of his lungs dragging behind him...hanging on by threads.

The running people on the sidewalk dodged away from him as instinctively as sheep will turn from a dog or coyote. He grabbed at each flying pair of legs. "Joe, this kid, he's not dead, he's not dead, he's, oh God, what is he, what's happening...?"

On some level, she realized she wasn't making any sense, and she closed her mouth. She was scaring herself. Joe told her to keep the doors locked. Don't go outside. He loved her. "Maggie? Maggie- can- me? Ma- I love you- can- wrong with the train- but Maggie?"

A lady fell down, right in front of the young man. Had she been pushed? Maggie thought so, yes. The young man grabbed at the lady, grabbed her hair and pulled himself up onto her. Her arms flailed, and she must have been screaming, of course she was, but there was no sound from the television. The young man was...he was...Maggie slid to the floor, her back against the kitchen cabinets, until the television was above her, the picture distorted by the angle. She said, "Joe, please God, please come home, Joe, come home please." Her voice was high and thin. She couldn't tell if she was hearing herself from outside or inside. She didn't care.

That young man was eating that lady. Eating her face. Tearing great hunks from her throat. Then the camera must have been hit because the scene seemed to float through the air, revolving, toppling. Maggie experienced a strong sense of vertigo as the camera fell.

"Maggie? I- lov- hear me? Can–" Joe's voice cut off all at once, and Maggie vomited between her legs onto the kitchen floor.

~ ~ ~

Maggie sent Babygirl along with Randy and Bonnie and then stepped down into the little rowboat. ThreeBees had two rowboats tied to the back of it plus two jet skis tied up alongside. From her vantage point on the rowboat, Maggie looked back at the ThreeBees. It had once been something pretty special, someone's Shangri-la. *Barbra's Bay Breeze* was painted in gold across the boat's back end in a boasting, fancy script.

Now, after two months of serious habitation, it was looking much worse for wear. The boats and jet skis tied up around it gave the formerly sleek vessel a doddering, mother hen look. It (*she*, Maggie corrected herself, *she*) was a sixty-foot cabin cruiser, a weekender yacht for someone of moderate wealth. Three bedrooms and a bathroom (*head, Maggie, it's called a head,* she thought and another ghost of a smile crossed her lips…what Joe would have said about that!). The second level, the level she was looking at, consisted of the back deck, side decks, and front deck and inside, a big salon and a galley. The cockpit was one deck up…the staterooms one deck below.

There were nine people living on it now. Randy and Bonnie, herself, Babygirl (she and Babygirl shared a bedroom), plus Jade and Singer, a brother and sister from New York in their mid-twenties who'd been staying with family in Sea Isle. Mrs. Allen, who had to be at least eighty, and Denny and Brian, roommates from Stockton State who'd managed to find their way to the coast, just as Maggie had done. The three young men bedded down in the salon, and Jade and Mrs. Allen shared the remaining bedroom.

Clothing hung from a line draped across the entryway from the salon to the back deck, drying in the wind. *Classy*, Maggie thought to herself, *very, very classy. Bet the former owners never thought to dry their underthings on a line this way as they cruised from port to port.* Of course, they had to conserve resources. Most important thing out here: resources. Her eyes slid with unconscious resentment to *Flyboy*, floating serenely out on the waves about a half mile away.

Flyboy was a yacht, too, but the former owners of *Barbra's Bay Breeze* might have gazed upon *Flyboy* with envy so deep that it would almost have been a physical itch. *Flyboy* was a super yacht: somewhere just over two hundred feet, Maggie would guess. Eight guest rooms, six crew's quarters, two salons, three heads, six decks–four above the water, two below, two galleys, a crew's mess, a gym, a media room, an elevator (which wasn't put to use), a grand circular staircase, a garage that could hold a runabout and jet skis, or even a car. Everything the seafaring billionaire would need to be comfortable.

Talk about using resources, Maggie thought, *what got used on that sucker in just one week could run the ThreeBees for a year!*

Flyboy also held over eighty people right now. Maggie had been on it last about a week ago for the general assembly. The formerly elegant appointments on *Flyboy* were looking even worse for wear than their own little ThreeBees. Cabinets had been chipped, and countertops stained. Hand-stitched leather upholstery had been snagged and gouged. Gym equipment had long since been heaved overboard to make room for beds. The luxurious owner's quarters had been occupied by at least ten people camped out in nests of blankets and couch cushions filched from the once glamorous salons. What once had been the private domain of some rich oil executive, was now actually the least desirable area on the boat–kind of a cattle pen of humanity. The marble floor was dull and dirty, the bathroom caked with the evidence of hard habitation. If the former owners could see *Flyboy* now, they'd probably faint dead away in a blue-blooded swoon.

Maggie dragged her mind away from resenting *Flyboy* and put it back on task. She was being a real bitch today–if not outside, then certainly inside. She needed rest and time alone: a bath, a drink, a magazine that hadn't been looked at eighteen times already. All of those things were near impossibilities in their new world.

She got a firmer grip on the fishing net and scanned the floor of the rowboat. Two fingers lay under the seat, and she scooped them up and over the side, her face set in lines of disgusted determination. She had to hunt for the third, as it had made it to the front of the little boat. She was reminded of snakes and chickens, both purported to 'live' quite some time after being divided from their heads.

She shuddered, hoping it wouldn't twitch when she touched the net to it. That grossed her out. She finally got up enough nerve to reach forward and with one smooth movement, flung it up and over the side. It made a little 'plip' sound when it hit the water. She sighed and sank down onto the middle seat, blowing out a held breath.

She scanned the horizon, as had become habit, her eyes skimming from beach to road to the little motel and its surrounding cabins. They hadn't seen any new survivors for weeks now. But you never knew.

"Maggie?"

She jumped and turned, her heart racing, but it was only Babygirl. She stood at the edge of the deck and looked at Maggie with worried eyes. "Did you get rid of them fingers?"

Maggie nodded and smiled. "All gone, Babygirl." She scrambled up onto the deck and took Babygirl's hand. "Want to eat?"

Baby's eyes went past Maggie, and her face clouded. "What man is that?" she asked.

"Man?" Maggie echoed, confused, then turned to the starboard side. A yellow life raft floated twenty-five feet out. A man lay spread-eagled in the center, unconscious or sleeping–Maggie couldn't tell which–but she could see that he was covered in blood.

Chapter Three

Maggie dropped Babygirl's hand and gave her shoulder a small nudge. "Go get Randy. Tell him bring the walkie."

Baby nodded and trotted away.

"Denny! Brian!" Maggie called, and they stumbled from the salon, bleary-eyed. Napping again. Christ, those boys could sleep twenty out of twenty-four hours.

Denny was dark-haired and Brian blond, but beyond that, Maggie thought the two of them had an almost troubling similarity. She knew that was largely because she wasn't looking at people the same way anymore. Although once a warm and friendly woman, she'd become colder since...everything...had happened. She didn't give the other members of the boat the attention she would have in her past life. She didn't question them or think about the things they told her. She felt inner-turned, like a pill bug rolled tight onto itself, a hard shell protecting her from her surroundings. She didn't want to let anyone in. Babygirl was bad enough with her growing need for mothering.

"What's up?" Denny asked. His eyes slid down to Maggie's legs and then back up, over her stomach and breasts. *He isn't lecherous, he's young*, Maggie reminded herself, *and he can't help himself*. She didn't take it personally. She found it ironic that she probably looked better now than she had for much of her life. She was thin and fit from the extra exercise and lack of excess food, and she moved with a physical confidence she had never realized came from having muscles.

"Dude," Brian said from just behind Denny and pointed, "there's a dude out there, man."

Randy huffed up, walkie-talkie in hand. "What's going on?"

"Dude in the bay, dude," Brian said.

Randy blinked at him and then turned to Maggie. "Dude in what? What is he talking about?" Randy liked to act as though Brian and Denny spoke a completely different language from himself.

In a way, they did kind of, Maggie thought.

She pointed past Randy. "There's a man out there on a raft. See him?"

Randy turned and squinted out over the bay, then nodded. "What do you think? Sinker? He's covered in blood."

Maggie shook her head. "I don't know. We have to go check. Call Steve, would you? It would be best if—"

Randy nodded, bringing the walkie up. He depressed the button. "Hey, *Big Daddy*, you guys there? *Big Daddy*? This is ThreeBees, and we have a, uh…a situation over here, over."

"What's up, ThreeBees? Over." The voice that came through the walkie-talkie was thin and tinny. Almost as one, Randy, Maggie, and Denny looked in the other direction to the fifty-foot tug sitting pugnaciously between them and the *Flyboy*. The words *Big Daddy* were spray-painted across the black hull like dripping, pirate graffiti. A man stood at the rail outside the engine room, walkie in his hand.

"Yeah, hey, Steve," Randy said. "We have a man floating on some kind of raft. He's uh, he's pretty bloody, and not moving. Over."

"Sinker? Over."

Randy shook his head. "We don't know. Can you send someone to check? Over."

"On it, ThreeBees, over and out."

Randy grinned a little sheepishly, letting the walkie fall to his side. Brian sank down onto a deck chair, running his hand through his hair. Denny was red in the face. "Dude, I could have taken a jet ski and checked it out. Brian would have gone with me, right, dude?"

"Yeah, man, 'course," Brian said, but there was little conviction in his voice.

Denny blew out a disgusted breath and turned, hands on hips, as three jet skis whined away from *Big Daddy*. They sounded like apocalyptic wasps.

Denny hated being stuck on the ThreeBees. It was old people as far as the eye could see, he felt, and he and Brian were only nineteen. Maggie was at least kind of hot, but she was old, too. Jade was hot, with her long black hair and exotic black eyes, but Jade rarely came out of the room she shared with the old lady. Her brother, Singer, would join the two of them in there, and they played mahjong or something equally boring all damn day.

Fuck, I wish I was on Big Daddy, he thought. *Or even Flyboy would be better than this floating retirement community we're on now. Big Daddy* was a sausage fest, but it still would have been better than this. His eyes tracked the jet skis as they went by. Steve was on the front one, and he gave the ThreeBees a short wave as he went by. Steve was a pretty big dude, blond hair kept very short, sharp blue eyes, and very much in charge on the *Big Daddy*. But he was a fair guy, from what Brian had overheard. He was calm and decent. Not like the dude that ran *Flyboy*, that dickhead, Adam.

Twenty-three of the men in the twenty-five to fifty-five age range had ended up with Steve on the *Big Daddy*. It took a lot of muscle to manage the tug. It was a big, bulky boat, powerful, but lacking grace. Sometimes at night, Denny would look across the water and listen as they played music and laughed the loud, raucous laughter of men out of the censorious hearing of women. Denny was petty sure a bottle would be passed around, too, adding to the fun. It was true, too, that many of the men over there had been single before the event. They'd had few ties and now were quicker to recover their equilibrium. For some–the ones who'd felt uneasy in a technology-oriented society–this brave new world came almost as a blessing, and they lived out the fantasy of seafaring warriors–Vikings or maybe even pirates, a little boy's dream finally come true.

Denny wished fervently that he and Brian were part of it, but fuck no, they were stuck on the ThreeBees. Christ, even the name was homo.

The three men on the jets neared the life raft.

Steve put up one hand, signaling the other two drivers to stop about fifteen feet from the raft. It bobbed harder in the small wake thrown up by the jet skis. The man inside lay on his back, and his head rocked uneasily side to side, as if telling them not to rock him so hard. He looked young–early twenties at the most. His eyes were closed, there was a long gash across his forehead, and most of his face was covered in blood: fresh near the wound but drying to a brownish maroon in the creases of his neck and in his hairline.

It was hard to judge how long ago the man had been hurt. Steve had seen a lot of injuries in that frantic week it took to attain the shoreline, and quick assessments of the injured had become a habit. Taking into consideration the sun and wind, the man's wounds could be relatively fresh. Steve scanned the horizon in all directions. He could see no other boats save their own small armada. Where had this guy come from, if there wasn't another boat around? He could have cast off from land before he passed out and been carried by the current, but that seemed a long shot considering the distance–and it wasn't a large raft.

The one sure thing was that this guy wasn't a sinker, because sinkers didn't bleed. If they were somewhat fresh, you might get a coagulated dark red jelly from them, but if they weren't fresh, then the most you might see from their veins would be a brownish, dried up crumble that looked almost like coffee grounds.

Steve reached out with a gaff, hooked the rope threaded through cleats around the raft's edge, and pulled it closer. He scanned the interior, seeing if there was anything useful aboard. That scavenger mentality had already become so ingrained that he hardly noticed he was doing it. Another condition of the times.

A hunting knife–big with a serrated section across the back of the blade–lay near the man's hand. A twitch of unease went through Steve's mind. The placement of the knife was off...somehow fake looking. Something was missing. As though someone had gone to some trouble to–

"Hey, little help?"

The man's eyes were open. They were bright, bright blue, and the whites looked very white, contrasting strongly against the mask of blood. His voice was raspy, barely there.

"Can you move?" Steve said, and the man closed his eyes again. He nodded slightly and then struggled to sit up, bringing a hand to the gash on his forehead. He opened his eyes again, but they were slitted in pain.

"Can you make it across to a jet ski?" Steve motioned Carl forward. Carl's jet was a two-person job, big and roomy. "Can you climb up with Carl?"

"Come on, man," Carl said, leaning forward and offering his hand. "Ease on up here." Carl was big, bigger than Steve, and dark. His wildly growing mass of curly hair and beard made him look like a virile pirate. He looked as though he should have been riding some kind of sea dragon of yore rather than the ubiquitous jet ski.

The man in the raft scanned Carl up and down with a look of unease. Then he reached forward shakily, coming onto his knees. Carl's hand was like a bear paw, covering the other man's entire hand and when he slipped, Carl was able to lift him bodily across to the deck of the jet ski.

Steve had another twinge of apprehension. There was something off about the guy, something...Steve shook his head. *There's something off about all of us*, he thought. *Nothing seems exactly right anymore. Because nothing is exactly right.*

"Get him to ThreeBees," Steve said, raising his voice to be heard over the jets. "Maggie can see about that cut and then we'll get him sorted." He watched as Carl started away, the man holding fast to the giant's back.

"Dave, tie that raft up to ThreeBees and then head back to *Big Daddy*, okay?"

Dave hesitated. He and Steve had met up three days after the shit hit the fan and had been together ever since. Dave had seen the hesitation in Steve's eyes.

"What is it?" Dave asked, raising his voice, reaching for the raft with his gaff, and then grabbing for the rope curled untidily at its bow. "What did you see?"

Steve shook his head, but his gaze went involuntarily to the departing jet. He shook his head again more firmly. "Nothing. It's nothing. I'll see you back at *Big Daddy*. Hour at the most." Even as he said it, Maggie came to his mind. He might be longer than an hour.

Dave started away, the yellow raft bouncing jauntily in his wake. Dave was young and handsome in a clean-cut, college way, his brownish blond hair blown sharply back from his face. The scene would have been set if the raft had carried two pretty coeds in bikinis with beers in their hands, laughing and squealing at the speed.

World isn't like that anymore, Steve thought. He powered off his jet, and the silence that fell was a relief. Even the imaginary laughter of the pretty coeds faded off to the horizon.

Water lapped the edges of the jet, washing up and over his feet. Despite the sun, he shivered, and the sky seemed to darken. The swamp. That had been the worst and not because of wet feet, either.

Because of Amelia and what had happened to her. That's why the swamp had been the worst.

~ ~ ~

Steve had lived in central Jersey, just outside of Princeton, and he taught at the university. He liked the dichotomy of the bustling, townie atmosphere of the campus, only a fifteen-minute drive away from the secluded silence of his little house in the woods. When he was home, he couldn't even see his nearest neighbor.

Best of both worlds.

The campus had become a very uneasy place during that last week. The rumor among the students was that lots of people were dying of a strange new flu, and it wasn't just the really old and the really young this time–it was everyone. They were hearing (and repeating) that the government was covering up the numbers and trying to soothe everyone with the platitude of get rest, stay hydrated, and you'll be better before you know it.

The rumor persisted: if you got sick, you died, and that wasn't even the worst part of what was said to be going on.

The rumors had begun in the spring and had been mere blips on the radar at first. A few mentions on Twitter and Reddit, a couple of uneasy Facebook posts. Someone had posted a ten-second video clip to YouTube of police in riot gear beating a small group of students outside a California university infirmary. They might have been protesters, as there was a lot of that going around lately. Something was happening behind the students, something impossible to see clearly in the shaky, obviously hand-held, low-quality video. Something–some*one*–staggered down the stairs from the infirmary, and the students had surged away from it like panicked sheep, looking over their shoulders and screaming, almost overwhelming the police line. The police had pushed back, batons swinging, and then the video had cut out, but not before an astute observer could have noticed the rally cry from the students: "Dead! Dead! Dead!" which they yelled over and over. The video had more than three hundred thousand views within an hour and then mysteriously disappeared, leaving only the warning 'owner has not verified content.' The comment portion remained for a day longer, becoming more strident, and then that was gone, too.

Steve looked at the iPhone in his hand. The screen had gone dark, so he pushed the button again to check the date. Tuesday, June 7th. He sat on the edge of his bed and rubbed his hand through his hair. It didn't make any sense. He reached behind him and shoved at the mound under the covers.

"Amelia, hey. Wake up. Wake up, love," he said.

The cocooned Amelia moaned and kicked back, but he jumped up, smiling and momentarily distracted from the message he'd just retrieved.

"Come on, Am, rise and *shine*." He slapped her ass through the covers. "Up and *at* 'em." He slapped again, a muffled whump on the downy quilt. He didn't get how she could sleep bundled up like that. She looked like a mummy. Didn't she get hot?

"Kill you," she said, her voice muffled and still half-asleep, but he knew she'd wake up now. She'd reached–as she called it–the point of no return.

He went to the kitchen to start coffee and once it was perking, he looked at the phone again. The voicemail had been left by one of his former students, Melanie Ransome. She'd been yelling–screaming, really–but it had been muffled. The phone must have been in her purse. He only knew it was her because it had been her name on the caller ID.

He stood looking at his yard from the window over the sink and listened to the coffee pot chortle behind him. He rolled a mug between his palms as he thought about Melanie's message.

She'd screamed something like "they've come back"–though his mind wanted to insist that he'd heard "please come back", because then, she could have been yelling for a dog or even a wayward boyfriend. "*They've* come back" didn't mean anything. He shook his head, recalling her tone. It had been panicked beyond reason. He shivered.

"I'd rather have tea."

He jumped and turned sharply, nearly dropping his empty cup. Amelia stood in the doorway, the comforter still wrapped around her shoulders. Her hair was a riot of honeyed curls, and one side of her face was lined. Her cheeks glowed with hot pink fire.

She sniffed, and one hand emerged from the swelter of blankets to rub her nose. Despite her thirty-two years, she looked about twelve.

"Not feeling well?" he asked and bent to kiss her.

She turned her head. "I'm getting a cold, don't kiss me."

He contented himself with a kiss on her temple. Her skin was very warm. Almost hot. The flu rumors floated into his mind, but he shooed them away. He'd been teaching too long to let drama-addicted students excite him.

"You should get out of that blanket," he said, filling the kettle. "You're gonna give yourself a fever."

She collapsed into a chair at the little four-person table. "I think I already have one." Her hand emerged again, this time to rub at her eyes. "It started yesterday in my throat. My throat feels okay now, but my nose is stuffed. See?" She sniffed extra hard, and he could see her nostrils close as no air was getting through.

"Very nice," he said and tipped the water over the waiting tea bag. "You're angelic, love, you know that?"

She grinned. "Yep, I know. That's why you love me."

He smiled. It *was* one of the reasons he loved her: her openness, her *realness*. At thirty-seven, he'd had plenty of casual girlfriends, even a handful of one-night stands, and had been pretty content with the mostly solitary direction his life seemed to be taking.

Then Amelia had stopped him in his tracks.

Funny, bubbly, and passionate, she'd reminded him of Meg Ryan...not a bad accompaniment to his somewhat dour Tom Hanks, he'd thought that first night they'd met. It had been at a bar, a mutual friend's fortieth birthday celebration. He'd seen her arguing with the birthday 'boy' about the recent firing of a near-tenured professor. Even as she'd argued, she'd been funny, wagging her finger in the birthday boy's face while her other hand steadied him on his bar stool–the man was *very* drunk.

Steve had pulled her away, disregarding the shocked expression on her face. "I think he was about to get violent!" he'd said over the crowd noise.

She'd looked back at the birthday boy, who sat jollily swaying. He was singing something. Auld Lang Syne? Then she'd turned back to Steve.

"Violent, huh?" She gestured to the happily singing drunk.

Steve's eyes never left hers. He'd smiled and nodded. "Yes, I'm sure of it. I think I just saved your life." He knew it was a gamble because she was very obviously a woman with a mind of her own, but the slow smile on her lips had convinced him that his gamble just might pay off.

They'd found they had a good deal in common. Each had no immediate family. They'd both never married. Neither of them wanted children anymore. In the big things, they were eerily compatible. He had been planning to ask her to marry him and had already started shopping for a ring.

He looked at her flushed features as she sipped the tea. She wiped a hand under her nose and sniffed hard. She must have sensed his gaze because she turned and smiled, then shrugged.

"Too sexy for you, right? It's killing you, isn't it?" Her eyes were red-rimmed, and the left eye was crusted at the corner.

He laughed and nodded. "I think it's the quilt that's doing it, actually. All that down...it's making me really horny...all those ducks...mmmm." He fingered a corner of the quilt and gave her a lecherous wink.

Now it was her turn to laugh, but it turned quickly to coughing. "I might go back to bed. I'm not due in to work until four." She was an artist and worked at a local screen-printing shop. "I feel awful."

He took her cup and turned back to the sink to wash it. "Good idea. I might come with you. Maybe I'll just call out today, what do you think?" He put the cup in the dish drainer and glanced out the window. "Maybe we could–hey...that's weird, Jerry is in the yard. What the hell is he doing?" Alarm filled Steve's stomach with sluggish butterflies as he noticed three things at once:

Jerry, his neighbor, was running full tilt toward the back door.

He was in pajamas and one slipper, and had a small axe in his hand.

Jerry's wife, Carol, was running just behind...chasing him?

"Jesus Christ, what's going on out there?"

Now Jerry was closer, and Steve could hear him through the old, single-paned windows.

"She's trying to kill me! She's dead! She's trying to kill me! Help! She's dead! She was dead! Help! Help me!"

"Guy's lost his mind," Steve said, his voice dropped almost to a whisper. His eyes switched to Carol, and his blood ran cold. The side of her neck had been laid open, and a blackish sludge coated her shoulder and arm. She seemed unable to lift her head completely. She was running clumsily, listing badly to one side, and he saw that her foot was gone. She was running on the ragged stump, bumping clumsily along.

"Jesus, Steve, what happened to Carol?" Amelia had crowded up against his back, and she was looking over his shoulder. Steve could feel the heat coming off her even through the blanket.

He shook his head. "I don't know–oh shit!"

Jerry had glanced over his shoulder, perhaps to judge the distance between himself and his rampaging wife, and he stumbled over a plastic lawn chair. He struggled to right himself, but he must have sprained his knee, or even broken it, because even as he stood, his leg collapsed back under.

Then Carol was on him.

She never slowed, just ran right into him, and they both toppled forward over the chair. Carol's mouth was on Jerry's neck as if she were kissing him, but then a grimace of panic and pain split Jerry's features, and Carol's head came up. Her mouth was covered in fresh red, and a stringy material jittered as she chewed. She was biting him. No, not biting...she was *eating* him.

"Carol, don't bite Jerry!" Steve said, his voice a startled roar. He banged the window with a fist. Even in his cold haze of shock, he realized how ridiculous his words sounded. He went for the back door. He had to do something...help out.

Amelia stood with her back to the door, covering it. The comforter had puddled around her like heavenly clouds, and her white face glowed with color. She looked like a feverish angel. She was shaking her head. "You can't go out there. I won't let you."

Steve stopped, nonplussed. "What? Why not? I have to help–"

She reached up and put a hand on his face. "Call the police, but *don't* go out there."

Jerry's screams went on as Steve stared into Amelia's bright and frightened eyes. She shook her head, slow and deliberate: *no.*

Steve wheeled and grabbed the phone from the table. He thumbed it alive and dialed 911. It rang five times before he depressed end. He dialed again and went to the kitchen window. Jerry wasn't moving anymore. Carol had managed to turn him over and he lay awkwardly on the chair, his head hanging upside down. White knobs of spine were visible above his chin where she'd eaten his throat literally to the bone. His head rocked and shifted each time she tore another chunk from him.

The phone rang and rang against Steve's ear. After a while, it cut off.

"Lock the door, Amelia, okay?" Steve said, his voice thin and soft, but Amelia was sitting at the table, her head in her hands, and she didn't move. Steve locked the door himself and pulled down the roller blind. Before it was all the way down, he'd taken a last look.

Another neighbor had joined Carol at her feast. They worked at Jerry's corpse like wolves. A whimper worked its way up Steve's throat. Carol's head came up. More gristle hung from the side of her mouth. Her face was smeared with blood.

She seemed to mark him with her glazed eyes.

~ ~ ~

He and Amelia waited until Carol and the other neighbor had wandered off before turning on the television. Every channel was either a special news report or blank. One station showed a map of the United States, and they were highlighting the areas of the heaviest 'breakouts' and urging people to keep calm. They cut to a reporter on a street that Steve thought was maybe Philly. The anchorman asked her if she'd been able to get the mood of the community, were residents scared? Worried? She nodded, looking serious, and just as she opened her mouth to speak, she was attacked from behind. A kid, fifteen or sixteen, tore a hunk from her cheek. The reporter screamed and tried to throw him off. "Tony, help me!" she yelled, grappling with the kid. "For Christ's sake, put the fucking camera down and–"

Another figure hurtled in from the side, knocking the reporter and her attacker both to the ground. The camera seemed to fall with them, and then it focused on the reporter's face. Her eye hung almost to the level of her mouth. If she'd put out her tongue, she could have licked it.

Then the shot went blank.

They panned back to the anchorman, and he sat, mouth agape. Then he stood and walked from the newsroom.

None of the other stations seemed to be doing any better. Finally, they caught one channel with a live feed from the shore. A reporter stood on a dock yelling, "Go to water, go to water, it's the only safe place, go to water, I repeat go to–" before that shot, too, went blank.

Amelia and Steve had looked at each other in the deepening gloom as night fell. They'd been afraid to turn on any lights for fear of drawing attention to themselves.

"How far are we? From the shore?"

Steve had rubbed his face, rubbed his tired eyes. "I don't know. If we take 33, I guess about forty minutes. Maybe more."

After deliberating, they decided to go after midnight. Neither said why it felt better to wait; it just seemed safer, somehow.

They were on the outskirts of a small town less than ten miles from the shore when they were confronted with crowds of the walking dead. The dead were everywhere…in the road, in yards, in parking lots. Everywhere. When the dead spotted the headlights and heard their engine, they swarmed like sluggish, cold-struck moths.

Amelia's screams filled the car like shards of falling glass, but Steve felt a calm settle over him like a cold cloak. He turned over their options, but it seemed to him there was only one. He swerved in and out, loathe to hit anyone, not understanding–not yet–the extent of the devastation. He had to get rid of the car. They'd do better on foot, bringing less attention to themselves.

He turned his lights off and doubled back to where the woods had ended. He told Amelia to be ready to go when the car stopped rolling. Just get out and head for the woods, he'd be right behind her. She nodded, her eyes enormous, her cheeks bright red with fever. He'd taken her hand and squeezed it. Even her hand was hot.

Steve waited for a clear stretch and let the car roll to a stop. They bolted from it and into the woods. The ground was marshy and soft in spots, trying to suck them down. It was like running in a bad dream where your legs and feet are leaden and unresponsive.

They'd gone about three miles in silence before Amelia's coughing forced them to stop and rest. They huddled against the base of a tree, panting with exertion, listening intently for sounds of pursuit–none came.

Steve berated himself silently for never once using his gym membership…his legs were burning with exertion. He was miserably unprepared for this nightmare.

Amelia coughed steadily. He bundled her to him even though her heat was making him uncomfortably warm. He was furious with himself for not thinking to pack water and food. He better get his shit together and start thinking, or they were going to end up as someone's dinner.

He felt Amelia relaxing in his arms and he tilted his head back against the tree. What had happened? The people walking around had died, he would swear to it. They all looked like corpses. Except ambulatory. He thought about the coagulated blackness coming from his neighbor, Carol, her missing foot, her glazed eyes. She had been dead, but somehow not. She had died, but been reanimated in some way.

But that wasn't possible. It wasn't.

He slept.

~ ~ ~

The first thing he thought as he came awake was that Amelia was better…she wasn't nearly as hot. In fact, her skin was a bit chilly. He snapped all the way awake. Amelia was dead in his arms. Stiff. Her eyes were open, but unseeing.

"Amelia?" he said, laying her flat. Knowing already that she was too dead…too far gone. "Amelia? Wake up, okay? Wake up, my love." He patted her cheeks. He pulled three pine needles from her tangle of curls. Her lips were so white.

He held her hands, rubbed them. Hesitantly, he felt for her pulse, already knowing what he'd feel beneath his fingers. Stillness. Nothing. Her heart was not beating. "Amelia, come on, baby, come on. Wake up, sweetheart, wake up."

He bent to kiss her white, gently-parted lips. A spider crawled out from between them and scuttled across her chin. Steve yelped and sat back, knocking his head into the tree. Crazily, he dug his phone from his pocket. It was dead. He took her phone from her pocket, flipped it open, and had dialed the 9 before he stopped himself. It was no use. The phone tumbled from his shaking hands and landed next to her ear in a nest of golden curls.

He put his head in his hands, but he was too shocked to cry. He thought about curling up next to her and waiting for it–the sickness–to take him, too. Hoping with all his heart that he would go quickly.

He lay down next to her, shoulder to shoulder, hip to hip, and closed his eyes. He felt calm wash over him, but even in his shocked state, he knew it wasn't a good calm. It was more of a numbing. A deadening.

The wind began to sigh around him. The pines seemed to call his name, gently and with love. "Steeeeeehhhh…" He tried to smile, tried to tell himself it was going to be okay. He just needed to rest. Maybe none of this was real, and he'd wake up at home, in bed with Amelia.

"Steeeeeehhhhhh…"

The sound was coming from next to him. He opened his eyes and turned his head.

Amelia lay supine, but her throat was working. Her lips pursed by millimeters. "Steeeeehhhhhhh…" She was saying his name.

He sat up and stared into her dead, unfeeling face. As he watched, another spider scurried across her unblinking eye. Her throat worked again. "Steeeeehhhhhh…" Her diaphragm lifted and settled, not as with breath, but as a simple muscle contraction.

She began to sit up.

Steve scrambled back, trying to gain his footing, but his hands landed in marsh mud, and he sank to his elbows. Amelia was on him before he could get his hands free. She swarmed up his body like a clumsy wraith, the expression of dead blankness never leaving her features. Her weight was that of the dead.

"Amelia, no! Please, God, please no…no, Amelia!" He scrambled up and she tumbled off, rolling onto her back like a beetle. Her hands and legs waved sluggishly, and then she found the ground again and righted herself. He took two shaky steps backward and sank almost to his knees, the marsh mud cold and sucking on his feet and legs. "Amelia, stay back, stay away from me, please, stay back, Amelia…we have to…we have to get you help."

She stood, swaying, and turned in a confused circle. Then she found him again. She started forward, her arms raised, mouth hanging open. Now she had an expression: hunger.

"Amelia, no! Stay back! No, Amelia, no!"

~ ~ ~

The water lapped up the sides of the jet ski, chilling his legs as he thought about what had happened out there. How he'd had to…to put Amelia down. He shuddered, and then the cold cloak descended, pushing regret and guilt to a dark recess where (he hoped) they'd have no effect on future decisions. He keyed the jet ski to life and headed for ThreeBees to check out his newest charge.

The wind dried his tears so quickly that he didn't even have to acknowledge them.

Chapter Four

Adam stood on the deck of *Flyboy*, the walkie-talkie crackling in his hand. He watched the scurrying jet skis. They'd found another survivor. *Another immune, most likely*, Adam thought, but he'd have to be watched. It was possible–if only slightly–that a non-immune had made it through. There were three ways to go: get the airborne sickness, die from the fever and reanimate, get scratched or bit, get the sickness and die and reanimate, or get killed by some sort of accident, die and reanimate. There were a lot of people who hadn't contracted the illness in its airborne state, but would still succumb to a scratch or bite, but some people, it seemed, were completely immune to getting the sickness in any form.

Adam felt a presence at his side and knew that Dr. Sami Rafiq had joined him at the rail, but Adam didn't turn to acknowledge him.

The jet with the survivor went to the *Barbra's Bay Breeze*. Adam felt a dig of irritation, even though he preferred the survivor be contained on the smaller vessel. The irritation came because, instead of *asking*, Steve had *told* him that they were taking the survivor to ThreeBees.

Adam thought again about getting everyone aboard *Flyboy*, but knew it wasn't the best idea; it was just ego. Especially since it was he who had suggested that Steve split off onto the *Big Daddy* in the first place. He couldn't let his ego get the best of him. Not this time.

People crowded the rails, chattering, speculating. Some had binoculars, while others had walkie-talkies. It had been weeks since a survivor had been found, and it had become an exciting anomaly all over again.

"Do you want me to go and check the survivor?" Dr. Rafiq asked, his voice soft and deferential.

Adam shook his head. "No, Maggie can do it. Just in case. You're too important, Sami."

Dr. Rafiq felt himself pulled two ways at once: flattered by being called 'too important', but embarrassed that Adam refused him the honor of his title. But Sami felt obliged to take a certain amount of Adam's insolence because Adam was protecting Sami's secret. If the survivors knew that Sami could have prevented this whole thing…he'd be lynched.

Everyone else had taken to calling him 'Doc'…it was something that Steve from the *Big Daddy* had started. It tickled him and brought to mind the handful of American westerns he'd seen as a child in India. Cowboys, as he'd seen them then, were in some respects also how he'd come to view his adopted country: brusque and somewhat crude, but also incredibly brave and noble.

"If something should go wrong, I don't want us affected," Adam said. He didn't lower his voice. He wanted the people closest to him to hear what he had to say. They would take it and tell the others. That was how he'd maintain loyalty. "We're the core group. No one here is expendable." He didn't believe that, of course. Everyone was expendable, but it made people feel good.

Dr. Rafiq turned troubled eyes from Adam back to the ThreeBees. What made the people over there 'expendable'? How were they different from anyone on the *Flyboy*?

His eyes caught the look of a woman two people down on the rail. She was staring at him, her gaze steady. She shook her head, and although Sami knew it was in response to Adam's comment, he could imagine she had read his mind. *They're no different from us*, she seemed to be saying. *So, aren't we all expendable, then?*

Sami looked quickly to Adam and was glad to see he had not noticed Candy's head shaking. Then Sami looked back at Candy. Ridiculous name, but she did resemble candy, even if it made him uncomfortable to think it. Her hair was soft, blonde floss, and her lips and cheeks a bright pink. Her lids were shadowed in an energetic blue that eased to baby blue by the time it reached her artificially arched eyebrows. Sami knew that other men (and women) judged her to be stupid, vapid, and–worst of all to Sami–loose, but for Candy, it was a sort of camouflage. She was intensely bright and just as brave as any of the fictional cowboys he'd ever seen in the movies, maybe braver. He loved her very much.

~ ~ ~

Dr. Rafiq had met Candy in Philadelphia, in January of this same year. He'd come to the University of Pennsylvania from his hospital in Princeton to attend a speaking engagement. He was there to listen to the engineers of a new gene therapy treatment that was being hailed as a cure for HIV/AIDS. A research facility in Nevada had developed a way to turn off the gene that was a gateway for the virus. It had been nicknamed 'Lazarus', since it had saved patients who'd seemed, quite literally, to be at death's door. It had a restorative power that had only been seen so far in stem cell therapies, but the best part was that it could be administered as a nasal spray. Once it came in contact with the mucous membrane, it went to work without further prompting.

Dr. Rafiq was there to try and meet one of the experts. He had a question about the findings of their trials. It seemed to him that there was a disturbing 'back door' to this new gene therapy, and he wanted to question someone on it. As he sat listening to the main speaker, he burned with anxiety and agitation–what if he was very off base? What if he looked foolish when he asked his question? His eyes scanned the auditorium. There were hundreds of doctors in attendance–many of them his superiors from the hospital. Surely, someone else would have noticed the same discrepancy as he had...if there *were* such a discrepancy. Dr. Rafiq was twenty-eight and had only been a full-fledged doctor for two years. He was intimidated to see so many doctors and researchers together to celebrate Lazarus. How could he *possibly* know something that thousands of others had overlooked?

When the lights came up and they called for questions, he stood, but then had an almost fainting sense of relief when he was passed over. His knees shook, and for a brief instant, he was light-headed. The engagement adjourned with his questions unanswered.

He found the hotel where the research group was said to be staying and went to the bar. He was still in a sweat of conflicting emotions, but the strongest was his sense that–if he was right about what he'd seen–the implications might be rampant transfer of disease. As he waited to confront the visiting scientists, he bolstered himself with two whiskeys when he normally didn't drink. Ever.

The combination of alcohol and nerves turned him into an unfortunate, incoherent mess.

That's where Candy found him.

Candy had been at the lecture, too. Her brother was dying of AIDS, and she'd read about the Nevada group in one of the physician's magazines she subscribed to. She came to the hotel to talk them into taking her brother on for the next trial. She knew she could persuade them–she was as rigorously convincing as any trial lawyer could ever hope to be. Plus, she was really, really cute. She had found that being cute helped quite a bit in life. Born into rough circumstances, she'd learned to use what she had to get what she needed, and right now, her brother needed a miracle. He needed Lazarus.

She entered the dark bar, expecting to find members of the group there–doctors were hard drinkers, she'd found–but it was empty save for one young Indian man. She'd just wait, then. They were most likely at Capitol Grille or The Palm…surely they'd stop in here for a nightcap after dinner.

She sat halfway down the bar, keeping one eye on the lobby and one on the young Indian man. She ordered a club soda. She waited.

The young man was talking to himself, quietly but vehemently. One hand was fisted, and he hit himself in the chest several times, as if to punctuate what he was saying. Candy thought she saw a gleam of frustrated tears in his warm brown eyes.

Just like that, she liked him.

The bartender's face showed annoyance, and Candy knew he was on the verge of asking the man to leave. She went to where he sat and put out her hand.

"Hi, I'm Candy," she said. She'd always found it was best to get that out of the way up front…to acknowledge her ridiculous name and put it right out there, without apology.

He looked up in surprise and then touched the tips of her fingers with his–it was the barest, most hesitant handshake she'd ever encountered.

"How are you?" he said, but she knew it was perfunctory. His voice was soft, his accent exotic, and to her, beautiful. She slid onto the stool next to him.

"I'm okay," she said. "You didn't tell me your name."

"I am Doctor Sami Rafiq and it is a pleasure to meet you, miss, uh, Candy."

"Doctor? Are you here from Nevada by any chance?" She hadn't recognized his name from the study or the lecture, but these things tended to involve a lot of people. "Are you working on Lazarus?"

It was like a secret code, the way it lit his features. He shook his head and almost tumbled off his stool. She steadied him with one hand.

"You know about Lazarus?" he said, astonished.

She nodded, completely unperturbed by his tone. She'd been underestimated plenty of times before. "You're here for that, too, then?" she asked.

He nodded and nearly fumbled his almost empty drink. The bartender whisked away the glass without offering him a refill.

"What is your interest in it?" he said. "If you don't mind me asking."

They each revealed their reasons for wanting to talk to the Lazarus scientists. Sami, simultaneously bolstered and befuddled by whiskey, admitted his conflicting feelings, and Candy told him about the struggles she'd had with her brother. Before they knew it, that day had become the next.

The Lazarus scientists never showed up, or they had never left their rooms in the first place. Either way, it amounted to the same thing: neither Candy nor Sami got what they came for. But they did leave with something they hadn't expected: each other's numbers and hearts.

~ ~ ~

Sami watched discreetly from the corner of his eye as Candy left the railing. Hiding their relationship had been necessary before everything happened. Sami's parents would have been disappointed in his choice of an Anglo mate, and Candy's family and friends would have taken every opportunity to ask why she wanted to date a terrorist.

As far as either of them knew, those people were all gone now. Or sailing in some armada of their own somewhere. So, why did they keep hiding their relationship? Habit?

Sami ducked away from Adam, excusing himself, and followed Candy.

Adam kept his eye on the ThreeBees, thinking. Maybe he should insist on having the survivor brought over, even if it was just to show Steve who was boss. Maybe that was reason enough. He brought the walkie-talkie up, but before he could depress the button, a voice came blasting through the speaker, obviously panicked.

"*Flyboy*, this is Mitch. We've got trouble, over!"

The screaming whine of an engine ran counterpoint to the voice, adding to the sense of immediacy. "*Flyboy*, do you hear me? Over!"

Adam felt his stomach twist in a knot of shock, and his hand froze on the walkie, squeezing it convulsively.

"Mitch, this is Steve, what's the trouble? Over."

Steve's voice over the walkie-talkie was concerned but not panicked. Adam looked across to ThreeBees and spotted Steve standing on the deck, facing the shoreline.

"We've got about eighty corpses on our tail, over."

"Just shag ass, then, Mitch. How far out are you? Over."

"We're not far, but that's not the problem, over."

"Well, don't get shy on me, Mitch, what's the trouble? Over."

There was a long space of static. Then it smoothed out, and the engine whine was back. "Uh, it's Mohammed, Steve. He was, uh…the fucking things got him, and…" Engine noise over the open line and then a choked off sob, and then silence again as the line cut off. Around the railing of the *Flyboy*, people's faces had gone white. They began to wander away. None of them seemed able to look at Adam.

Steve's voice across the walkie: "What happened, Mitch? How bad is he? Over."

An even longer silence and then the engine whine as the line opened back up. Mitch's voice was calmer now, bled of emotion. "We had to, uh…we left him. We had to. We…"

The line cut off again. Adam stared at the walkie, open-mouthed, and then his eyes lifted to the deck of ThreeBees. Steve had turned to face the *Flyboy* and he seemed to be looking right at Adam. His stance was either that of anger or shock.

Behind Adam, a woman began to scream.

~ ~ ~

The first thing Adam did when he got to work every day was to mark off the day on the calendar, and today was no different. He put a black line through June 6th. He dropped his lunch into his bottom desk drawer and docked his laptop. Carl and Anita were already tapping away in the cubicles across from him, logging into the help desk queue.

Adam hated the queue–hated it. He hated being part of the help desk for a pharmaceutical company. He despised the other employees who didn't understand their computers. At thirty-six, he felt he should have been in charge of the department. Even though he hated it.

He never got a break. Everyone was always against him. He'd seen it time and time again how he was passed over. He'd complained about it to Carl and Anita (both in their early twenties) back when they were new to the department and they'd all gone to lunch together on a regular basis, but those two would just shrug it off and change the subject. Couple of losers.

Adam had stopped going to lunch with them. He didn't acknowledge to himself that they had stopped *asking* him to lunch. People came and went pretty quickly from the help desk, and maybe he'd have more luck with the next person who came to work here.

His current manager had actually started out in the cubicle right next to Adam, and now was his direct supervisor. Just goes to show you what an ass-kisser can get away with.

He logged into the queue. Only fifteen complaints so far today. Strangely light. Although, maybe people were already starting to take long weekends. It wasn't unusual in the summer in a town so close to the shore. A hand descended on his shoulder.

"Got a minute?"

Adam turned. His supervisor, Toby, was smiling at him, but it was a tight, perfunctory smile.

Adam nodded. "Yeah, sure. What's up?"

From the corner of his eye, he saw Carl and Anita glance his way. Were they snickering?

"Let's go into my office, okay?"

"Uh…sure."

Adam followed Toby to his 'office' as he called it…that was a laugh. It was just another cubicle, really. The only difference being it had four walls and a door, but the walls didn't even go to the ceiling, for fuck's sake, and they shook any time someone walked past. Some office.

"I'll get right to it," Toby said and then contradicted himself by spending five minutes sneezing and blowing his nose. "Man, this cold is kicking my ass, and it came on so fast! I wasn't even sick yesterday, but today…bam! Probably got it from my daughter. Her class is a cesspool of germs, and…"

Adam stared at Toby, expressionless.

"Well, but anyway…we got another complaint about the department," Toby said and shuffled through sheets of paper on his desk.

Adam didn't say anything, just crossed his arms over his chest.

Toby looked up. "About you specifically, I'm afraid."

"Look, if it was that dingbat in marketing, that Carrie or Cassie…" Adam said, but Toby shook his head. Adam tried again.

"Teshay? In accounting? Because she was the one who…Alan in accounts payable? DeShawn in–"

Toby continued to shake his head, but had closed his eyes, a pained expression compressing his features. Adam closed his mouth with a snap.

He'd ended up with another warning in his file. Had to sign it and everything. Fuck. They wouldn't leave him alone. But this is what happens when you're (figuratively) the tallest man in the room, he told himself. It's jealousy, pure raging jealousy that kept everyone after him, wanting to pull him down. Bastards.

At home that night, he called his mother and raged to her about how unfairly he was being treated at work. She listened, but Adam got the impression her mind was elsewhere. Well, everyone else was shitting on him, why not his own mom, too?

"Ma. Are you listening to me?" he said. "Ma?"

"Yes, I am, dear, but it's just…" She paused, and Adam listened as she blew her nose. Disgusting. "I'm worried about your father. He's very sick with this flu, and now it looks like I might be getting a bit of it, too."

"Ugh, I hope I don't get it. Did he get sick this past weekend? 'Cause I was over there on Friday, and he was probably still catching on Friday. I wish you'd thought to warn me, Ma."

"Well, but…he *wasn't* sick on Friday and not Saturday or Sunday either. He woke up sick this morning, and he's gotten a lot worse just in this one day," she said and then coughed. Adam thought about his supervisor, that asshat, Toby, coughing and blowing his nose…he'd left around ten and never came back.

"Well, I guess there's something going around. Get rest or whatever." His mind wasn't on it, though. He wanted to talk about the warning he'd received. Well, not about that specifically…he didn't want to tell his mom about that part. He just wanted to express how he was *constantly* tagged at that place.

"I think I should change to another industry. Banking maybe, some kind of finance. This pharma shit is for the birds anyway." He sighed, not hearing his mother sigh on the other end of the line. "So, can I talk to Dad? If you've got nothing to add to this? I know, I know, it's just my shit, right? You could at least have an opinion." Impatient rage was heating up his face. "Is Dad there?"

"Well, he is, but like I said, he's in bed, and…I really don't think he should get up."

Adam sighed again. "Okay, well, whatever. Take care, then. I hope *you* feel better. Don't worry about *me* at all, okay? Don't bother yourself."

"Oh, Adam, dear…it's not like that, of course I care, we both care about you, but…"

"Whatever, Ma. I'm hanging up. I have more important things to do than chat with you all night about your problems." His voice had gotten higher as he spoke, petulant and whining.

"See you on Friday?" she asked.

"Maybe, maybe not," he said, clipped and cold. "We'll have to wait and see. Goodbye."

"All right, dear, goodbye then," she said, and the phone clicked off.

She'd hung up on him.

God, his mother was horrible. A horrible monster. So selfish! Sometimes, Adam wished he could just take off, move across the country and have nothing more to do with anyone on the east coast. Just start over. A fresh start.

That night, he watched a wholly unbelievable pay-per-view romantic comedy and went to bed with a very sour stomach.

The next morning, he was awakened by pounding on his apartment door. His heart raced in his chest. He'd never even had a visitor here, save his parents…why would someone be pounding on the door?

"Please, let me in! I need your phone. Hello?" Pound, pound, pound. "Hey? I need your phone! Do you have a cell?"

Adam peeked through the peephole. It was the girl that had the apartment under his. She was crying and jittering in an impatient way. Probably a junkie, a meth-head bent on robbing him.

"What is it?" he yelled.

Her head snapped up at the sound of his voice. "Thank God! Can I use your cell phone? I need an ambulance!" Her eyes were huge blue marbles, wet and frantic. She wasn't very pretty.

Adam hesitated and then unlocked the deadbolt and opened the door. She started in, but he blocked the doorway with his body. She pulled up sharply and shock crossed her features. It made him feel powerful. Plus, he didn't want her to see his apartment. He knew the jokes people made about adults who collected action figures. His apartment was full of them.

"What's this about?" he asked, his voice impatient. Chicks like this thought the world was their oyster. He knew her type. Well, he, for one, wasn't going to jump through her hoops.

"It's my son…he's very sick, and the landlines aren't working. Can I use your phone? I only want to call an ambulance." She shifted from foot to foot, more tears welling up in her eyes.

"Yeah, okay, I guess so." He dug his phone out of the laptop bag that sat on a table by the door and handed it to her. He watched as she dialed and then raised a shaking hand to cover her eyes. She was skinny, but older than he'd thought at first. She was likely close to his age. No ring–probably lived on child support and goofed off with her kid all day. Women had it made in the shade.

She flipped the phone closed. She stared at him, confused. "No answer? At 911? Is that…how is that possible?"

He sighed. "I'm sure you dialed it wrong. Here, let me." He took the phone from her, shaking his head. He punched in the numbers. Obviously, this chick was too stupid to work. She probably never had a job in her whole life. He shook his head again.

The phone continued to ring. No answer. He pulled it from his ear and checked the screen. 911, right there. He hadn't misdialed.

He put the phone back to his ear, but the call had dropped.

He dialed again, but this time he only heard a series of clicks, and then the call dropped.

"That's weird," he said. "Something must be wrong with the towers in this area causing a service disruption."

Irritation flitted across her features, and she lifted the phone in his hand to her face and then turned it to his. "Five bars. It's not cell phone service that's out; it's 911 that's out."

His face colored with embarrassment.

She'd turned away and was trotting down the steps that would take her back to her apartment.

"Hey, genius," he called after her, "why don't you just drive him if you're so concerned?"

41

She'd stopped and stared back at him in disgusted astonishment. "I don't have a *car*. We've been neighbors for five years, Adam. You've never noticed that I don't have a car?" She shook her head and continued down the stairs.

He was taken aback by her use of his name. How had she known his name? Had they really been neighbors for five years?

He went to his kitchen to start the coffee. It was earlier than his norm, but he might as well stay up now.

A muffled scream came from below him. Then another.

Fear slipped around him, pulling his skin into gooseflesh. He flipped open his phone and began to dial 911 before he remembered that it was out.

The scream came again. Was she screaming his name?

He slipped on sneakers, tucked his phone into the waistband of his pajama pants, and descended to her apartment. The door stood open three inches.

"Adam, help me! Please help! Can you hear me? Adam!" Her voice was a frantic sob.

She was somewhere in the back of the apartment, where the bedroom was. He went in, noting the swirl of blankets on the couch–is that where she sleeps?–feeling creepy and oddly ashamed.

"Uh, hello? I'm here."

"Oh, Adam, oh, thank God." She came down the short hallway, sobbing, a child bundled in blankets in her arms. He looked way too big to be carried. "Can you take us to the hospital? He's not...he's unconscious, I think, and..." She stumbled as she got closer to him, her arms giving way under the weight of her son.

Adam stepped back, and the boy nearly fell between them before she recovered herself, hefting him more solidly against her chest.

"Is he sick? I don't want to touch him!"

"No, you won't have to touch him. Just drive us. I'll hold him...in the back...please just, please drive us to..." Her sobbing overcame her words. Mucous ran freely over her top lip. Adam felt his stomach turn.

"Fine, okay. He's not gonna puke, though, right? I don't want anyone puking in my car."

~ ~ ~

The emergency room at the hospital was bedlam. Eighteen people waited in the line to sign in, and the chairs were all full. People were lined up against the walls. Everyone seemed to be coughing and vomiting. Nurses with fatigue-white faces ran back and forth, handing out kidney-shaped pans to the heaviest pukers.

Adam was about to turn around and leave when his neighbor shoved the boy into his arms, her face a white mask of determination. "Hold him. I'm going to find someone to look at him *right now*. Just stay right here." She spun away before he could even voice a protest.

The kid was heavy, dead weight heavy.

Adam searched for an empty chair, but there were none. He shifted the kid and scanned the waiting room. It was like a crazy version of hell–all that vomit! He decided to wait outside. It wasn't too hot or too cold, and he'd be able to see inside to the waiting room when his neighbor came back. When this was all over, he was going to give her hell over making him wait like this. Some people needed to be reminded that the world didn't revolve around them.

The doors whooshed open before him, and the fresh air was all the sweeter for not having the tang of vomit in it. And it was so much quieter! He'd never realized how loud the sick were.

He put the kid down by the wall, where he'd be out of the way of anyone coming by, and then scanned the parking lot. There was an ambulance parked at the curb about sixty feet away. How come they were parked there and not out retrieving sick people? It was obvious now that something was spreading like crazy, some new epidemic.

He looked down at the kid. No movement. Adam felt a twinge of unease. Well, but...he was just asleep. That's all. It's not like the kid's dead or anything. It's just the *flu*. Nobody dies of the flu, not *really*.

He decided to jog over and check out the ambulance. The emergency room entrance was at the back of the hospital and relatively secluded. No one would bother the kid, and if his mom came out, she'd see him lying right there. He'd be back in a sec. The uneasiness rolled through him again like distant heat lightning. He ignored it.

He jogged quickly to the ambulance and peeked in the back, through the windows. No one in there. He went quickly to the front. He was so strongly anticipating two paramedics sitting in the front seat that for an instant…he saw them. Then he realized it was just EMT jackets slung over the backs of the seats. Maybe they were in the hospital helping out. He scanned the dash. Man, there was a lot of extra shit in there. Big radio. Some kind of screen, maybe GPS or something. Huh.

He turned at a light, scraping sound from behind him.

The kid was up and coming toward him. Adam's first thought was *Geez, he's an ugly fucker*. The kid's hair was plastered down on one side and sticking straight up on the other. His tongue was swollen and peeking out between blistered lips. The worst were his eyes: they were glazed looking, almost as though he'd developed cataracts.

His second thought was: *Kid looks dead!*

That thought stuck and began to swirl like a slowly accelerating tornado. Once that thought got its full strength, it would be the only one left in his head.

"Yo, kid," he said, "your mom is right inside. She's coming back for you, okay?"

The kid never hesitated, just kept coming toward him at a shambling walk. His eyes never left Adam's face. Adam watched in surprise as the kid's bare foot went right over the curb edge and his ankle twisted with a snap, but still he continued his sluggishly steady pace.

"Kid, you better lie down," Adam said, and the tornado was accelerating, accelerating, kicking up wind and beginning to fan the flames of his panic. "Stay back, man, I'm telling you."

He wasn't aware of his switch from 'kid' to 'man', wasn't aware that it was part of his mind leveling the turf. All he knew right now was that his stomach had tightened and his legs were telling him to *move!*

But he didn't, and then the kid was on him.

At first, Adam was able to bat him back, pushing roughly at the kid's shoulders. He wasn't aware of a high-pitched yelp that was coming from his mouth every time he shoved. Panic was wrestling the blinders down over his conscious actions, readying him for the unthinkable...should the unthinkable occur.

The kid's efforts doubled and re-doubled; his arms like pistons, he kept coming on. He was snarling and chomping, and Adam saw that he had bit off the first half inch of his own tongue. There was no blood, just a blackish jelly that slicked the kid's lips.

Adam felt his gorge rise. "I'm warning you, man! Stay the hell back!" He pushed again, and the kid stumbled, the weakened ankle snapping again. Adam shuffled backwards, but then the kid was on him, his foot turned under, the skin scraping off onto the rough sidewalk.

"What the *fuck*?" Adam demanded, his voice both loud and weak. How could this be happening? That kid looked dead, he looked dead, but he was still coming, still coming on. "Stay the fuck *back*. I'm not *telling* you again."

The kid's hands were on his arms and then on his stomach. Adam tried to hold him back, but the arms turned in his hands like muscular snakes and slid forward. The kid was reaching for his shoulders, reaching for his neck. His little hand made a grab at Adam's windpipe and squeezed, and for a brief second, Adam had no air. Reflexively, he kicked out, connecting with the boy's stomach, sending him back and over. The kid's head hit the big side mirror of the ambulance with a sound like a melon hitting concrete.

He crumbled silently to the ground. Adam put his hands on his knees and leaned over, a panicked whistle in his throat, trying to catch his breath.

"Danny!" A scream, high and despairing, came across from the emergency room doors. His neighbor was running over, an EMT running behind her. Adam's mind cleared, and he saw the sad bundle under the mirror for what it was. A little kid, he's just a little kid, and I killed him. Now what was he going to do? Get arrested? Go to trial? Go to *jail*?

No. No way.

As his neighbor fell to her knees at the wreck of her son, Adam said, "Some guy...he came and...he tried to get your kid." He heaved in a breath. His eyes skittered from the EMT back to his neighbor. Her eyes were as big as tennis balls it seemed, swimming with watery blue tears. "I stopped him, but then he, he pushed your kid, and–"

To his horror, he saw the bundle of kid twitch and then one of his arms lifted, swaying. Shit, oh shit, the kid was alive...he would tell them the truth, the kid would tell everyone that Adam had kicked him and then...

His neighbor looked down, smiling in relief. "Danny! You're okay, oh baby, oh my baby, mamma's here, honey, and everything–" The kid reached both arms up as if for a hug, and she raised him to her, to her neck, and then she must have seen the eyes and the tongue, and a shadow passed across her face. It was too late...the kid's mouth was on her neck, tearing. A great gout of blood welled out around his questing mouth. Her eyes shifted to Adam's in mild shock, and then they rolled up to show only the whites. The EMT said, "What the *fuck*?" and leaned forward to try and get his hands on the kid's head. The kid turned, snake-quick, and the EMT's hand was in his mouth. The EMT screamed in mingled shock and pain. Adam's neighbor fell over backward, blood jetting from her throat, raining down on the EMT and the feasting boy.

Adam ran.

~ ~ ~

Adam clicked off the power on the walkie-talkie.

The despairing screams went on behind him.

Mohammed was the first time Adam had publicly and forcefully overrode Steve in a decision, and now this had happened. Not good.

Mohammed was thirteen and the third youngest person in the group of survivors. He was here with his aunt; she had saved him. Very few children had made it and although everyone knew why, it was rarely discussed. Children and the people with children had been more vulnerable at the time of the panic.

Mohammed had wanted desperately to go out on one of the scavenging runs. Two months on a boat was a long time, and he didn't consider himself to be a little kid. He thought he should be on *Big Daddy*, with the men.

Steve had said that Mohammed was too young for a scavenger trip, and he'd put a hand on Mohammed's shoulder, giving him his *Big Daddy* smile. Adam, seeing that look of certainty in Steve's eyes, the way Steve didn't even *bother* to check with him...Adam had said that Mohammed *could* go. That, in fact, he *should* go. He was hardly a kid and after all, shouldn't everyone be involved in the group's survival? Mohammed's aunt had been very uneasy, but Adam–who'd made himself over to some degree since the panic– had convinced her otherwise. He'd been very pleased when she had come around to his way of thinking. He mistook the concern in Steve's eyes for jealousy. Jealousy of Adam's position and place on the largest of the boats.

Now the kid, Mohammed, was dead. People were going to lose their confidence in his leadership abilities if he didn't do something, but how can you fix a situation like this? Can't bring the shitty kid back, now can you? No.

He'd just have to think of something else.

Chapter Five

"I should have stopped him," Steve said. His voice was equal parts anger and anguish. He was standing behind Maggie as she leaned over the survivor from the life raft, stitching the gash on his forehead. Brian and Denny sat nearby, ready to spring forward if the guy woke up struggling. Randy and Bonnie had taken Babygirl into the salon.

She looked around and then bent back to her work. "You tried."

Steve shook his head, watching the Jeep that careened along the shoreline. Two people were in the front seat. Only one in the back. They were too far away for Steve to see the expressions of the Jeep's occupants, but he read fear and despair into them anyway.

"I could have tried harder."

"It isn't your responsibility…Mohammed wasn't your responsibility. His aunt let him go. Not you."

Steve's hands balled into fists at his sides. Maggie, sensing his tension, glanced toward shore. Then she looked back down. "They'll make it. Don't worry."

She felt his movement and assumed it to be a nod. She and Steve had become close. She liked him and sensed his willingness to have things between them progress beyond friendship. But she missed her husband.

"*Big Daddy*, you have eyes on them? Over." Steve's shadow slipped over Maggie as he stepped past her to the bow.

"We're all set. Ready to roll. No worries, man. Over." Carl's voice over the walkie was calm but somehow still burly, as though his beard were a testosterone amplifier. Steve's eyes went from the racing Jeep to *Big Daddy*, which sat idle, fifty feet from the end of a long pier. The Jeep rounded a turn and shot down the pier, headed right for the water.

A shambling crowd of corpses slogged their way onto the pier behind the Jeep. Many were forced to the sides, and they tumbled down the steep shoreline and rolled into the water. Big, angry, Atlantic waves rolled them like bundled sticks, bashing them into the pylons under the pier. Some of them broke apart like poorly constructed dolls.

Others dropped off the sides and plopped into the water further down.

The Jeep reached the end of the pier and turned in a tight circle, facing the onrushing hoard. Two people in the Jeep jumped out and ran in the direction they'd just come…straight toward the advancing line of corpses.

They kneeled in unison and threw ropes over their shoulders. The pier developed a split as the section with the Jeep began to move with the waves. Big plastic barrels revealed themselves under the raft as it rocked. The third person raised his hand in an all clear to *Big Daddy*, and her monstrous diesel engine roared to life. *Big Daddy* chugged forward. She was powerful, not fast, but still fast enough to put a gap of five feet between the Jeep's raft and the crowd of dead.

The first several rows of corpses never broke off their painful, shambling run, and they dropped straight off the end of the pier, still reaching for the people on the departing raft. The crowds behind continued to push forward and more of them plopped into the ocean. They looked like the arcade game where you drop a coin down a chute and hope for a shiny cascade of quarters to reach a tipping point inside the machine, making you arcade rich.

On the deck of the ThreeBees, Steve lowered the binoculars. Part of him–the scared, despairing, *flagging* part–wanted too much to laugh at the tumble of reanimated corpses. To laugh at their flailing, their insectile stupidity. He wanted to see them as the enemy and revel as each one became a sinker, chum, fish food.

You may as well curse the rain, he thought. *May as well give a tornado the finger, or tell a tsunami to go fuck itself.*

It didn't help, and it didn't stop them.

On *Big Daddy*, a winch whined, dragging the Jeep raft close. The railing was clustered with men. Normally, they would be cheering and the people on the raft would be celebrating, hands clasped above their heads. The unpacking of each new treasure–food, water, clothing–would have been greeted with fresh cheers.

There was no sense of celebration this time.

No one counted this run as a victory.

Not after losing Mohammed.

Steve turned back to Maggie. She was laying a bandage over the guy's forehead and taping it down. She worked quickly and economically, wasting nothing.

Steve had been part of the boats for ten days before Maggie showed up. She had come through the Pine Barrens. She was bedraggled and too thin, but she led the little girl she called Baby, having found her in a trailer park near the shore. When Maggie was finally on the boat, she'd been invaluable because of her nursing skills.

It was Adam who had told her to stay on ThreeBees instead of joining the community on *Flyboy*. She preferred the smaller boat anyway, and although ThreeBees was *substantially* smaller, it still seemed to her less claustrophobic.

"Okay," she said and sat back. She stripped off the latex gloves. "Denny, would you and Brian grab a blanket? I want to get him out of the sun."

As they trotted away, she looked at Steve, bringing a hand up to shade her eyes. "Do you think we should restrict him in some way? Restrict his access to the boat?"

"Why do you say that?" Steve was surprised that she seemed to have the same mixed feelings about the survivor, especially since his own misgivings were so vague.

She shrugged, glancing at the man she'd just bandaged. His eyelids fluttered slightly. He could be coming out of his faint, or he could be faking unconsciousness. Maggie looked back at Steve, shaking her head.

She stood, and her voice dropped to a whisper. "I don't know why I say that. There's just something…" She put her hands on her hips, staring with consternation at the man she'd just stitched up.

"Off," Steve said, supplying the word she needed. She turned to him and smiled briefly.

"Off, yeah. Something just isn't quite right," she said.

Now it was Steve's turn to shrug. "Yes, I felt it, too, but I don't know how much of that is just us…I mean, nothing feels exactly right, does it?"

She nodded her head in acknowledgement and sighed. The boys were back with the blanket, and they rolled the man onto it.

"No restrictions, then?" Maggie said.

"Well, I wouldn't say that. We don't know him, but the circumstances of him being here are odd. Better to be safe than sorry, especially with…" he trailed off and nodded toward the salon doors where Babygirl stood holding Jade's hand. Baby's angelic lightness was in sharp contrast to Jade's jet-black hair and black eyes. Both were beautiful, and vulnerable.

Maggie hated that being female, being young, *made* them vulnerable.

"Can you take him to *Big Daddy*?"

"Yeah, we'll do that. It would be for the best. Let me get over there and get a bigger jet…yours are all one seaters, right?"

"We'll come with you," Denny said, standing. "Me and Brian. We'll help you keep an eye on him."

Steve laughed, not unkindly. "That's okay, Denny, we need you here, on ThreeBees. If you and Brian left, who would protect her?"

Another dig of annoyance jabbed Maggie, made worse because she knew it was true. She'd be much more fearful if she didn't have Denny and Brian on the boat. She liked that they were in the salon. Anyone coming aboard would have to go through them first, and they were young, strong, and fit.

Singer, Jade's brother, was young, too, but he didn't come across as strong and fit. He was almost as thin as his sister, with the same lithe, graceful body type. The two of them could pass for twins.

Maggie's smile was rueful. "Come on, Den, you don't really want to leave us, do you? For *Big Daddy*? I hear it smells like dirty socks over there. Besides, who would I train if you guys left?"

Maggie had been giving the two of them what she called EMT training. Denny enjoyed it and not just because it passed the time, but because it made him valuable. Denny was smart enough to see that 'valuable' would be an outstanding commodity in their new world. Just look at that guy Adam. He was a total tool, but he ran the show because he'd been able to figure out some of the things on that big boat, *Flyboy*. Now he douched it up, and everyone just said 'yes, sir' to him all the time.

Not that Denny wanted to be a tool or a douche. He just didn't want to be one of the shuffling multitudes like most of the people on *Flyboy*. When he found his parents someday, they'd be really proud of him. Especially his dad. Denny never admitted to himself that he might *not* find his parents, but his bad dreams were ones where he found them floating (inexplicably together) next to the boat. In the dream, he bent over to try and pull them into the boat, but then they reached up, their mouths opening and their eyes deadly empty, and pulled him over into the water. He'd wake shivering from that one.

Steve jet-skied off, and Denny and Brian carried the guy into the salon to wait for Steve to come back with the two-man jet. At their entrance, Jade faded back down the stairs to her stateroom, taking Babygirl with her.

Maggie stayed on deck, tidying and wiping blood from the teak boards. The guy had bled a lot. *Head wound*, she thought, *they bleed like crazy*. It had been a clean cut–surgical, almost–and straight across his forehead. He was lucky half his face hadn't folded over on itself.

"Maggie, this is Steve, you there? Over."

Maggie sat on the bench that curved around the inside of the hull and picked up the walkie-talkie. "I'm here, Steve, what's up? Over."

"Listen, Maggie, we're having some problems over here; will you guys be okay for a bit? With your passenger? Over."

"We're fine; take care of business. Over."

"Over and out."

She sighed and looked across to *Big Daddy*. *Big Daddy, what a name*, she thought, *but fitting, I guess, for its purpose*. Tugging and nudging, putting boats where they were supposed to be. Keeping them from harm. Providing.

She smiled.

A gunshot echoed across the water. Maggie recoiled in shock, almost as if she had been hit.

Someone had fired a gun on *Big Daddy*.

~ ~ ~

"*Big Daddy*...Steve, what happened? We heard a gunshot. Over." Maggie's voice warbled from the walkie-talkie on his belt, trying for calm, but Steve heard the panic that wanted to break through. He felt Maggie's panic himself, but was trying to quell it.

He stood with his hands up, looking at Sujon, Mohammed's aunt. Tears coursed down her cheeks, and her teeth were bared in rage. She held a gun in thin, trembling hands. Her entire body shook. The gun was pointed at Steve. Light smoke curled from the barrel.

Carl rolled on the deck between them, cursing and holding his leg.

"Where is Mohammed?" she said. Her voice was shaking, choked.

"Sujon, you have to put that gun down. You don't want to hurt anyone else," Steve said, but he didn't move, not yet.

"Where is he? Where is his body?"

"He was...he was left behind. Sujon, they had to leave him behind." Steve heard the despair in his voice, the guilt. They should not have had to leave Mohammed behind because Steve should have done more to stop his going.

"Who?" she asked, and her gun traced the line of men who stood behind Steve on the deck. "Who left him? Who left a little boy to be torn apart by the dead?"

A man's head fell as a sob escaped him. Sujon's gun swiveled to him as levelly as if she were a twenty-year sniper veteran. "It was you? You *left* him? You left a *child*?"

53

Steve heard the loathing in her voice. He stepped neatly between her and the man she'd targeted.

"It's not his fault, Sujon. Don't aim that gun at him. You know it isn't his fault."

"It's *your* fault," she said, her voice a shaking ruin in danger of imminent collapse. "*Your* fault." Tears coursed steadily from her red-rimmed eyes. Steve had a distant twinge of surprise that she could even see. Everything must be a blurred swirl to her.

Her hands shook, and her finger gripped and relaxed reflexively on the trigger. If he didn't do something quick, get through to her, she was going to shoot again. This time, it might not be a grazing leg wound.

"Sujon, it isn't my fault; it isn't anyone's fault. It just happened. It's terrible. No one wanted it to happen, but it did, it did happen. We're all upset about it, Sujon, but no one is responsible. No one is at fault."

Sujon blinked rapidly. Steve noted how slack her clothes lay against her skin, how dry and malnourished she looked. *We all look like that now*, he thought. *We are all like the sinkers except just not dead. Not yet.*

Abruptly, Sujon's tears stopped. "Yes. It is *someone's* fault. Someone was responsible for Mohammed." Her eyes were alight with a terrible inner fire. She stepped back three quick paces until her back was to the rail. "*I* was responsible for Mohammed," she said and turned the gun to her own face. She pulled the trigger.

The top half of her head disintegrated, blowing blood and gobbets of brain and bone into the air. Steve and everyone else nearest her were peppered in gore.

Steve had stepped forward when he'd realized her intent. But his hand closed on nothing as her body toppled over the rail and caught in the lines crisscrossing the side of *Big Daddy*. She dangled, half headless and twitching, one bare foot kicking.

Steve stared at Sujon's sandals on the deck. They were light green with sparkling faux gems on the straps. Very pretty. She'd been blown right out of them. He cocked his head at a strange patter, like rain, and realized it was her blood raining into the ocean below.

He felt his gorge rise, and he stepped forward, drawing a knife from his pocket and flinging it open. He cut Sujon's bonds in two furious swipes, nearly cutting off his own thumb in the process. Her body tumbled into the ocean below.

He turned away and stared at his men. Each set of eyes that met his were round with shock. All faces had drained of color. A few of them had bent over themselves, crying or trying not to vomit, Steve couldn't tell which.

In his despair, his eyes went to the deck of ThreeBees, which was facing the side where Sujon had shot herself. Maggie stood at the rail, utterly still. Steve raised a shaking hand to her, and she raised hers back.

What a fucking mess, he thought. *Is this our world, now? Is this our only option?*

He wiped a tickling drip from his cheek and stared at the smear of gelatinous gray matter shivering delicately on his fingers.

Yes, most likely.

~ ~ ~

"That was Sujon, wasn't it? Was that Sujon? Mohammed's aunt? She just shot herself. Didn't she? Didn't she shoot herself?" Denny's eyes were feverish.

Maggie put a hand on his arm, trying to calm him. "Yes, I'm pretty sure she did."

"Well, but why? Why would she? Why did she...I mean, it doesn't make sense. For her to...to kill herself." He dropped his head, thinking, considering.

"I think it was just too much for her," Maggie said, patting Denny's back.

Brian turned away, embarrassed but also near tears. It's strange, Maggie reflected to herself, these people who had seen so much horror in that first wave of panic are *still* not immune. None of us is immune. We've had two months of relative calm, and we're ready to pat it on its head, call it good, and assume it's here to stay.

How complacent.

How stupid.

"She just couldn't take it, Denny. She was..." Maggie trailed off, realizing she couldn't put herself in Sujon's shoes. She didn't know what it was like. She'd had no children of her own, no nieces or nephews, no one she was solely responsible for. Babygirl flitted into her mind, but Maggie pushed her aside. It wasn't the same thing. *Maggie* was not solely responsible for Babygirl, *everyone* on ThreeBees held a responsibility to the child.

Not just me, Maggie thought, and the thought was touched by a tinge of resentment. Then she pushed that aside, too.

"I think we should probably plan on having our visitor stay the night," she said and turned away from the railing, away from her view of *Big Daddy*. "I think they're going to be distracted over there for a while."

Denny stayed at the rail, his head down. Maggie thought about going back to talk to him, comfort him some more. But this was life now, she decided, and he'd just have to face up to it. He was old enough. He was an adult.

There had been a furious burst of chatter over the walkie-talkies as the people on *Flyboy* wanted to know what had happened. Maggie had ascertained that the shot fired had mostly just grazed Carl's leg, so she wouldn't be needed. There were questions of retrieving Sujon's body, but most people took a 'what for?' attitude on that. They'd only end up burying her at sea anyway, right? Let her rest, poor thing. At least she wouldn't reanimate, not with half her head gone.

Severe damage to the brain, it turned out, was the key to dropping the walking dead.

Adam had addressed and readdressed Steve several times over the walkie-talkie, the tone and pitch of his voice escalating through the octaves until he'd seemed to realize that Steve wasn't answering the phone, so to speak. There had been no more from Adam, but Maggie found the silence ominous.

Adam had, in Denny's words, 'a kink in his dick' for Steve.

Thinking of the term now, Maggie smiled, but it was brief and unhappy. She surveyed the deck in the fading light. All cleaned up. She looked back to *Big Daddy*, almost expecting (hoping?) to see Steve at the railing, but he wasn't there. No one was.

Everything seemed too quiet as the darkness fell.

Chapter Six

Maggie eased herself into the double bed next to Babygirl. Baby's lips had gone slack around her thumb, and she was covered in a light sweat. Maggie brushed a hand over the girl's forehead and marveled that her skin could be so cool despite the uncomfortable heat in the stuffy cabin.

Maggie thought she was probably going to have a hard time falling asleep. When she closed her eyes, she saw Sujon tumbling from the railing, revealing Steve where he stood, knife in hand. Funny how no sound accompanied this image, only the light breathing of the girl next to her and the ubiquitous whap, whap of waves against the hull. ThreeBees rocked. Maggie felt consciousness waning.

Sujon fell again.

A small gasp escaped Maggie's lips, and her eyes fluttered halfway open before shutting more firmly. She slid into sleep, watching Sujon fall, watching Steve revealed, his face a mask of revulsion, shock, and grief.

Sujon fell again. Maggie felt the sensation in her stomach, felt herself falling through blank space, and she jerked without waking.

Above her, the boards creaked as someone walked through the galley.

Maggie slept.

~ ~ ~

"Denny is gone. Maggie? Denny is gone." Hands shook her.

Joe? was her first, semi-coherent thought. *Stop shaking me, hon, I'm up.*

It wasn't Joe, Joe was dead. Her eyes opened. Bonnie sat on the edge of the bed, and everything had tilted toward her weight. Maggie felt herself being pulled implacably to her as if Bonnie exerted her own weird gravity.

Bonnie shook her again. "Maggie? Denny is gone."

"Gone?" Maggie sat up, trying to clear her muzzy head. "Denny?"

"Yes, Maggie, like I told you. Denny is gone. Are you awake now?" Bonnie leaned over to peer into Maggie's sleep-puffy face, and Maggie felt the force of her pull increase. She pushed herself further back to keep from toppling onto Bonnie.

"Yeah, I'm awake. I am." She scrubbed her hands over her face and looked automatically to her side for Babygirl. She wasn't there. A tendril of unease whispered around her heart. "Where's Babygirl?"

"She's up on deck with Randy and she's fine. Look at you, mama bear!" Bonnie chuckled but then remembered her original business. "Denny is gone."

"Well, geez, Bonnie, he's probably just over on *Big Daddy*. You know how he's always crabbing about being stuck over here with us. Back up, okay? You're blocking the whole damn room." The space in the cabins was extremely limited. Maggie wouldn't be able to get out of the bed until Bonnie retreated almost all the way to the door.

Bonnie surveyed Maggie one more time, her face grave, almost watchful. It didn't sit well on her happy, blowsy features. She stood and backed to the doorway.

"He's not on *Big Daddy*. Randy already radioed them," she said. "We're old, Maggie, not stupid." She exited the room.

Maggie sat for a moment longer, nonplussed. *Whatever Bonnie's problem was, she could go take it out on someone else*, she thought. *I'm not the boat's whipping boy, am I?* But even as she thought it, she cringed. None of them were, and so none of them should act like it, but that doesn't stop any of us from being human, does it?

She sighed and stretched her way out of the bed. Then her thoughts went to Steve. Would he come for their visitor today? She quelled the small thrill of anticipation in her lower stomach and chided herself for her fickle grief.

Joe deserved more than two months of mourning.

She went on deck, and Babygirl ran to her, wrapping her arms around Maggie's legs. She looked up, and her blue eyes held a scrim of worry. "Denny is gone," she said. "We can't find him."

Maggie put a hand on Babygirl's head and glanced automatically over the side. Both jets were still tied up. Both rowboats were tethered neatly at the back of the ThreeBees.

Randy was sitting on the deck bench and the survivor sat on a deck chair, his eyes closed and face to the sun. Brian moved back and forth in the galley, and Bonnie was in the salon, tidying the boys' beds as she did every morning. The 'boys', as she called them, were the perfect age to be substitute sons and for her to be their substitute mom.

Bully for her, Maggie thought, feeling that uncomfortable itch of pique run through her again. What was wrong with her today? Why was she being so mean?

Babygirl's small hand curled into hers and squeezed, but it was impatient, not reassuring. She seemed to be telling Maggie to forget about nonsense and focus on the important things.

"Hi, Maggie."

Maggie was startled and then realized the voice was that of the survivor. He had opened his eyes to slits and surveyed her from his half-reclined position. His one leg was crossed over the other at the ankle. She could see now that his hair was an ashy, almost mousy, blond.

She nodded in his direction. "You know my name, so what's yours?"

He merely closed his eyes and leaned his head the rest of the way back. A small, tight grin surfaced on his features.

"His name is John," Randy said and leaned forward to pat the man's knee. "John Smith, isn't that funny? You hear all the time how common it is, but you never meet one! Now we have one here, in the flesh!" He grinned at Maggie, inviting her to share in the humor.

Maggie wasn't humored. She found the man to be creepy in some way she couldn't put her finger on. Maybe it was the bruising around his eyes and forehead that was so off-putting, but face it, she'd seen worse. She shifted her attention to Randy.

"Bonnie said Denny's gone? And you already checked with *Big Daddy*?"

"Yes and yes. I'm kind of worried, to tell you the truth. Where would he have gone?" He flung an arm out to indicate the expanse of ocean around them.

Maggie shook her head. "Maybe someone came and got him from *Flyboy*. Like you said…where else could he be?"

Inside the boat, a thin, tremulous cry arose. Maggie tilted her head, confused. It sounded almost like a teakettle or something mechanical. Then she realized what it was: Jade was screaming.

Randy and Maggie looked at each other, startled, and Randy was the first to act. He jumped up and raced into the salon. Maggie was behind him but glanced back once at John Smith…he sat still as stone, unconcerned, and the small grin had not left his features.

They followed Jade's tremulous cry toward the front of the boat (*Aft? Or fore? What's it called?* Maggie asked herself distractedly), and they pounded up the short flight of stairs to the cockpit. No one ever went up there. No reason to, really, since it had been decided by the group that they would stay at anchor and collect survivors until they figured out how to pilot *Flyboy* and head south.

Randy nearly knocked Jade over in his haste. She stood just inside the doorway, hands clasped under her breasts like an opera singer. Her mouth was an almost perfect 'o' as she screamed that one, unwavering note.

Denny was in the main captain's chair. His face was covered with thick plastic, taped fast to his neck with duct tape. Behind the plastic, his eyes had bulged nearly from their sockets, and the whites had turned a shiny red. His tongue had swelled, and it jutted from between his lips. Vomit had congealed at the bottom of the bag all around his neck. Traces of bright red blood threaded the vomit, and a foamy pink layer floated on it. Maggie nearly gagged at the smell in the tight cockpit. Her nostrils were assaulted by the fetid stink of feces. He had most likely lost control of his bowels at the end.

Randy put a shaking hand on Jade's shoulder and her scream cut off. She looked at Randy, her beautiful black eyes consuming her face.

"I wanted somewhere to read in private, that's all…"

Her eyes rolled up to whites. Randy caught her as she fell forward.

"I'm going to put her in the salon," he said, puffing. The girl could not weigh much, but she was still too heavy for him. He turned and Singer, Jade's brother, was already there. His eyes widened in alarm.

"Is she—"

"She's okay, she just fainted," Randy said. "Can you take her? Put her in her room?"

Singer nodded, stepping up and taking her from Randy's arms.

"Wait," Maggie said and reached past Randy. She pinched Jade's wrist in her fingers. She looked up for a brief second and then nodded. "She's okay. Strong heartbeat. She'll come around in no time."

Obligingly, Jade moaned, and her eyelids fluttered. Maggie smiled reassurance to Singer, and he left with his sister already beginning to wake.

Maggie glanced at Randy and then reached a hand to Denny. She knew he was gone, she was positive…but she had to check. She placed her fingers at his throat, just under the tape and pressed. No pulse.

He was gone. Long gone, by the stiffness of his skin. She wasn't a coroner, but she knew that rigor started setting in after three hours. The only thing she didn't know was how far along he was. Not that it mattered.

"Dead?" Randy said behind her, and she nodded. He cleared his throat. "Killed himself." It was halfway between a statement and a question. Maggie shrugged.

"I guess so, yeah, but it's so…Jesus, it's so brutal."

"Randy?" Bonnie's voice floated tremulously up the stairs.

"Stay down there, Bonnie. Don't come up here," Randy said.

"Bonnie, who has Babygirl?" Maggie asked.

"She's fine. She's right here next to me. Why was Jade screaming? Did you find Denny? Is Denny okay?"

"No, honey bunny, he's not," Randy said, surprising Maggie with his honesty. "Go tell Brian to call Steve. See if he can get a few guys together and come over here. Keep Brian out of here, too, Bonnie, okay?"

"Yes, Randy," Bonnie said, and then there was silence.

Maggie stared helplessly at Randy. He looked older today than he had yesterday. He looked older than he'd looked ten minutes ago on the bright, sun-washed deck. She wondered if her face was just as shocked, just as haggard.

She looked back at Denny, and her stomach somersaulted, forcing hot bile into her throat. She grimaced over the acid taste of it.

Most likely it was, yeah, she thought. More likely than not.

~ ~ ~

Steve put a hand to Denny's neck then looked apologetically at Maggie. "I just have to check for myself, okay?"

She nodded, but it was stiff, perfunctory. She crossed her arms over her chest. The movement was not lost on Steve. He sighed.

"I'm sorry," he said. "I just get used to doing things a certain way. I double-check everything. Forgive me?"

"You don't have to apologize, I'm just…I'm just kind of in a little bit of shock myself. I'm not seeing things right. What are we going to do?"

Steve shook his head and shrugged. "Burial at sea. What else is there to do?" He glanced back at Denny's unintentionally leering face. Steve's eyebrows drew together. "Look at the plastic, Maggie," he said. She looked and then looked at Steve.

"Yeah?" she asked.

"It's not ripped...not torn at all. Is it possible to kill yourself by suffocation? Wouldn't you fight at the end? Even involuntarily?"

Maggie nodded, thinking. "Yeah, it would be...well, but unless he took drugs, too. We've got lots of sleeping pills on the boat. He could have taken something...it would explain the vomit."

Steve glanced around the tight bridge. "Where's the pill bottle?"

"Maybe he threw it overboard. Who knows?" She felt herself getting angry again. "Who cares? He did it to himself, and that's all that matters." She swallowed against the tears tightening her throat. She was remembering her conversation with Denny the night before when she'd come up so woefully short in the comfort department. If you spun it a certain way, hadn't she almost *advocated* suicide as a way out? Maybe. Anyway, maybe that's how Denny had taken it.

Steve moved toward her, but then the walkie-talkie at Maggie's hip crackled to life.

"ThreeBees, what's going on over there? Over."

Adam.

Maggie unhitched the walkie and threw Steve a despairing glance. "Hi, Adam, it's Maggie. We do have a problem, but I'm not going to go into it over an open line. Over."

Maggie stared at the speaker of the walkie-talkie, and she could almost feel the annoyance coming from Adam on *Flyboy*.

"Steve's there?" Adam's voice was just shy of a hiss.

Maggie waited, wiping the sweat from under her eyes. Then she realized he was too perturbed to remember walkie protocol. He'd forgotten his 'over.'

"Yes, he's here with me. Over."

"Tell him to report to me on *Flyboy*." The walkie went blank for a split second, and then Adam's voice snapped through the speaker. "Immediately."

Blank line.

Maggie glanced up at Steve. He stood very close. A small thrill of butterflies coursed rapidly through her lower stomach, and she stepped back, confused and angry with herself.

He stared at her intently and then took her upper arms in his hands. "Maggie…" he said. His voice was low, bordering on rough.

She stepped back again. "You better go."

Steve's hands dropped from her arms. She could still feel the heat where he'd gripped her, as though he'd burned some trace of himself into her.

He studied her for a moment more. Then he glanced at Denny. "I'll be back in a half hour at the most. I'll help you with him then." He turned back to Maggie. "Keep an eye on your passenger, okay? Keep Brian and Randy near him. I'll send someone from *Big Daddy* if you think–"

Maggie had a flash of impatience at the mention of an enforcer– a babysitter, really–being assigned to them. "Why?" she asked, even though she'd felt it herself…something was off about that guy, but murdering off? No. No way.

"I just don't trust him."

Just then, Jade's thin, teakettle whistle of a scream wound up the stairs and onto the bridge.

Maggie turned in alarm.

What now?

~ ~ ~

"She was old, Jade. In her eighties? At least that." Maggie rubbed Jade's thin back as the girl huddled over herself, crying. They were both crammed in the stateroom Jade shared with Mrs. Allen.

Mrs. Allen was dead.

"I was resting, listening to her breathe. It helped to calm me. But then…" Jade had an odd way of speaking, almost foreign in her intonation, but with no true accent. She had told Maggie this same thing three times already. Maggie looked back at Bonnie standing in the doorway. Babygirl peeked out from behind her, and Bonnie was absently trying to keep her hand over Babygirl's eyes.

"Then she stopped breathing," Jade continued. "I couldn't wake her."

Maggie patted Jade's back, at a loss for what else to do. Jade must be at least in her twenties; she shouldn't be taking this so hard. She'd only known Mrs. Allen for two months, just under. How could she have so much grief?

"She lived a long time, Jade. I'm sure she had a good life, lots of good times and family and friends." Maggie shrugged and looked at Bonnie with a 'help me out, here' expression.

"Jade," Bonnie said, her voice slightly sharp, commanding.

Jade looked up, wiping the tears from her cheeks.

"It's better for her; you know it is. She was an old lady, vulnerable and not fitted to…to what we're going through. Be happy for her that she's out."

Maggie was shocked that Bonnie could be so blunt, and she expected a fresh wave of hysteria from Jade, but Jade sat straighter. "Yes, you are right, of course. It was hard on her, being on this boat. Everything she knew was gone." Jade sighed. "It is better for her, I know, but I will miss her."

"I know you will, sweetie," Bonnie said and gave Jade a warm smile. "We all will."

Maggie stood, glad to have it settled. "We'll get her…buried…have a nice ceremony of some kind, maybe, and then–"

"Not at sea," Jade said, her voice steely.

"Well, but, Jade, how else? We can't bury her on land," Maggie said. "You know that."

"She hated this boat! She was terrified of the ocean! Why do you think she never came out of this cramped room?" Jade's voice lowered with vehemence. "She told me many times how much she hated being surrounded by the water. She was terrified of everything in it. Now you want to throw her in there like…like a piece of trash. You want her to be pissed on when the men piss off the side of the boat? Is that right for an old woman who…who only wanted…to live out her life with…family and grandchildren…but ended up…" Jade's sobs wrenched Maggie's heart.

Singer pushed past Bonnie. "We'll bury her on the land, Jade, of course we will." His eyes raked Maggie and Bonnie as he pulled his sister's head to his shoulder. "Do not worry, dear sister."

Jade hung on her brother, the sobs wracking her thin body. Maggie shuffled past them to the doorway.

"Singer, you know we can't," Maggie said.

He curled his sister into his arms and said: "Yes. We will."

~ ~ ~

"This is ridiculous," Maggie said. She and Steve stood on the deck of ThreeBees, watching as Singer and Brian brought Mrs. Allen's body up from her room. She was wrapped in two sheets, and to Maggie, the rolled form resembled a large white maggot.

Steve glanced at her, eyebrows raised. "I agree, but I can't let Singer go alone, and there's no way to stop him. I'm not the police, you know?"

"We should have just taken her body and given her a ceremony and then..." Maggie trailed off.

"And dumped her in the ocean? With Jade screaming bloody murder and Singer fighting us every step of the way? You *really* think that would have been better?"

Maggie felt stung. "Better than risking more lives, yes!"

But she could picture the scene as Steve described it, and even if they did just dump that poor old lady overboard, then what? What would Singer and Jade do and how would they feel?

This isn't a dictatorship; it's a boat full of random survivors, Maggie thought, missing her unintentional pun. There was no policy, no procedure to follow. "We're going to do that to Denny...put him in the ocean...why don't you carry him to land, then, too?" She was still angry, but not sure at who.

Steve's jaw tightened. "Because no one is asking us to."

Maggie sighed, deflated and a little bit ashamed of herself. It wasn't Steve's fault...no one person was deciding what was best for them all.

Adam crossed her mind at that thought...he was the closest thing they had to a leader. No one on ThreeBees or *Big Daddy* had informed him of their decision regarding the disposition of Mrs. Allen's remains. Partly because it seemed a somewhat private matter, but also because–Maggie had to admit to herself–the people on *Flyboy* had become superior under Adam's watch. As if they truly believed themselves at least slightly more important than the people on the other boats.

She glanced across to *Flyboy*. There were lights on over there, too many. They were getting lax with resources. Why not? When you always had a ready supply that had been provided to you without any personal risk, it held a lot less value.

ThreeBees was intentionally dark.

"I wish we had Carl here," Steve said, but the big pirate was still nursing the gunshot wound on his leg. Steve had accepted Singer's demand that Mrs. Allen be buried on land, but only on the condition that he–Steve–dictate the scope and boundaries of the mission.

His first decision was that Jade was not allowed to come with them. It would be himself, Dave, Singer, and Brian. The less people, the better, but Jade had insisted she go, and Singer had backed her on it. Steve told them they were being ridiculously and dangerously short-sighted, but they wouldn't budge. Jade was going with them.

Steve had relented, but now, seeing Jade on the deck, a slip of a shadow amongst the other shadows, he had another uneasy twinge.

"Jade," he said, his voice calm, "are you sure you want to do this? Go with us? You could say goodbye to her now. Not put yourself at risk."

She looked at him, her eyes glittering eerily in the dark. "We are all at risk, all the time."

Steve nodded and then turned to watch as Singer and Brian lifted Mrs. Allen's body down into the rowboat. They would take both rowboats, using the small electric motors until they were close enough to paddle. Silent and dark, they should be able to get in and out without alerting any of the walking dead.

Or so Steve hoped.

He turned to Maggie. "Wish me luck."

Her face was full of an emotion that Steve didn't know how to interpret. "Good luck," she said, and then faded back into the doorway to the salon. Steve turned to Dave.

"Giddy up," Dave said, his face a grave mask.

"Yeah, let's go. I want to be in and out before dawn." Steve looked at his watch. "We've got no more than four hours, but we need to keep it to three to be extra safe."

"Shallow grave, then," Dave said, leaning in and whispering, a strange grin on his face. He raised his eyebrows comically high and it perfectly complemented the black humor of his comment.

Steve's laugh was a startled snort. He glanced back to the salon doorway, embarrassed, but Maggie was gone.

"Come on, dumdum, let's get this show on the road," Steve said.

He and Dave would take the smaller rowboat and the lead. The other three–Singer, Brain, and Jade–would take the larger rowboat with the body and the shovels.

They skimmed across the black water, engines humming. Steve scanned the shoreline. Everything looked quiet. They would tie up at the same shallow pier that had held the Jeep raft and go inland from there. Steve wondered briefly if Jade would consent to burying Mrs. Allen right on the beach, but knew she wouldn't. She'd lost all perspective.

Or maybe *I* have, Steve thought, feeling unnerved. Maybe it *is* important to bury the dead and I've just forgotten why.

He leaned lower and cranked the engine another notch.

Fifty yards from the pier, they cut the engines, rowed the rest of the way in and tied up. The water was rougher near the pier, tossing the small boats. They got the body up onto the pier. Brian was about to toss the shovels up, and Steve stayed him with an outstretched hand. He shook his head at Brian. "No sound," he breathed. Then he looked around at everyone assembled. "No sound, follow my lead, and don't separate," he said, meeting the eyes of each person. "If we do get separated, come back here, try not to lead the walkers back with you, wait with the boat. If the boats are gone, hide, use your walkie-talkie–don't forget that you have to switch it on–a jet ski will come for you. Don't jump in the water under any circumstances. You know what's down there."

They all nodded.

"Okay, here we go," he whispered.

They turned and began trotting down the pier, Steve leading, Brian and Dave next with Mrs. Allen between them, Singer behind them with the shovels, and Jade bringing up the rear.

They got to the place where the pier disappeared into the sand, and they stopped, crouching and watchful. There was a fifty-foot stretch of beach glowing in the moonlight, edged by a two-lane highway. On the far side, a small motel office sat surrounded by miniature log cabins that served as the guest's rooms. Behind the motel and cabins was the expanse of woods known as the Pine Barrens.

The woods were dark with pine trees, mountain laurel, blueberry bushes, and scraggly pin oaks. Nothing stirred; even the wind off the ocean had trouble penetrating the dense boughs of the pines and died at the edge of the forest.

Steve knew that the combination of dirt and sand of the Pine Barrens floor would be ideally suited to a quick internment. Plus, there were fewer walking dead in the woods. Or at least that had been the case when he'd arrived. Amelia flirted into his mind...as she had been before everything and then as she had been that last morning.

He pushed the memories aside and scanned the cabins. They were dark blobs against the darker forest, and nothing moved there. Colorful mounds littered the beach and the area around the cabins–ten or twelve that Steve could see–the survivors of the flu who had not survived the rampaging dead.

Steve didn't know why some people (most) got back up after dying and others never did. He also didn't know why the handful of survivors that had made it to the boats had never gotten the flu. They had to be immune. Did that mean they were safe from reanimation? Like the sad bundles around them?

Would he rather reanimate or rot?

He pushed all extraneous thoughts from his mind and concentrated on the task at hand: get the old lady buried, and get the rest of his people safely back to the boats. He double-checked that the walkie on his hip was powered off–it would be a disaster if someone (Adam) radioed him while they were on land. The reanimated corpses seemed to have pretty good hearing.

He stood and started across the beach, the others following behind. Brian was puffing under Mrs. Allen's weight, and Steve heard each hiss and gasp like a shout. When they reached the road, he turned to Brian and pointed to his own chest and then to the wrapped body: *do you want me to take your side?*

Brian shook his head, but lowered his eyes. Sweat had broken out across his forehead. He was still panting. Steve tapped his shoulder, and he looked up. Steve put a finger to his own lips. Brian nodded and took a deep breath. He gave Steve a thumbs up.

They trotted lightly across the highway and skirted the motel's gravel parking lot. The cabins stood dark and ominous, the twin windows of each looking like blank, accusatory eyes. Steve paused between two of the units and waited for the group to reform. There were too many of them. It was too unruly, too chaotic. He passed a nervous hand over his eyes. Then he took a breath and slipped from between the cabins and into the woods.

The forest floor was soft and forgiving, a layer of pine needles covered the sandy soil, making their passage noiseless. Steve led them about fifty feet in and stopped when he found a small clearing. There would be roots, because pines sent their roots wide, not deep, but they should be able to dig a good grave.

Singer, Jade, and Brian watched the woods on all sides, searching for movement while Dave and Steve grabbed the shovels and went to work. Mrs. Allen glowed whitely, like a pill-shaped apparition. Steve tore his eyes away from her and concentrated on digging…looking at her body was creeping him out.

They dug the grave long and thin and within a half hour had dug down four feet. Steve tapped Jade's shoulder and armed sweat from his eyes as she turned to inspect it. Steve raised his eyebrows at her: *Good?*

She nodded, and he saw the glitter of tears in her eyes, the thankfulness. She put a light hand on his arm. She nodded again.

Brian and Singer lifted the body into the grave, but Jade made a furious, rotating gesture with her hand. Mrs. Allen's face was in the dirt. They hastily turned her, and a small sob escaped Jade's lips. The front of the body was covered in black soil and pale sand.

Jade kneeled at the edge, trying to brush away the dirt, and then Steve put a hand on her shoulder and squeezed. *Doesn't matter, please hurry.*

Jade sat back, and her lips moved in a silent prayer. Then she leaned over, placed a small object on the corpse, and stood, turning away with her face in her hands.

Dave shrugged at Steve: *Is that it?* Steve shrugged back and nodded. *Guess so, yeah.*

They advanced to begin filling the grave, but first, Steve leaned over to look in. A small picture frame sat at the level of Mrs. Allen's bosom. Three beautiful, tow-headed children were held in the frame. Her grandchildren. Steve felt a wave of black depression sweep over and into him, like cold cement filling every inch of his body. Is this what it had come to? This poor old lady buried in the woods with a picture of her (most likely) dead grandchildren? What were they doing? Why didn't they all just lie down and die?

He drove his shovel furiously into the mound of carefully piled dirt and threw it down into the grave. He turned for another shovelful and felt his throat close with an ache of unshed tears.

He hadn't been able to bury Amelia. He had...at the end...when she wouldn't stop coming at him...he had...

Chunk! Another shovelful of dirt. He was working like a dervish, the dirt flying in an arc as he turned with each load. He didn't notice the look of concern in Jade's eyes, the pity. He didn't see Dave lowering his head in embarrassed silence.

He saw Amelia. Amelia of the beautiful, honey-colored hair. Her adorable bare feet now covered in swampy black mud. She was on her stomach, but her head was turned around, facing him from between her shoulder blades. Her head twitched, and her mouth worked, opening and closing, but the rest of her was still. Her eyes rolled, searching for him, accusing and alive but still dead. Dead and alive. Then he had...in his panic and disgust he had...

A hand on his back made him jump, and he dropped the shovel. Jade was looking at him; they all were. He ran his hand over his eyes and shook his head. "I'm sorry," he whispered. "Sorry about that."

Dave reached forward and thumped him on the shoulder; Jade squeezed his hand in hers.

"Let's go," Steve said. "Let's get back to the boats."

They were almost to the beach when it happened.

They had moved quickly back through the woods, making better time on the way out because they weren't burdened with a body. Steve was in the lead, Dave behind him and then Brian. Singer and Jade ran side by side, holding hands like young children.

They neared the edge of the woods, and Steve felt a rise in his spirits: he could see the pier from here. They were almost home free. He slowed and signaled for everyone to stop as he searched the area around the cabins, looking for signs of undead movement. Singer squatted next to him.

"Let's go. What are we waiting for?" Singer whispered, his voice laced with impatience. He, too, had felt a hopeful lift at the sight of the pier, but it was still tinged with electrifying anxiety. On the way in, he'd been bolstered by the fact that they were doing the right thing, the thing that Jade wanted, but now that it was done...he was chafing at the possible foolishness of the act. He wanted everyone to get back safely.

Steve hushed him with a gesture, his eyes never leaving the cabins. They were squat and spooky, surrounded with black shadows that could have concealed anything. Anything at all.

The five of them were crouched in a rough line, using the scrub and blueberry bushes for cover, watching the cabins. No movement; no sound except the eternal shushing of the waves lapping the shoreline.

Singer shifted again, bringing one knee up, and leaned to put a hand on Steve's shoulder. "There's nothing there," he whispered. "Come on, let's–" A sharp, searing pain burned into his calf.

Reflexively, Singer threw himself forward into the clearing, bellowing. Steve looked back just in time to see the black pine snake that Singer must have kneeled or stepped on slide away in the other direction.

It was gone in a second.

Singer rolled, still bellowing, grabbing for his calf, and Jade jumped up. "Singer!" Her voice rang out, a panicked and breaking bell, as she watched her brother writhe in pain.

Steve threw himself toward Singer.

"Listen to me," he whispered, trying to grab Singer's terrified face in his hands. "It was a snake, just a snake, please calm down, it was just–"

Behind him, Jade continued to scream. Dave grabbed her from behind, putting a hand over her mouth as his eyes went wildly to the cabins. She panicked and bit his hand. He jumped back, hissing, and Jade stumbled away from him, panting in harsh little bursts.

A low, sighing moan froze them all into stasis. The sound could almost have been the wind, passing through tree branches, but they all knew better. They'd all heard that sound, so distinctly and disturbingly human, and yet not…it was the sound of the living dead.

Brian, who had been the last to react to Singer's screams, stood in the scrub and bushes, frozen with shock. Then he saw a shadow that seemed to coalesce from the deeper shadow between the two closest cabins…the undead had found them.

"Guys…guys, it's…" His voice was breathy, shaking. "It's one of them…a sinker." He pointed, unable to take his eyes from the shuffling horror that had now come fully into the moonlight of the clearing.

It was, or had been, a kid…maybe six or seven. A little boy in footie pajamas detailed with red, cartoon cars. One of his arms was gone, but the shoulder under the flannel bunched and rotated in imitation of the arm that had risen, grasping. The boy's face was gray and beginning to peel at his hairline.

One of its eyes was gone.

Its mouth hung open, and the curious breath of unlife coursed over its spongy, rotting vocal chords. It was less than twenty feet from Singer and Steve.

Steve saw the boy and stood, pulling Singer with him. "Get to the boats," he said, his voice a harsh whisper, and shoved Singer in the direction of the beach.

Singer only turned in a half circle, favoring his leg, and saw the undead boy. He felt a crazy free fall of fear in his stomach and searched automatically for his sister. She stood next to Dave. They both stared at the boy, and her hands were laced over her mouth. Her eyes were large and swimming with panicked tears.

Brian was still standing a few feet back in the woods.

Another shadow lurched to life from between the cabins.

Then another.

Now there were three corpses between them and the beach.

Now five.

Steve felt the cold cloak of decision-making descend, washing away the panic. He turned to the others, his voice a harsh and commanding whisper sawing through the dark.

"Run!"

That broke everyone's paralysis. They all ran, dodging the sludgily moving dead, whose numbers were growing at an alarming rate. Steve broke left, and Dave followed while Singer and Jade ran shoulder to shoulder between another set of cabins with Brian not far behind.

The sighing moan became louder, a chorus of rot and ruin, of despair so great that it existed even without the consciousness of those souls in despair. They sighed with both hunger and longing, some deep primal need encouraging them to possess what they now lacked.

At least half were children.

The children and caretakers of children had not fared well in the plague that had decimated the world.

They were past the cabins and across the highway, and Steve felt a triumphant lift that pumped his legs harder. They were going to make it.

He pounded down the pier, counting the footfalls behind him: Dave, Jade, Singer, Brian...they were all going to make it.

The boats bobbed complacently at their tethers. Steve stopped ten feet short, ushering everyone past him with a wave of his arm, and looked back the way they had come. The first of the walking dead were just now shuffling onto the pier. They had time. Enough. He turned in time to see Dave and Brian lifting Jade into the larger boat.

Dave jumped into the smaller boat and stationed himself at the oars while Brian did the same in the larger boat. Jade had gone to the rear, her hand on the engine, ready to push the button that would bring it to life.

Singer looked back at Steve. "Come on!" he said and moved forward. He missed his footing and stepped between the pier and the edge of the boat and sank, hitting his chin on the way down.

Steve stared in shock at the place Singer had been a split second before. He'd gone down so fast; it was like an optical illusion, a pratfall.

Then Jade's scream sliced into his shocked consciousness, and he was moving, throwing himself belly down on the pier, reaching down.

Singer's head broke the water, and he reached for Steve's hand, but in his panic, he missed his grip and flailed wildly.

"Singer, take my hand!" Steve said, aware of the rowboat rocking furiously as Brian advanced to help. Singer's panicked waving finally put his arm within Steve's grasp, and Steve pulled, dragging Singer from the water. Brian pulled too, and Singer slid like a leaded eel into the rowboat.

Then Steve felt hands grasping greedily on his outstretched legs.

He rolled, kicking and cursing. A woman was chewing on his jeans over his heavy work boot. He kicked reflexively with his other foot, connecting with her face. It sloughed off like a thick, spongy mask, taking her nose and lips with it. She lifted her head, her face a blackish ruin, her jollily rolling eyeballs seeming to bulge from their black sockets.

Her teeth were soft, chalky ruins that crumbled and fell across Brian's leg. She bent to bite again.

Rough hands gripped Steve's shoulders, and a scream ripped its way into his throat. But it was Dave, pulling him into the safety of the rowboat.

Dave threw off the line and kicked out, his foot connecting with the wood decking, sending the rowboat skittering crazily away from the pier. The woman that had been gnawing at Steve's leg tumbled head first into the water, and then three more corpses behind her also went in, becoming sinkers.

Steve grabbed the oars and pulled, taking them further from the pier. He glanced behind him and saw the boat with Singer, Jade, and Brian cruising steadily in the direction of ThreeBees.

Good. They had made it.

He glanced back at Dave, and Dave was huddled over himself, arms crossed over his stomach. He was moaning.

"Dave, are you bit? Did they bite you?" Steve's arms went slack on the oars. "Dave?" he said. "Hey, man…are you…are you bit?" His voice had dropped, chilled and aching.

Dave glanced up, grimacing. "No, they didn't bite me. You fucking kicked me in the nuts, you asshole. I think I'm gonna fucking puke." He moaned again.

Steve was shocked to feel laughter bubbling up from his stomach, and he laughed despite himself. It was a short bark of amusement, and then he threw a hand over his mouth.

Dave looked up again, his face sour. "You sound like a goddamned seal, you know that?"

They both broke up laughing. It carried across the water to the ThreeBees, and at the railing, Maggie tilted her head in confusion.

Across the water, at the end of the pier, the undead did the same.

Chapter Seven

Jade sat on the deck bench of ThreeBees, shivering.

Maggie draped a sweatshirt over Jade's shoulders and took her chin in her hand. She tilted Jade's face up and looked into her eyes.

"Do you feel like you're going to faint? Do you feel lightheaded?" Maggie's voice was calm but detached as she felt for Jade's pulse.

Jade shook her head 'no', and a tentative smile trembled on her lips. "I'm all right. We are all…all okay." Tears spilled over her lids. "It was not right of me to…to insist on burying Mrs. Allen. I apologize." Her voice had dwindled to a sad whisper, and she cast her eyes down.

Maggie, who agreed with the girl that she shouldn't have insisted on the foolish formality, merely patted her shoulder. Then she moved on to Singer. It was automatic for Maggie to get a pulse, and she did so with Singer, picking his wrist up almost absently as she looked into his eyes.

"How about you, Singer? Any dizziness?" Maggie asked and then frowned at his wrist in her hand. "Do you have low blood pressure?"

He shook his head no to both. "I'm not dizzy, but my leg hurts where I was bit by the snake."

Maggie nods. "Yes, we'll have to get that cleaned out. At least it wasn't poisonous." She placed her fingertips at his throat, palpating. "Heart murmur? History of arrhythmia?"

He shook his head no again, and Maggie frowned. She wished once again that she had at least a stethoscope. They had yet to find one on any of the scavenger missions. It would help to find this kid's heartbeat because it seemed pretty weak at his pulse points. That could be indicative of many underlying conditions, and besides, it didn't matter at the moment.

There were other things, worse things to be concerned with.

"Lie on your stomach on the bench. Let's see that bite."

Singer did as he was asked.

Maggie rolled up the leg of his thin, cotton pants and then stood abruptly. Panic flashed across her features.

Steve and Dave were sitting in deck chairs nearby, and Dave was still grimacing, but he was chuckling, too. Steve kept up a constant stream of jokes, partly to keep Dave distracted from his pain, but also in part because, although his own relief was immense, it was still shaky. The jokes were bolstering his spirits.

He looked up as Maggie stepped away from Singer, and the smile faded from his face.

"Maggie? What is it?"

She glanced at him and then gestured to Singer's exposed leg. Then she looked over at Jade, but Bonnie and Babygirl surrounded her like protective flanking. Maggie was glad to see it because there was no telling what was going to happen next.

Steve was next to her in an instant, his face grim as he looked at Singer's leg. Almost as though he could feel their terrified scrutiny, Singer started to sit up, but Maggie put a restraining hand on his back. "Just...lie still. Don't move, Singer, please."

Dave had caught their concern, and he hobbled over. He pulled in a breath. Singer's calf had an oval bruise, mottled from dark red to purple–a bite mark–it had to be a human bite. Dots of blood were still welling up where the skin had been broken. Further down, closer to his ankle, the ragged, two-hole snake bite had already stopped bleeding.

"What is it? What's wrong with my leg?" Singer's voice was laced with panic barely held in check.

Jade heard and looked over, her face falling. "Singer?" she said, beginning to stand.

"Jade, stay over there," Maggie said, her voice flat and commanding. Jade plopped back down. Bonnie put her arm around Jade's back.

"Is it...what it looks like?" Steve said, his voice low.

"Was he near them? I thought you said that you were the last one on the pier...how did he–"

"The water. He fell in the water. It's shallow near the pier."

"Singer," Maggie said, "when you fell in the water...did anything happen to your leg? Did you feel it get caught on anything?" Singer shook his head in violent denial, but his eyes cut back toward Steve, rolling frantically.

"No! Nothing got me! Just that snake!"

Maggie put a hand on Singer's forehead. "He's hot, and his pulse is...it's odd. Not strong."

Singer scrambled up, pulling his pant leg down with a wince. "I'm not hot. You're crazy. If I'm hot, it's because of the snake...the snake bite."

Maggie and Steve looked at each other, and their gazes were deeply troubled. If Singer had been bit by a sinker, then he might get the disease himself. If he got the disease, and died, and reanimated...it wasn't a chance they could take.

No one was one hundred percent sure how the sickness worked. The people who had made it this far *seemed* immune...but what if they weren't? What if an individual just hadn't yet been exposed?

"We have to get him off the boat," Dave said and stepped away from Singer.

Singer's face flew open in panic and fear. "I'm not leaving this boat. You can't make me."

"Singer?" Jade said. "What's wrong? What's happening?"

"You can't stay! What if...what if you–" Dave said, his voice rising.

"Singer? What are they saying?" Jade tried to rise, and Bonnie, almost instinctually, grabbed her tighter.

"You can't make me! You can't make me!" Singer chanted, his voice furious and filling with tears. "You c-can't m-make me!" His face was red.

"You can't stay here!" Dave said, and now he loomed over Singer, furious in his panic, shouting. "You might be a goddamned sinker!"

Jade, who'd been struggling in Bonnie's arms, fainted.

~ ~ ~

Jade stood forlornly at the back of ThreeBees and stared at Singer, who was tethered in the smaller rowboat, a hundred feet out. The boat had been stripped of oars and motor. Dave sat in a deck chair, and he, too, faced the rowboat. He held a shotgun across his lap. Being motorless and oarless wouldn't stop Singer if he decided to use the tethering rope to hand over hand himself back to ThreeBees.

This situation, in Dave's opinion, was barely better than the honor system. There was too much at stake to trust anyone who might be coming down with the sickness. He glanced at Jade, feeling both ashamed and angry...he wasn't the bad guy here; he didn't need her doe eyes following him around accusatorily. He shifted his gaze to *Flyboy*.

He hoped Steve wasn't getting too much shit from Adam.

~ ~ ~

"You just...went? To land? Without *notifying* anyone?" Adam's face was red, agitated. He was very aware of the people nearby who could overhear this conversation, and he very much wanted the conversation to go a certain way.

Steve sighed inwardly. He wanted to keep the peace, above all else he wanted it, but Adam made it hard. He reminded Steve of the attention-seeking fanboy students who waited, tense and alert, for any sort of misstep so they could pounce, triumphant, with their trivial corrections.

"Maggie knew where we were going. I thought if something happened, that–"

"That what? She'd *save* you? She'd *cure* everyone of the disease that we have *no firm knowledge of*?" Adam liked the tone he had adopted; he thought it sounded sharp and demanding. He didn't notice the eye-rolling that went on around him.

Steve noticed.

"No, I just meant, if something went wrong, then she could alert *Big Daddy* and–"

"*Really*? *Big Daddy*? Alert *everyone* on *Big Daddy*?" Adam looked around theatrically, raising his arms. "And what are *we*? Nothing and nobody? You don't *care* if the disease comes back to *Flyboy*?"

Steve shook his head, frustrated. "No, I didn't say that, I just meant…look, it was no big deal. We were going to bury the old lady and then be back before anyone could–"

"So you admit you did it secretly? To circumvent me?"

"What? No. You're twisting my words. Now, listen to me…" Steve stepped up close to Adam, getting right in his face. Panic flew across Adam's features. "You aren't the king. We have no king. You run your business, and I'll run mine."

"Oh, now you don't want to work together, is that it? We're not good enough for the *Big Daddy* ThreeBees crowd?"

Steve was disgusted by the shimmer of tears that appeared in Adam's eyes. "Of course we want to work together, haven't we been? We just wanted to get the old lady buried. That's all. No big conspiracy, okay?"

"No conspiracy, huh?"

"No. None."

Adam nodded, but Steve saw the nasty, triumphant gleam come into his eyes. "Then why didn't you tell us about the other dead guy?" Adam stepped forward at the confusion in Steve's eyes. Now *he* was the one in *Steve's* face. "What, *exactly*, did that guy die of, Steve? Was it anything…*catching*?" Adam's eyebrows were raised almost to the level of his slightly receding hairline. In his mind, he'd just delivered the incriminating blow…the dramatic line that puts an end to all the bullshit. He imagined everyone sitting, breath held, waiting for Steve to crumble out a confession.

To his chagrin, Steve laughed bitterly.

"I fucking hope it's not catching…he committed suicide."

People surged forward to huddle around Steve, asking about Denny, visibly shaken. Steve had no doubt that probably a quarter of these people, maybe more, had contemplated it for themselves at some point during the cruel festivities of these last two months. He remembered lying down next to Amelia in the woods, waiting and hoping for a quick death.

Adam had been moved back by the crush of people wanting to hear about Denny. He felt angry and frustrated, as though Steve had gotten the better of him in a test of wills. He felt Steve was always doing that…undermining him and trying to short-circuit his authority over *Flyboy* and the people on it.

He hadn't been the first person aboard, but he *was* the first one who was starting to figure out the complicated controls on the bridge. *Flyboy* wouldn't be much good to anyone come cold weather if she couldn't be sailed south, he'd been fond of telling everyone, patting himself on the back. No one bothered to point out that, eventually, they would have gotten the bridge figured out. Everyone was too panicked, too tired and distraught to think clearly. Most everyone had lost someone. It wasn't a time of great clarity.

Except it had been, for Adam. He'd been pretty clear-headed once he got on *Flyboy*. Calculating, even. He'd begun to shape his new society, bending the tired, sad people to his will. Most of them had been more than happy to let someone else take control, but not everyone…not Steve and a handful of men that followed him around like lovesick skunks.

That's when Adam had floated the idea of expanding to a tug…ostensibly for protection and maneuverability because they hadn't gotten *Flyboy* figured out as far as sailing her. The bridge was a complication filled with gauges and screens that no one currently aboard had enough degree of nautical experience to work. They had found her here, anchored like a small island, and here she still sat. That was okay for now as they waited to see if there were more survivors, but come cold weather, they'd need to pull anchor and sail south. Without YouTube, without the internet, learning *Flyboy* was catch as catch can.

Adam really just wanted Steve and his merry fucking men on another ship. Out of his hair and out of his plans.

He didn't want them to leave entirely. They were good protectors and good providers, and Adam considered himself way too important to make the harum-scarum land runs. Who would step in if something happened to him? These people would be done for.

When *Big Daddy* had found *Barbra's Bay Breeze* during a scouting trip, and Adam had seen how Steve looked at Maggie, he'd decided that the people already on board her should stay on board. There was nothing wrong with their accommodations, he'd pointed out...they were safe and relatively content. Why not leave things as they were?

In the back of his mind, he'd begin to imagine an armada, an entire fleet with *Flyboy* in the lead, with *himself* in the lead. It would be glorious.

He just had to make sure he stayed on top. Of everyone.

Adam waited until the crowd had dispersed and Steve was on the low platform that ran across the back of *Flyboy*, ready to mount his jet ski. Then he approached him.

"I want that mystery man, that John Smith, brought back here to *Flyboy*. I want to meet him. To determine where he should go."

Steve shifted uncomfortably. "Listen, Adam, I think we should be cautious with that guy. There's something off about him, and Maggie thinks so, too. I'm going to put him on *Big Daddy* where I can keep an eye on him."

Adam felt his impatient rage bubble up. "Oh really? *Maggie* thinks so, too? You and Maggie agree that there's something *wrong* with the guy?"

Steve opened his mouth to speak, and Adam shushed him with a brisk, chopping movement of his hand. "I don't care what you and Maggie think. You're both horrible judges of character, based on who you each associate with." Adam felt a cruel giggle wanting to rise, but he forced it down, forced his face to stay passive. Probably Steve was too dumb to get his meaning, anyway. "Bring him to *Flyboy*. Today."

~ ~ ~

"Any change?" Steve asked and waved to Singer, who sat in the distant rowboat. Singer gave him the finger and turned so that he was facing the shore, showing ThreeBees his back. Steve sighed and pulled a chair up next to Maggie's. The gun was lying next to her, just in reach. It made Steve uneasy, and he wanted to say something about it, tell her to pull it in closer, but he knew she wouldn't. He was surprised she had it near her at all. She didn't like guns.

Maggie glanced at Steve and then at Jade, who had fallen asleep on the deck bench. Jade's hands were fisted together under her chin as though she had fallen asleep praying.

"No, no change. He still seems sick, but it's hard to tell from this far away." Her tone was mildly scolding. "Are we just going to wait and see if he keels over?"

Steve sighed and shook his head. "I guess so. I don't know what else to do. With everything else going on, I just..."

At the honest despair in his voice, Maggie reached out and squeezed his hand. "It has gotten kind of eventful lately." Her tone was dry but not unsympathetic.

Dave had driven John Smith to *Flyboy* that afternoon, and while he did that, the rest of the people on ThreeBees had buried Denny at sea. All they'd done, really, was wrap him in a sheet and slide him over the side while Randy said the Lord's Prayer. Steve had been heartsick about it, and he felt cowardly, too. He'd glanced out to the rowboat at Singer–to see if he was watching–and then doing so struck him as morbid. So he turned back around.

It didn't seem right, tipping this young man's body into the ocean; it made it seem unimportant, too much like tossing garbage.

Jade had been right about that.

They'd have to think about doing things another way if (when) someone else died.

Maggie squeezed his hand again, and then she left her hand in his. "We're all struggling. No one knows what to do about anything. We just have to figure it out as we go along."

The thought depressed her. Is this what it will be now until she dies? This boat? These people? No, actually, it's going to get a lot harder. They are going to run out of fuel, they are going to run out of canned food. Eventually, they may run out of water...what then? They can't stay on the boats forever, anchored out here like small islands of sanity. It wasn't permanent; none of it was permanent.

The thought of permanence depressed her, and the thought of change scared her. For the millionth (billionth?) time, she found herself wishing for her old life back. She wanted her house, she wanted a shower, she wanted to do laundry on a bright Sunday morning…she wanted Joe. That, most of all.

She took her hand from Steve's and stood. "Take over for a minute?"

"Sure," he said, "you okay?"

She didn't answer.

He watched after her until she was out of sight in the salon and then leaned down and scooted the gun closer.

"She likes you," Jade said, startling him. Her voice floated across the deck in the gathering dark. She sat up, stretched, and looked to where her brother sat, forlorn and rocking on the late-afternoon waves. As if he sensed her gaze, he looked over his shoulder. He gave her a small wave, and she raised her hand in turn. "He's not sick. I'd know if he were."

Steve looked at her a moment more, and then his gaze returned to Singer. "It won't be too much longer before we know for sure." He didn't ask if she understood or if she was okay with any of this. He knew that she didn't and she wasn't. Would he be? If it were Amelia out there in that rowboat? If it were Maggie?

That's why someone else needed to make the decision, he thought. Loved ones are not always the best arbiters of our fate. That brought Amelia to mind again, what he had to do to her at the end. Had he been the arbiter of her fate?

So far, no one had ever recovered from being sick. Not that anyone on the boats seemed to know of, anyway. If you got sick, you died, and if you died from the sickness, then you came back to life. If you happened to die from something else–car accident, say– then you didn't come back.

It was the sickness, itself, that was the trigger for reanimation, but what was the sickness? Where had it come from? Could it have been a natural occurrence? The final pandemic which scientists and religious nuts alike had posited at one time or another?

Possibly, but it didn't ring all the way true to Steve. Especially when you added in the fact of the dead coming at least halfway back to life. That was crazy, voo-doo shit. Or maybe, weren't there frogs that did something like it, too? Essentially dead until rain hit them or something?

Steve shook his head. He didn't know and felt pretty sure that no one ever would. Not in his lifetime anyway, and what was his lifetime going to be now? Drastically reduced, that was for sure. The means and ways for injury and death were doubled, trebled…and no hospital in sight. No one to save us, he thought. We are on our own.

A splash from the side of ThreeBees yanked him from his reverie.

"Jade?" he said, standing, automatically grabbing the gun, already knowing where she had gone. "Jade!" He saw her now, five feet from the boat and swimming in an easy breaststroke. She rolled onto her back, kicking. The water seemed to shatter around her as the light of the setting sun was splashed into a million pieces.

"You would go, too," she said, "if it was Maggie." Her low voice carried easily to him even though he couldn't see *her* anymore; she was merely the dark star around which the broken, sparkling water swirled.

"Jade, come back, please. What if it isn't–if Singer isn't–safe?"

He thought he caught a glimpse of white teeth, and then she must have rolled again, her arms and legs working in a languorous way. He watched until he saw her emerge at the rowboat, pulled aboard by Singer. She looked like an oil slick come to liquid life.

He considered his options and, in the end, decided to leave them be.

What right did he have to judge if Jade was willing to put herself on the line for her brother? What right did he have to decide if companionship was enough of a reward to merit such a risk?

Steve put the gun down and sat back in the deck chair, vowing that he'd not be the judge anymore. He'd learned his lesson. With Amelia, he'd learned it.

~ ~ ~

John Smith watched Adam with careful attentiveness. He studied his mannerisms and the inflection of his words. Adam was IN CHARGE, and John knew what that meant...it meant that he had to get close to Adam. He had to absorb some of Adam and reflect it back to him, because that's what made a man like Adam like and trust you.

He didn't care what Adam was saying and paid almost no attention to the words themselves. He just nodded, keeping a look of concern on his face while he thought about other things. He trusted his intuition to tell him if Adam was saying something that actually mattered. So far, nothing.

For Adam's part, he found that he really liked John Smith. Liked and trusted him, despite what Steve had to say. The guy was courteous and let Adam talk. He was really listening, Adam could tell, and he really seemed to like Adam...possibly even admired him.

"Steve runs the day-to-day stuff on the tug, *Big Daddy*. No one is really the leader on *Barbra's Bay Breeze*—we usually just call it ThreeBees, by the way—they basically just do what I tell them. They are kind of an annex to *Flyboy*...a castoff, if you will." He laughed, and John Smith laughed too, and stopped just before Adam did. Adam liked that...he and John were simpatico.

"What did you think of Steve? Kind of a dick, right?" Adam kept his tone neutral, testing John, trying not to lead him too much.

"Yeah, he was a dick. I noticed that." John's voice was smooth and calm. He crossed his arms over his chest and nodded just slightly. Adam nodded back, almost without realizing he was doing it.

"And Maggie, his main squeeze. What did you think of her?"

This time John raised his brows, and his gaze went to ThreeBees, although it was too dark to see anything. "They're a thing, huh? Got something going on?"

"Oh yes, they certainly do," Adam said and crossed his arms over his chest, in unconscious imitation of John. "Listen, we haven't talked about you at all. How did you end up in that life raft? Where did you come from, before?"

Everyone knew 'before' meant before the sickness, before the dead had started to come back. Before the world had turned upside down.

John glanced at Adam and away. Heavy sorrow flowed over his features. "Boat I was on sank...before that, well...I guess my story's pretty much the same as everyone else's. I lost everything." He turned back to Adam, and there was a kind commiseration in his gaze, more acknowledgement than pity. "I guess you did, too."

Adam lowered his head with a sigh. "Yes, my parents. I talked to them the night before everything, and my dad was already sick. I'm sure my mom got it, too." His voice was thick with pain, but he heard the edge of theatrics and dialed it back. He was overdoing it. Sounding fake.

John nodded. "Did you try and get your mom out, or did you just count it as a lost cause?"

Adam sat up, stung. "There was nothing I could have done for her. I told you, she was sick already, or at least...probably she was, since my dad was sick." His voice bordered on strident.

John merely nodded again, calm as calm water. "Nope, nothing you could have done, then. What was done was done, wasn't it? You had to make the hard choices." He stared out over the water, thoughtful and sad.

Adam found himself nodding. "Yes. It...it was a difficult choice...but the right one. I know it was the right choice."

"Course it was, because here you are, and look at everything you've done! Doesn't sound like they'd have much of anything going on without you to lead them, isn't that right?"

Adam nodded again. He stared at John's profile, almost hypnotized by the wonderful, soothing flow of words. "Yes, that's right. They couldn't even figure out how to get *Flyboy* started." Of course, there had only been a handful of people here at the time, and chances were that someone would have figured it out eventually. Most likely.

"These people must worship you," John said, and the admiration in his voice was unmistakable now. "It takes a lot to step up in these circumstances. To be a man, be the hero. Most won't do it."

"No, they don't worship me. They don't need to! I'm here to serve, really, more than anything. I just want to help out."

John smiled at him, and Adam felt himself growing warm from the admiration.

"What else you got going on over here?" John asked. "Who're your best friends? Your right hand men? Anyone else as important as you I should know about?"

Adam missed the slight hitch in John's tone, the wink of insincerity. He was too busy thinking how he was going to tell Steve what a truly lousy judge of character he was.

"Well, there's Sami: Dr. Sami Rafiq. I keep him close. He's useful. The rest of them," Adam shrugged, "they're okay, each good for something."

"How about a lady friend? Got anyone in your bunk or in your sights?"

Maggie came immediately to Adam's mind, and he colored in embarrassment. "No, not really. No time," he said, mumbling. He was glad for the dark. His mortification must be written all over his hot face.

John *did* see the color in Adam's cheeks, and he noted it and then put it aside.

"Plenty of time for that later. After everything is settled," John said and yawned.

Adam nodded, not really paying attention, still embroiled in his conflicting thoughts about Maggie and Steve. The ominous tone of John Smith's last statement passed by him entirely.

Chapter Eight

"We can't keep this from Adam forever. Especially now, with both of them out there," Maggie said to herself, watching the rowboat tethered behind ThreeBees. There was no movement on it, but she could just make out the huddled forms of Singer and Jade…they must have fallen asleep leaning against each other after Jade swam out there last night.

It was very early, the sun just beginning its ascent, and the colors in the sky were beautiful. Light blues and light pinks, deeper salmon gradually becoming a hot orange right where the sun was about to crest. It was a sunrise that bespoke of a good day, weather-wise.

Maggie checked her own internal barometer. How would her day be? Calm? Changeable? Stormy?

The rowboat rocked gently. *It must be nice*, she thought, *to have someone so close to you, so close by.* She missed being physical, hugging, cuddling. Just the comfort of an arm around her shoulders, a known arm, a comfortable weight. She missed having a man. She missed her husband.

Light as a butterfly, a hand tickled into hers, and Maggie smiled, turning. Babygirl's pale skin was washed sweetly in the pinkish orange glow of sunrise, but her eyes remained anxious.

"It's okay, honey," Maggie said and gave the girl's hand a gentle squeeze. "Want to pull up a chair? Sit next to me?"

Babygirl looked at the scatter of deck chairs and then looked back at Maggie, shaking her head. She pointed to Maggie's lap.

"You're too big to sit on laps," Maggie said, mock scolding, but dismayed at her internal reaction to Babygirl's suggestion: reluctance with a dash of fear. Had she really become so emotionally stingy?

She relented and pulled Baby onto her lap, and the girl settled sideways, leaning against Maggie's chest, her head tucked under Maggie's chin. She plugged her thumb into her mouth and sighed. Maggie held her loosely; the girl was a warm, felt-covered bag of bones under Maggie's arms, but she wasn't that heavy, actually. No, not heavy at all.

~ ~ ~

The whine of a jet ski roused her from a half doze. She looked out at the rowboat and then glanced down at Babygirl still cuddled in her lap. Still sound asleep. Maggie hesitated, her hand on the white-blonde floss on the girl's head. Her hair was so soft it barely made an impression on Maggie's fingers. The word 'precious' slipped into her mind, unbidden, and she frowned. Then she stood, lifting Babygirl, and turned to place her on the cushioned deck bench.

The engine whine cut off, and Carl scrambled up onto the back deck of ThreeBees. At the sight of his giant's form, Maggie felt a shift of disappointment. She had been expecting to see Steve.

"Hi, Maggie," Carl whispered, glancing at the sleeping girl. Even his whisper was big—gruff and gravelly. "I'm here to spell you guys for a while." He glanced from the gun near the deck chair to the rowboat. "Everything quiet out there?"

"Yes, quiet as the grave," Maggie said and regretted her words instantly. There were very few quiet graves anymore.

Carl merely nodded. "Gotcha." He glanced again at Babygirl. "She need a blanket or anything?"

Maggie smiled to herself. Even this early, it was already close to eighty degrees; the girl would roast under a blanket, but everyone was solicitous toward Babygirl. Part of it, Maggie knew, was pretty standard...most everyone felt protective of a child this age, but there was more to it than that. There was a sad and certain feeling that children were rare, now. Each one was (*precious*) to be guarded with extra caution, extra vigilance.

"She'll be okay. It's warm enough out here," Maggie said and smiled at Carl. "Want me to take a look at your leg?"

"No, that's okay. It's not even bleeding anymore." He shook his head, and his eyes were drawn back to Babygirl. "I can understand why Sujon did it. Why she was so crazy at...at what happened. I don't even blame her for shooting me." He sighed, and it sounded like a minor brushfire, filtered through his beard. "Mohammed was her actual family. Not many of us have that anymore, but for it to be a kid...someone you're responsible for...well." He shook his head again. "I'd a shot somebody, too, I guess."

"She shot the wrong guy, though," Maggie said, surprised at the bitterness in her own voice.

"Yep, that's the truth," Carl said, still unperturbed. "I feel like that guy–that Adam–is going to have a lot to answer for once all this is..." He trailed off.

Maggie knew why, it was the backlash. It was hard to get your mind wrapped around the fact that this was–most likely–a permanent state of affairs. No one was going to be held accountable for bad decisions.

Unless Carl meant he'd be judged in Heaven, in which case Maggie heartily disagreed. Heaven would soon be closed for lack of participation, in Maggie's opinion. Not that she actually believed any of that stuff anymore, anyway.

"How long are you staying?" she asked.

"I dunno. Till whenever, I guess. Who watches next?"

"Brian. I'm glad you came because he's pretty racked up. Between Denny and Mrs. Adams...well, let's just say I think he could use some catching up on his sleep, you know?"

"You, too."

"Me, too, what?" she said, honestly confused.

"You could use a rest. It's been hard on you, too, hasn't it?"

"Oh well, yes, of course, but not as much...I didn't go on shore, and Denny wasn't...I mean, Brian and Denny were friends, they came together from Stockton State, so you can imagine that Brian would be more upset about everything."

"But you'd been on this boat with him, with both of them—Denny and Mrs. Allen—for what? Two months? That's enough time to develop a friendship, a bond. I know the guys on *Big Daddy* feel as close to me as my own brothers did, back before all this."

Maggie stared at him, open-mouthed. The words he spoke seemed to have no connection to his brusque, biker's exterior. He sounded like a therapist, not a pirate.

He smiled at her surprised expression. "I was a psychologist, before everything. Well, technically, I guess I still am. I've let myself get a little carried away, I think, with the whole seafaring thing. Avoidance, a little, plus using fantasy to cope with a bleak reality, would be my diagnosis of myself." He smiled again. "Want me to diagnose you?" His tone had a slight teasing quality, but underneath was warmth.

Maggie laughed and shook her head. "No, thanks. I prefer to remain ignorant to my inner workings."

"Ah…classic avoidance!" he said. "Something we all seem to be practicing to one degree or another."

Maggie shook her head, still smiling, and bent to pick up Babygirl. "I'm going to lie down. Brian is in the salon, right through there, okay? Just give him a shake when you need a rest."

Carl nodded and settled into the deck chair facing the rowboat.

At the entrance to the salon, Maggie hesitated and turned back. "Carl?"

"Hmm?" Carl looked at her over his shoulder.

"Did you help Steve take John Smith to *Flyboy*?"

"No, why?"

"Nothing. I was just wondering if you'd had a chance to talk to him."

"To John? No," he said his features pulling down in concern. "Something about him bother you, Maggie?"

She frowned and opened her mouth to respond but was stopped by a splash and a scream.

Jade was swimming back to ThreeBees, her strokes frenzied and ungraceful, churning the water. She was screaming her brother's name, her voice choked and breaking, her face a panicked white disc.

Behind her in the rowboat, Singer stood, swaying, staring dumbly after her. Then he stepped off the side, and sank.

~ ~ ~

Jade shivered under the big towel Maggie had thrown around her. She sobbed, her face buried in her hands. She had not stopped sobbing since Carl had pulled her from the water. Maggie wondered absently if tears could ever be used up.

Carl sat across from Jade, patient as a mountain, waiting for the fury of her emotional storm to pass.

Maggie tied the rowboat up at the back of ThreeBees as the diesel engine rumbled to life beneath her feet. She had asked Randy to move them a few hundred yards away. He'd wanted to know in which direction, and Maggie had replied simply: any.

Any direction would do as long as it got them away from the presence that seemed to lurk beneath ThreeBees. Denny's body down there had been bad, but the thought of Singer down there, too, staring up in silent despondency at the underside of ThreeBees…that gave her the creeps. It also saddened her in a way that the deaths of Denny and Mrs. Allen had not. They had died and *stayed* dead.

They were lucky.

She glanced back at Jade, scanning automatically for any sign of injury. Maggie had looked her over after Carl pulled her back on board, but Jade hadn't been cooperative. She was too distraught to be cooperative.

Maggie had to be sure, because there was no question now that Singer had been overcome by the sickness. He wouldn't have slipped out of sight like that if his body had held any air. It meant that people on the boat weren't automatically immune–at least not from direct contact.

Scary thought. Especially if it meant that Jade might now be a carrier.

Maggie's eyes went to Babygirl, who sat next to Jade, her small hand making circles of comfort on Jade's back. ThreeBees jolted, pulling forward, and that moment of disorientation seemed to color Maggie's thoughts.

"Babybirl, come over here," Maggie said, more harshly than she'd intended. Babygirl looked up in surprise then slipped from the bench and trotted obediently to Maggie.

Maggie took Babygirl's face in her hands. "I think you should go take a nap, okay?"

Babygirl shook her head, not in defiance but in confusion. "But I just woked up!" she said, her little voice like that of a bird peeping.

"I know, honey, I know you did. Just go in there and look at the picture books, okay? Stay in our room and I'll ask Bonnie to come sit with you. Keep you company. Will you do that for me, Baby?"

The little girl nodded and trotted toward the salon. She waved one hand to Jade on the way. "Bye, Jade, I hope you feel better."

Jade never looked up.

~ ~ ~

Steve stood next to Maggie on the back deck of ThreeBees. They both looked at Jade, who'd fallen asleep on the deck bench right where Babygirl had slept that same morning. Carl had told Maggie that Jade wasn't really asleep, not in the sense of the restorative state we are accustomed to. He said that she was in something called a fugue state, on the verge of catatonia, overwhelmed with guilt and sorrow, completely unable to cope. He said they'd have to watch her very closely.

Maggie had agreed, but not for precisely the same reasons.

"Has Adam asked you why you're moving?" Steve said, still not taking his eyes from Jade.

"I told him we wanted to try to get out a little deeper, test the waters for fish. He didn't question it beyond that."

"No, he's preoccupied. That John Smith seems to have him a little in thrall."

Maggie frowned and looked at Steve. "What do you mean?"

"He's made the guy his right-hand man. Already. I mean, that's some pretty short acquaintance, wouldn't you say?"

Maggie nodded, and her eyes went back to Jade, where she lay curled on the bench. She looked like an exhausted child, but Maggie did not feel moved. She realized she was assessing Jade with a coldness she would never have thought herself capable of prior to the events of the last few months. In her mind, she had already classified Jade as potentially 'other' or 'undead'. At least in possibility, if not in actual fact.

The possibility was enough to justify the caution. It's the reason they had put Singer adrift in the first place, wasn't it?

"We have to put her out on the rowboat," Maggie said, her voice calm, her eyes never leaving Jade.

Steve shifted uncomfortably. "Was she bit or scratched or marked up at all?"

"Maybe. Maybe not. We're all so cut up and banged up and malnourished...who can tell if her cuts and scrapes are from yesterday or this morning? We can't take the chance." Babygirl flashed into her mind, all big eyes and vulnerability. Was that what was making her feel so adamant? Babygirl's safety?

Primarily, yes, it seemed so. It seemed she'd developed some sort of maternal instinct after all.

She didn't want it, but she couldn't deny it.

"Help me with her," Maggie said. "Be careful in case she comes to and struggles."

Steve felt a cold reluctance trying to fill his limbs with lead. They couldn't put that exhausted, skinny, run-down girl out by herself in a rowboat. She'd get sunburned; she'd die from exposure.

"Can't we lock her in her room?" Carl asked. "At least she'd have the bed."

"Well, but then what? What if she changes?" Maggie whispered furiously, and tears danced at the edges of her eyelids. "Escort her out? Abandon the boat?" She took a deep breath, steadying herself. She wiped under her eyes. "What choice do we have, guys? Tell me. I'm willing to listen."

Steve realized that Maggie *did* understand the consequences...and the possibilities. She'd just thought it through quicker than he and Carl had. He looked at Jade again and shook his head.

"None, I guess. You're right. I just wish..." He trailed off, shrugging.

"Yeah, me too," Maggie said. "Everyone else, too, but this is where we're at. This is what we need to...to deal with." Her eyes were full of grief and an aching exhaustion that Steve thought was probably mirrored in his own.

"Yes, you're right," he said. "Let's get it over with."

With Carl's help, they placed an unresisting Jade in the rowboat. They covered her with a white sheet and packed in a waterproof canvas tarpaulin, water, beef jerky, and hard candy—some of the staples of their diets.

"Three days at the most. That's all. Then we'll know," Maggie said, and Steve and Carl nodded, as if making a pact.

Steve played the line out, hand over hand, until Jade floated a hundred feet away.

The three of them stood watching the rowboat until Maggie took up her post on the deck chair. It had been too much like a wake, the way they were standing there. Jade wasn't dead, she told herself.

Not *yet*, anyway, she answered herself and shivered.

~ ~ ~

"What's the deal with this John Smith guy?" Carl asked Steve. They had moved to the side of ThreeBees, sensing that Maggie needed some space. "Maggie thought there was something off about him?"

"Yeah, I don't know what it is. He's a sycophant, but a discreet one. I don't think Adam would ever recognize that about the guy."

Carl snorted. "Not likely. Not when your ego's as big as his. Takes a lot of stroking to keep that sucker inflated."

"Is that your professional assessment?"

Carl laughed. "No...that one's all personal. All *kinds* of personal."

Carl had had a few run-ins with Adam back at the beginning, when everyone was still getting their shit together. Carl didn't like Adam, didn't like his manipulations and fits of pique. He recognized a God complex but also an almost ridiculously stunted sense of self worth…a strange combination. Possibly dangerous, especially in light of the power he'd been able to achieve. Adam had been lucky so far that most people were too tired and depressed–still trying to recover themselves as people–to take issue with very many things.

Look at a situation like Sujon and Muhammad…that was poor decision making at its finest and it had gotten Muhammad killed. Sujon, too, if you followed the line of reasoning out to its bitter end.

A bad decision that had cost two lives, and it had been based on anger, and bruised ego, and fear. Fear of someone else getting the upper hand. Fear of being pushed aside. Now Adam had acquired a genuine toady.

Something might have to be done, sooner rather than later, but who would do it? Who had the authority?

No one, that's who. It was troubling.

"Maybe I should take a ride over there today. Talk to the new guy," Carl said.

"Not a bad idea. I'd like to hear your assessment, and hopefully, you'll prove me wrong. Maybe I'm just adding worries to my worries," Steve said and sighed. "I think I'll stay here in case Maggie needs me. In case anyone here needs me. I mean, if they need help with anything." He fumbled and stumbled his way through his last sentences and then glanced at Carl.

"Huh," Carl said and crossed his arms over his chest. The barest hint of a grin sat comfortably under his beard.

Steve's face soured. "'Huh' nothing. Hey, listen, why don't you go look under someone else's hood?"

"Will do," Carl said, and grinned.

Steve punched him on the shoulder.

~ ~ ~

"I can't get Brian to wake up. He is *out!*" Randy said, coming across the deck. His shorts were strapped across his shrinking but still big belly with what looked like a length of clothesline. He looked like a hillbilly or a homeless person. *Bonnie must not have seen that get-up yet*, Maggie thought, amused.

"Let him sleep," she said. "He probably needs it. I'll make sure he gets up in time to eat something for lunch. You know he's only nineteen?"

Randy dragged a chair across the deck and stationed it next to Maggie's. He nodded a hello to Steve, who sat on Maggie's other side. "Yep, I know. Nineteen, Jesus Christ almighty, that's young. I barely remember it." He tilted his head back and closed his eyes. "Sun feels good."

"Is Bonnie sitting with Babygirl?" Maggie asked.

"Yep, looking at picture books. That little one is sweet, isn't she?" Randy cracked an eye open and glanced at Maggie.

Maggie nodded, but then her gaze slipped back to Jade out on the rowboat.

Brian stumbled from the salon, scrubbing his face with his hands. His eyes were red-rimmed and sunken into the dark circles surrounding them. He shuffled like a drunk. He looked more like a man emerging from a coma than a restful night's sleep. Maggie felt a wrenching tug of pity in her heart. They'd all been through so much. It seemed there was no end to the misery.

"What's up?" Brian said, seeming to address his own feet. He shoved his hands into his pockets and squinted out at the rowboat. "Singer okay?"

Chapter Nine

Sami and Candy were in bed, but they weren't sleeping, not anymore. Sami had wakened them both with his silent struggles. Another nightmare.

"Same one as before?" Candy asked, cradling his head in her lap and caressing his thick, black hair.

"Yes. Always that same one. Always that same ending." His voice was slightly muffled. Despite the terror and sweat, he was already falling back to sleep. His hand opened and closed on the bunched-up hem of Candy's baby-doll nightie.

Opened and closed.

Like a baby, she thought. *All men revert when in distress.* She'd noticed this before. She sighed and tipped her head back against the hand-carved, teak headboard. Sami had a nice room. One of the nicest. Most people had to cram four or six to a room, but not Sami, because he was Adam's right-hand man.

Or had been, anyway. Until that Smith guy showed up.

Candy didn't like him, and Candy was a good judge of character. *Very* good. Maybe because her own manner of dressing was camouflage...she could see out, but no one could see in. People tended to reveal themselves around her.

She had noted the glittering lack of humanity in Smith's eyes as he'd surveyed the other passengers. This guy had just been dragged from a life raft? Not likely. Most of the people on *Flyboy* had been here for at least two months, safe, warm, fed...and they *still* looked like recent refugees from hell. Candy didn't know what John Smith was selling, but she surely wasn't buying it.

She'd have to make sure Sami didn't make a purchase either. In her own practical, unromantic, clear-eyed way, she loved Sami, and more than that, she protected him. She didn't know if it was his given nature or the fact that he was a foreigner or a combination of both those things, but Sami was too vulnerable. *Emotionally* vulnerable, she amended to herself. Physically...he did okay. She felt a fluttering of lust in her lower belly as she raked her fingers through his hair.

He was already back to sleep, and she was tired, too. So she thought about Sami's dream instead. It was a lust killer, for sure.

He had it almost every night, but it started differently each time. He'd be eating in a restaurant, riding a bus, or hailing a cab, and everything was prosaically normal. Mundane. Then a hand would grasp his ankle, and he would turn, and holding onto him would be a half-body: a head, a torso, and an arm. Its face was rotted almost to the bone, the muscles brownish and crumbling, veins and arteries darkly purple, the lips gone, the nose twin holes under a bridge of yellow cartilage. He couldn't tell if it was–had been–a man or a woman, but its eyes were blue, bright with life and tortured awareness...nothing like the dead eyes of the walking corpses they'd all encountered at the end.

In his dream he would panic and try to yank his foot away, but the half-body held fast, its grip like that of a vise, ten times as heavy as half a body should be. It would twist, rocking itself toward him, closer and closer. He would become aware of a susurration emanating from its throat...*aaallll...oooorrrrr aaauuuuuuuuullll*...and its mouth would begin to snap open and closed, even as it whispered. It got closer and closer, and Sami would see that his pant leg had pulled up, exposing his shin, his calf, his ankle. Then the teeth were on him, sinking in, searing like a brand, and he would hear the accusatory whisper as it cleared the channels of his deciphering mind: *all your fault*...

When he recounted the dream to Candy, his eyes took on a deep despondency that she didn't like. In Candy's view, the world was a cold, tenuous place, with little room for the fragile vulnerability of self-doubt. That was something she'd always known, even before the sickness, but Sami didn't know it. Sami didn't know that the real enemy is other people...not the sinkers and walking corpses.

Look at Adam, for example. He was more than willing to lord it over Sami even though Sami was–quite literally–a better person. Adam had a way of shrinking Sami, reducing him until Sami felt unsure of every decision, shrunken even in his own estimation of himself.

Adam had gotten a hold of Sami when he and Candy had first come aboard. At that time, they were still pretending to be coincidental acquaintances only. Old habits, dying hard. She hadn't been able to protect Sami from Adam's poisonous rap.

Adam had latched onto Sami almost immediately. He seemed to like everyone calling Sami Dr. Rafiq; he liked the automatic respect that title demanded. Adam acted as though he had discovered Sami, sponsored him in some way, and that Sami's title should somehow convey to him, too. If not the title, then at least the respect.

Candy had seen the dynamic before. She understood it. Sami was Adam's prize, the possession through which he would buy esteem. If you don't have a title yourself, the next best thing it to have someone with a title looking up to you. Standing on the shoulders of giants? Yes, that was some of it, but if Adam was standing on Sami's shoulders, then he was also shitting down Sami's neck at the same time.

Because it was obvious that Adam also resented the respect that Sami received...he resented and feared that people were drawn to Sami: to his kindness, thoughtfulness and calmly quiet nature. After something terrible had happened, who would you want to sit next to? The guy that would sit shoulder to shoulder with you in companionable solidarity? Or the guy that worried and fidgeted, discontentedly stirring up trouble and unnecessary worry?

Candy would pick a Sami over an Adam every time.

Sami had confessed to Adam the first night they'd been on board. There were just over a dozen people at that time...dazed and uncomprehending ghosts, each with a story of horrific survivorship that they seemed compelled to tell every new person who came on board.

Candy listened to each story with equanimity, holding them at a mental floodgate, but Sami's eyes grew rounder, more shocked, as if for him these stories were not only burdens, but cumulative.

Adam had been the one to assign them their rooms that night. He had put Candy in with three other women because they expected more survivors. Then he'd taken Sami aside, questioned him about his title, wanting to know what kind of doctor he was. He told Sami that everyone would feel better if they had a medical doctor on board. Candy didn't believe for a minute that Adam cared that much about the other survivors. She knew Adam's type, and she knew even then that Adam was looking at Sami like the candle that was going to draw the most moths. Candy would bet that, above all, Adam was a collector. A collector of insults, hurts, grudges…maybe even action figures, if he'd never found himself a woman. The women that would be able to stand his Napoleonic tendencies would be few and far between.

Sami–exhausted, miserable, separated from Candy and burdened with the stories of the other survivors–had broken down. Consumed with guilt and shame, he'd mistaken Adam's calculated interest for genuine human concern. He'd told Adam of what he perceived to be his failing, seeing the potential for just what had occurred and not acting on it. Not putting a stop to it. His cowardice, as Sami saw it, was the thing that had doomed the world to its current fate.

That's when Adam had stopped calling him Dr. Rafiq. Even though he corrected anyone else who tried to address Sami by his first name.

Now John Smith had come along, and Candy watched as he drew Adam in through flattery and manipulation. She knew it could be a good thing; or it could be bad. Either Adam's relationship with Smith would set Sami free…or Sami would become the low dog on the totem pole, the whipping boy for both of those psychopathic assholes.

Candy would watch and see which way it was playing out. She'd rescue Sami if she had to, she didn't mind. She considered herself more fortunate than most of the other survivors because she felt almost entirely the same now as she had before this whole shitty mess.

To Candy, the world was a terrible place, now *and* before. She'd seen her own brother into his grave due to a disease that had been largely ignored by mainstream society because of the perception of who, specifically, got the disease...and she'd seen even worse than that.

Walking corpses and sinkers hadn't made the world an endurance challenge.

The real people–the living–had done that.

~ ~ ~

Sami sat next to John Smith on the small upper bridge deck. John was staring intently at Adam and Carl on the lower deck. They were at the very back rail, away from anyone else, and Carl looked frustrated. Twice, he gestured to the main body of *Flyboy*. He wanted something, that much was obvious, but Sami wasn't able to determine what it was that Carl wanted.

Sami glanced uncomfortably at John Smith. All conversation had ceased as soon as Adam had walked away. It was as if Sami did not exist in John's world. It made Sami very uneasy. Very nervous.

"That Carl is a very big man, isn't he? He looks like a pirate! Very fitting for the boats, wouldn't you agree, John?"

John Smith didn't even bat an eye, only continued to stare at Adam and Carl.

"The funny thing is, he is a psychologist. You would never guess it, would you?" Sami laughed nervously.

John blinked once, closing and opening his eyes slowly. Then he looked at Sami. Sami felt a shiver of unease at John Smith's unblinking gaze. John's eyes reminded him of something...

"A psychologist?" John asked.

Sami nodded and smiled. "Yes, as I was saying...you never would have guessed, would you? He looks very intimidating at first blush, but as soon as you talk to him, you see that–"

"Talk to him?" John asked, cutting Sami off. "Who has to talk to him?"

"No one *has* to talk to him, I just meant...*when* you talk to him, in general terms...he is very kind. Very thoughtful and insightful. I am sure that he is...was...good at his profession."

John stared at Sami for so long that Sami became more and more uncomfortable. It was very rude, Sami thought, for someone to stare so forthrightly and without comment. What was wrong with this man? Candy was right. This John Smith was no shaken survivor with post-traumatic stress disorder as the rest of them seemed to be. In fact, this John Smith actually seemed very acclimated to this new world.

John Smith stood in one fluid motion and turned onto the bridge–the only way to get off the upper bridge deck. He didn't say goodbye.

Sami took a deep breath, aware only now that he must have been holding it. He looked out to where Adam and Carl had been, but now they were gone, too. Sami took another deep breath. He would go and find Candy. That always made him feel better. She was his touchstone in all things.

He stood to leave but as he did, Adam came onto the deck with Carl.

Carl came forward, grasping both of Sami's hands in his. "Dr. Rafiq. How are you? You look well. Everything going okay?" His smile was small but very warm. Sami had the impression that under normal circumstances, Carl was most likely a very jovial person.

"Dr. Fairfield," Sami said, "I am well. I hope you are, also."

"Just Carl, please, Dr. Rafiq," Carl said, his smile widening, "and I'm good. Doing real well."

"Sami," Adam said, irritation evident in his voice, "Carl wanted to talk to John...wasn't he just up here?"

"He left right before you came up," Sami said, and in a flash it came to him that was *why* John had left...to avoid Carl, but why?

~ ~ ~

"I think you should move into this room with me. Why do we care who knows of our relationship? There is no one here to disapprove."

105

Candy sat in the small chair near the bed, putting her shoes on in preparation for the trek back to her own shared room behind the engines...formerly the crew quarters. It was late afternoon, but people went to bed early, now, setting with the sun to conserve resources.

She looked up.

"I don't think that's a good idea, Sami," she said.

When they had met, their bond was immediate and strong. However, Sami's family was conservative, and he was less than a year away from his arranged marriage. There had been no way for him to pursue a visible relationship with Candy.

Candy's family...the ones she still associated with, the *less* rabid ones...would never accept an Indian into the family. Candy knew that as well as she knew her name.

Their feelings were undeniable, so they became each other's secret. The relationship was only five months old when everything had gone wrong in the world, and it had been five months of hyper-sexualized excitement, tinged by Sami's dissolving obsession with the Lazarus project. For Candy, the drug trials had become a moot point–her brother had lost his years long fight only weeks after she and Sami met in Philadelphia.

Neither of them contemplated a future for themselves, for being together, and sometimes Candy wondered if that was one of the things that stopped them from being more diligent about contacting the Lazarus doctors. Everything had seemed in a state of suspended animation. Days passed without acknowledgement. They couldn't see a future for themselves, so they simply didn't look in that direction.

She wondered how much that had contributed to Sami's guilt.

"Why is it not a good idea?" Sami asked, swinging out of the bed. Some instinct of self-preservation seemed to demand that he not be naked for the conversation to come. He slipped into his underwear.

Candy shrugged. "It just...it will make us vulnerable. Do you see that?"

"No. It will make us stronger."

You maybe, Candy thought. *Not me.* She lowered her head into her hands.

"Candy," Sami said, "I am not as fragile as you think I am."

"I don't think you're fragile, Sami. I just think it makes us both more…if everyone knew we were together, then they could use it against us somehow. I don't know. I don't know why I feel that way. I just do."

"It will not make us vulnerable, it will make us stronger. We love each other, don't we? That can only be a good thing. People will be happy for us."

Candy was astonished at his naiveté, but maybe she was just too jaded, too harsh?

She shrugged again.

Sami drew her shoes from her feet, placing them side-by-side next to the chair. He took her hands, pulled her gently to standing, and relieved her of the rest of her clothing. Then he guided her to the bed.

"We will stay together from now on." He curled himself around her, drawing the light sheet over their shoulders. "We will have this one happiness. There is no reason for us to be separated. Not anymore."

Candy shivered at his words. She knew that to ask for the good is to invite the bad.

There are always two shoes, after all.

~ ~ ~

"Why did he want to talk to me? Is he the one in charge?" John put an extra dose of innocence into his voice. He and Adam were on the bridge deck, overlooking the activities below them on the main deck. The sun was sinking into the scrubby pines at the shoreline.

Adam's face soured. "*That* guy? Jesus Christ, no. No way. I guess if you had to say anyone was in charge of *Big Daddy*, then it would be Steve, but even Steve is more or less a manager. Under me." He clapped John on the shoulder. He was able to do that because John had positioned himself on the deck, cross-legged, next to Adam's chair. "He doesn't need to talk to you. He can go fuck himself." Adam ruminated. His hand rested on John's shoulder.

John felt the weight of Adam's hand, the disgusting, meaty heat coming from it, and he contemplated turning his head enough to bite it. He could practically feel the bone in Adam's pinky finger breaking under his teeth, the hot blood slicking his chin. Just like the undead did. Man that was fan-fucking-tastic to watch when they attacked someone. Better than Discovery Channel even.

He controlled the desire to bite Adam's hand. He would bide his time. He had a good trick up his sleeve. Better even than the last time. A very interesting trick. He just had to work out the logistics.

"Carl isn't anyone," Adam said. "You know what? Fuck that guy for coming over here demanding this and demanding that."

"Do you think…" John put a twinge of embarrassed consternation into his voice this time. An 'aw, shucks, could it be?' tone. "Do you think they might be jealous of me?"

"Jealous of you? Why?"

John shifted, drawing himself millimeters closer to Adam's chair. "Because you've kind of…taken me in? Maybe they're jealous that I get to hang out with you? They've all been here longer than me."

A swell of hot pride suffused Adam's face with blood. He really liked this guy. *He gets me*, Adam thought.

"Before…before all this." Now John's voice broke with emotion. "I was just a blue collar guy, you know? Just doing my thing every day, punching the clock. The other guys, they all hated management…really resented them, you know? They thought that management were all sit-on-their-ass-pussies while we did all the *hard* work." John shook his head. "But I get it now. This…" He gestured to the crowd below them. "This is the hard part…the decision making. The responsibility." He turned to look at Adam, his chin tilted up in a posture of worship. "Their fates are in your hands, and they're all too dumb and ungrateful to know it."

Adam's stomach tightened. His throat ached with tears. *Yes*, he thought to himself. *That's just right. Their fates are in my hands.*

"You know something?" Adam said, squeezing John's shoulder. "I think they're getting a little too big for their britches over there on *Big Daddy* and ThreeBees."

"Maybe you should bring them all aboard *Flyboy*. Where you can keep a closer eye on them. They'd think twice about crossing you, then."

Conflicting ideas ran through Adam's mind. It would be good to scoop everyone up and bring them to *Flyboy* where he could keep a tighter rein, but at the same time–

His mind shied away from a difficult idea and settled on a more comfortable one: the resources. It was better to have the resources spread across the three ships. The idea made no rational sense, but it was an easier reason than the first one that had actually occurred to him…if Steve were on *Flyboy*, then somehow, Steve would take over as its leader. People just flocked to the guy. It was unfair, but it was the way things had always been. Fortune favored the assholes.

He sat back and crossed his arms over his chest. "Maybe. I'll have to give it some thought." Adam didn't see the look of annoyance that flashed through John's eyes.

Sami appeared at the doorway to the bridge. He'd left Candy sleeping in his…their…room.

"Adam," Sami said, glancing nervously at John Smith. It bothered him, the penitent's position John had taken, sitting practically at Adam's feet, his head lowered. "I wanted to speak to you. If you have a moment."

Without turning, Adam raised a hand and flicked his fingers in a 'come' gesture. Sami looked around for another deck chair, but they had been moved. Intentionally? It's a small deck, but still big enough for a handful of people to sit comfortably.

"Have a seat!" Adam said and gestured to the floor before him. "Sorry about the lack of chairs. I had John take them all below…so that everyone had a chance to use them down on the lower decks. I don't want it to seem like I'm trying to keep all the good stuff for myself, right?"

"No, of course not," Sami said. "I am content to stand. It is no problem."

Adam nodded in an exaggerated way. "What did you want to talk about, Sami?" Adam asked. He found himself feeling annoyed with his friend, he wasn't sure why. It was certainly irritating to have to stare up at him while he stood there like a…like…like he was the boss or something.

"I thought we could perhaps speak in private," Sami said, careful to keep a deferential tone. Adam heard it as dismissive.

His hand strayed to John's shoulder. "John can stay."

John's head came up, the bandage over his split forehead shining whitely in the gloom. He smiled at Adam, and the smile conveyed gratitude, maybe love, too. Sami felt a sharp twist of jealousy, irritation, and fear. His relationship with Adam had become complicated. Adam knew a lot about Sami, more than Sami would want anyone else to know. What if they ended up hating him for what he'd done, or hadn't done?

Then he remembered his most important relationship, and that buoyed him.

"I am going to have Candy stay in my room with me. She is…we are…we're a couple. We're together." Sami braced himself, raising his head and standing straighter.

Adam read it as arrogance. Blatant disregard for his opinion. His decisions.

"Well, congratulations, man. Lucky you. Candy is hot, man, a hot little mama…maybe we should all have some candy, huh?" Adam's gaze held a challenge that Sami couldn't face…he dropped his eyes. "Hey, I'm just kidding. That's great. I'm happy for you."

Sami smiled, relieved but still uncertain.

"She's down in the crew quarters, right?" Adam had an exaggerated 'trying to recall' look on his face.

Sami nodded and unease snaked delicately into his stomach.

"Well, it's gonna be tight for you guys down there, but I'm sure you can work something out, right?" Adam's grin stretched across his face like a cold meat zipper.

Sami opened his mouth to protest, but Adam stood abruptly, cutting him off. "John, come with me, would you?"

John stood quickly, but then staggered, his hand going to his head.

Adam reached out to steady him, and John gave Adam another look of grateful love. "Sorry, I guess I'm…still a little shaky. My head, you know?"

"I'm going to put you in Sami's old room. He won't need it, and I'm sure you could use the space to recover. You don't mind, do you, Sami? Now that you have Candy to bunk with."

Adam helped John out, and Sami stood for a second, shocked, then hurried after them.

They got to Sami's room, and Adam went in without knocking. Sami squeaked out a protest, but it was too late–Adam and John were in the room.

Sami closed his eyes and leaned against the wall in the tight corridor, waiting for Candy's scream of outrage, but nothing came. He heard the whump as a body fell onto the bed. Still nothing from Candy.

Sami put his head in the room. John was on the bed, and Adam stood over him, his expression almost parental.

No Candy. Sami was confused. When he'd left her fifteen minutes before, she'd been sound asleep.

"Ssst."

Sami jumped, startled, and looked at Adam in confusion, but Adam hadn't made the noise.

"Ssssst!"

It was coming from back the way they'd just come, down the corridor. Candy. It had to be.

Sami and Adam exited the room, and Adam headed further down the corridor to the last room, his...the biggest below-deck stateroom. Sami hurried down the corridor in the opposite direction.

Candy was at the juncture where you could go up to the bridge, down to the crew's quarters, or into the galley and from there into the salon. She smiled at him.

Sami didn't know what to say. He was ashamed of himself and confused as to her actions...her foresight.

"We're out, right?" she asked.

Sami nodded, his face clouding, but she smiled wider.

"Why are you smiling?" Sami asked. "Now we won't know where to go to be together. Candy, all the rooms are full."

"I'm smiling because you've been kicked to the curb, Sami! I'm so happy!"

She threw her arms around him. He didn't understand, not yet, but he would. He would see that it was better to be on your own and to fend for yourself. No amount of favor made up for allowing yourself to be treated like an unloved dog.

She took his hand. "Come on. Let's go see what we can get worked out."

On their way through the galley, they came across Carl sitting by himself. He had a gas lantern lit on the table in front of him, and he was making notes in a tiny notebook. He glanced up as they entered. He studied their expressions, their clasped hands.

"You guys going out?" he asked.

Candy laughed, and Sami blushed.

"Yeah, I guess you could say that," Candy said and squeezed Sami's hand. "Why are you here so late, Carl? Shouldn't you be headed back to *Big Daddy*?"

"Yeah, I should have been, but I got carried away with my note-taking. I'm leaving in a few minutes." He stretched, his hands at his lower back, and then he rummaged through his beard, scratching reflexively. "What are you guys up to? Heading to bed?"

Candy shook her head. "We haven't actually worked that out yet. My old room already had four in it, and Sami's room just got…taken over."

Carl noticed the hesitation, but let it pass. He was worn out and too tired to *look* for problems when there were enough obvious ones so readily available.

"You should go to ThreeBees. They have room over there," Carl said. He stowed his notebook in an inside pocket of his light vest.

"You think they'd have us?" Candy asked.

"Sure. More the merrier. I guess you heard they've had a good deal of trouble in the last couple'a days." Then he remembered Jade, and he remembered that it was…not a *secret*, exactly…but certainly private. However, Sami and Candy struck him as good people, really good. He liked Candy, especially. In his professional opinion, she was very healthy. He glanced around the galley, making sure there was no one to overhear. "You might want to wait a few days, though…"

He told them about Singer being bit and getting the sickness and that now they thought Jade might have it, too, and that they were watching, waiting.

None of them saw the shadow that lurked in the back doorway.

John Smith listened to every word Carl said.

Chapter Ten

Steve watched as a jet ski whined its way from *Flyboy* to *Big Daddy*. It was late for someone to be out, but the moon was bright enough to navigate by. It was probably Carl. Steve wondered if he'd come up with anything on that John Smith guy.

He settled back in the chair, the gun across his lap. He was getting tired. He'd have to get Brian up soon to spell him, but he didn't entirely trust that Brian would stay awake. That kid was almost as close to catatonic as Jade had been.

When they'd told Brian what had happened to Singer and why they'd had to put Jade back out on the boat, he had nodded in a resolute, almost unconcerned way. He'd sat with them for an hour but didn't speak, other than to say he thought he needed a little more sleep before stumbling back into the salon.

Steve wondered how long it would be, if ever, before anyone felt 'normal'. As long as you kept your head down and slogged through minute by minute, it seemed you could go on forever in that half-alive way. It was when you were brought up short by strong emotion—anger, fear, joy—that you had trouble reconciling the world as it is now.

Distantly, a dog barked. Steve reached down and grabbed binoculars. They had seen dogs at the shoreline on a few occasions, but once a dog started barking...it didn't usually end well for it.

He scanned the beach, left to right, looking for movement and then saw it–a big dog, lab or something like it, racing across the beach. It stopped and turned, barking, and then turned again to flee. Five of the dead were following; an entire contingent couldn't be far behind.

He wished they could do something to save the dog. Dogs were good animals to have, good companions, happy and uncomplicated. A dog in the post-apocalyptic world would be pretty much the same as a dog pre-apocalypse. Unless it had gone feral.

He lost sight of the running lab when it dodged inland and bolted for the woods. He lowered the binoculars.

"Were you looking at Jade?"

Maggie's voice was edged with strain. Steve turned in the chair and was troubled by her pallor and thinness; she glowed like a ghost on the dark deck. She wasn't doing enough to take care of herself. As much as she tried to act as though she could take or leave the people on ThreeBees, he knew that Maggie was damn close to saintly in how well she took care of them. She never put herself first, but you'd never get her to admit it.

"No," he said, "there was another dog."

Maggie's eyes searched the shoreline as if she'd be able to see the dog from here. Her hands twisted together. "Did it get away?"

"As far as I could tell," he said, erring on the side of kindness. "I didn't see any of those...those things get him, anyway."

She continued to stare into the dark distance, but her eyes had become unfocused. "I wish we had a dog," she, said and her voice was so wistfully sad, her wish so childlike, that Steve's throat tightened.

He stood and drew her to him.

She remained rigid, her arms across her body between them. Steve didn't pull back, and eventually she unclenched her hands and her arms dropped to her sides. Her body gave a violent shudder, then another...and she burst into tears.

He held her as she sobbed, and her arms came up to his waist, and she clung to him and turned her face into his chest. She shook against him, her grief almost violent.

He thought about Amelia as he stared at the dark shore. The woods beyond where he'd left her to rot. He felt his own tears, first hot and then cold, slide down his face. Guilt and shame ran through him like lava, heating him up and tearing down his defenses. His arms tightened on Maggie, and she jumped, startled.

His tears stopped her own, and she led him to the deck bench, clumsily stumbling in their embrace. His arms never left her as they sat, but now his head went to her shoulder. A hard twist of grief and guilt seemed to pull his stomach up to the base of his throat, and he choked on his words. "I...I left her...I left her to...in the woods, and...she was so, she just...didn't deserve it, and..."

"None of us deserved any of this...it's okay, it's going to be all right..."

"It's not...not all right...I left her, and she was still...she was moving and...oh God, Maggie, oh God help me, I left her there...and her head was...it was turned...around and..."

His words dissolved into shuddering tears.

She lifted his face to hers, his tears running hotly over her thumbs.

"You're right, it's not okay...none of this is okay. Amelia didn't deserve what happened to her, you're right. My husband, Joe...I don't even *know* what happened to him. I *think* I know, but..." She shook her head. "If he was on the train, then, I do know. He's probably still on that train." She sighed and dropped her hands into her lap. She looked past Steve, out over the water. It was moonlit and peaceful. She sighed again. "We don't deserve this, but this is what we have. It's better than the alternative...did you ever hear anyone say that? When they were talking about being in a bad situation? I think it's truer now than ever before. Because the alternative is..." She trailed off.

Steve wiped his face on his sleeve and watched her, the way the light lined the bridge of her nose, and dropped a kiss onto her forehead. Her eyes were dark and inner-directed.

"Maggie," he said, and she looked up, "I'm sorry. I'm sorry for what you went through."

She shook her head, confused. "You don't have to say that, we all–"

He leaned over and kissed the words away. Her mouth under his was at first startled and unresponsive. He persisted, drawing his hand up her arm and cupping her head gently at the base of her skull. He pressed his mouth to hers, parting her lips with his. The inside of her mouth was hot, and then her lips softened, returned the kiss.

"Here?" he said and ran his hands through her hair, drawing her head back to kiss her throat. "Okay? Are you okay? Is this good?" He murmured and whispered his way down her neck, his hands undoing the buttons of her blouse as she drew his shirt up and over his head.

"Yes," she said, her breath a drawn-out sigh. "Please...please. I want..."

They made love under the moon and the stars, the boat rocking gently. The sex was quiet, but desperately intense, and for a brief moment, they both forgot the circumstances that had brought them here.

Neither of them saw when Jade sat up in the rowboat.

~ ~ ~

"Maggie, this is Candy on *Flyboy*. You there? Over."

Maggie looked at the walkie-talkie on the table in front of her. She had told Steve she was going in to get water, but then she'd lit a lantern and sat down in the galley to think. She was already feeling guilty over what she and Steve had done together.

A large part of the guilt came from the fact that she didn't feel *bad*; she didn't *regret* it. She should...but she just didn't.

She reached for the walkie.

"Hi, Candy, this is Maggie. Over." She remembered Candy...blonde, bimbette-type, but there had been something to her, Maggie had surmised. Something that most people would miss.

"I'm sorry it's so late. I wanted to see if you had an extra bed over there on ThreeBees. An extra room, actually. Over."

Maggie looked at the walkie in her hand, her face a study in confusion. No one had ever requested to change from the huge, gorgeous *Flyboy* to the dumpy by comparison *Barbra's Bay Breeze*.

"Did I lose you, Maggie? Over."

"No, sorry, I'm right here. Listen, Candy, I'm not sure if…if we have a room or not. It's hard to explain. Over." What she meant was that she didn't want to explain, not on an open line. She hoped Candy understood the subtext. Then Candy confirmed Maggie's suspicion of a brain hiding under that cotton candy exterior.

"Loud and clear. Can we drop by tomorrow? After it's light out? We could talk. Over."

"Yes, of course. We'll see you tomorrow. Over and out." Maggie set down the walkie-talkie, wondering who Candy meant by 'we' and why she wanted a whole room. *I guess she hooked up with someone*, Maggie thought. *Good for her.*

"Seems so late for a call. I guess you could call it a call, right?" Bonnie crossed to the small pantry and took out a bottle of water with her initials on it. Everything was divvied, although they hadn't paid too much attention to the rationing. Not yet, anyway…not as much as they were going to have to.

"I guess you could," Maggie said, "but it's hardly late. What is it? Nine? Nine-thirty?"

"That feels about right," Bonnie said and sat across from Maggie in the banquette. "Nine used to be my bedtime, so it does still seem late to me." She smiled. "What time did you used to go to bed? Before?"

"All different times. It depended on the shifts I was working at the hospital." Maggie smiled at her hands. "My husband always went to bed at ten o'clock on the nose. He said he wanted to make sure he missed the news."

Bonnie smiled and then laughed. "'Miss the news.' That's a good one. He was funny, your husband?"

"Yeah, he was always joking. Everyone loved him for it."

"Especially you."

"Especially me, yes."

Bonnie patted Maggie's hand. "I lucked out. Got to keep my Randy. If I hadn't, well...I don't know what I'd have done. None of the kids showed up, you see, and..." Bonnie smiled, but her eyes shone with unshed tears. "I think I may have lost them all. I told you that already, didn't I?"

Maggie nodded but then reached for Bonnie's hand. "You can tell me again, I don't mind."

"No. It only does me so much good to cry...then it just gives me a headache." She sipped from her water. "Who was it on the walkie-talkie? No trouble at *Flyboy* or *Big Daddy*, I hope."

"No, nothing like that. Not as far as I could tell, anyway. Seems someone from *Flyboy* wants to come bunk with us on ThreeBees."

"You're kidding me. Why would someone want that?"

Maggie laughed. "Gosh, Bonnie...you got something against us?"

"No, honey, you know what I mean." Bonnie smiled warmly. "I wouldn't trade it for any of the others, you know that!"

"I feel the same," Maggie said. "I think someone from *Flyboy* has...uh...hooked up and needs a little private space, and we have that spare room now, especially if Brian stays where he is."

Maggie and Bonnie both glanced at Brian asleep on the far side of the salon.

"Word traveled kind of fast about the room, didn't it? What if Jade is okay? Where are we going to put her?"

Maggie nodded. "Yes, I know...I told them it was complicated. I didn't want to say too much over the walkie-talkie, though. We still haven't told Adam about Singer and Jade."

"Oh, he's not the boss of us, anyway. That prick." Bonnie clapped a hand over her mouth, her eyes round with shocked surprise at her own words. "Goodness!" she said through her fingers.

Maggie laughed. "You're right, though! He is a–"

"Maggie!" Steve's voice filtered in through the salon, past the still-sleeping Brian and into the galley. "Come quick!"

Maggie scooted past Bonnie and ran out the glass doors.

Steve was standing at the very back, the shotgun raised to his shoulder.

"Steve?" Maggie said.

He glanced back at her. "It's Jade. She's up. I'm not sure if..."

Maggie looked out across the water, and Jade was standing in the small rowboat, her hands on her hips. She was just a dark silhouette.

"I saw what you were doing!" Her voice rang across the water, thin but accusatory, verging on hysteria. "You're disgusting!"

Steve lowered the shotgun, and Maggie's face suffused with blood. She stepped away from Steve.

"You can't leave me out here!" Jade's voice was growing thinner, weaker.

"Jade, eat something!" Maggie's voice was a harsh and carrying whisper. "We put food out there with you! You have to eat or–"

"Fuck your food! Fuck you for putting me out here while you–" Jade raised her arm, no doubt giving them the finger, and the boat wobbled alarmingly. She dropped quickly to her knees, hissing out a breathy scream.

When they heard her again, her voice was choked with tears. It was too dark to see her face. "I'm going to jump in and swim over there. I'm going to...you can't...can't make me...stay out here by myself...I'm scared...please..." Her voice trailed away, and they could hear her faint sobs. Then she disappeared entirely. She must have curled back up in the bottom of the rowboat. "Please...please...I want..." Her voice carried weakly over the water, barely audible.

Maggie's face fell. Those were the very words she'd used with Steve when they'd made love. To hear them again, filled with so much pain...she was suddenly furious with herself. For not being careful, for not caring who...Christ, what if Babygirl had come out, and...she was an idiot! So thoughtless! She'd never forgive herself for what she had done.

"Jade?" Maggie called across the water. "Please eat and drink your water, all right? We're right here. We're not going anywhere, and *nothing* has changed." In her peripheral vision, Steve's face turned to hers, but she didn't look at him. Didn't acknowledge him. "As soon as we're sure, we'll bring you back. Jade, trust me! Jade? Do you hear me?"

Jade's thin arm, almost invisible, ascended from the rowboat and waved tiredly. "Okay," she said, and the two syllables rode plaintively across the waves.

Maggie dropped her head into her hands and stood motionless. Steve reached to put an arm around her, and she stepped away. "No," she said and seeing the startled vulnerability in his face, she said, "I'm sorry, but it's not…it isn't right. There's too much at stake."

"Maggie, there's nothing at stake. You're just using this as an excuse! We don't have anything to lose by–"

She held up her hand, palm out. "No…I can't. I can't do this. I have to…"

"You have to what? What? You don't have to do anything! You don't–"

"I have responsibilities! I can't just take up with you!"

"Nothing you need to be responsible for means that we can't be together." He grabbed her arms. "We'll be responsible together. We'll work together. Me and you."

Maggie shook her head, eyes closed. She wouldn't say anything more.

Eventually, Steve dropped his hands from her arms, turning her loose.

~ ~ ~

Early on the morning of August 10th, Sami stood on the back deck of ThreeBees, looking out to the rowboat.

"How long?"

"We put her out there yesterday morning. We didn't know what else to do." Maggie's voice was flat and worn.

Sami turned to glance at her. "It is difficult, but I am thinking you did the right thing. Did she have any symptoms?"

"No, Doctor, but Singer, her brother…he was symptomatic. He'd been bitten on the leg…a five-inch laceration, at least. Teeth marks, signs of bruising trauma." It was easy for Maggie to fall back into a doctor/nurse relationship. It helped straighten out her disjointed feelings.

"They were on the rowboat together?"

"Not at first. She swam out to him later that day."

Sami shrugged. "We can't judge it, can we?" His voice was sad but resigned.

"No, we can't," she said. She liked Dr. Rafiq. He was calm and courteous, if slightly too mild-mannered, too meek in his demeanor. The other doctors must have ridden all over him.

"I wanted to ask Steve something…is he here?"

Maggie dropped her eyes. "No. He left early this morning, before dawn. He needed to get back to *Big Daddy*."

"You don't have enough people here to stand watch?" It was both a question and a statement, and Maggie didn't know how to respond, so she shrugged. "Would it help if Candy and I came to ThreeBees?" Dr. Rafiq said. "We need a place where we can…be together. We'd like very much to join you here."

"I'm not sure what to do with Jade if she is okay; if she doesn't have the sickness. There's a good chance that she doesn't. This is really only a precaution."

"Might it not be better for her, and for you, if she moved to *Flyboy* after all this is over?"

"No! That wouldn't be for the better!" She tried to swallow the defensiveness she felt, but it came out in her tone, anyway.

Sami looked at her. "There might be some…resentment? When you bring her back in?" he suggested delicately. He could see that Maggie took it personally. Most likely she had put this girl's welfare on herself, because good nurses did that. "She might want a change of scenery. A wider selection of people might be a good thing for a young woman."

Maggie had opened her mouth to protest, but she closed it with a snap. There was more to Dr. Rafiq than met the eye, it seemed.

"Maggie!" Babygirl's voice peeped from behind them, and Maggie turned, expecting to see Babygirl running to her, arms wide to be swung into the air. She rode astride Candy's hip, and seeing them together, Maggie's heart stuttered in her chest. They could be mother and daughter. "Maggie, I love Candy!" Babygirl said and laughed delightedly at her own joke, hugging Candy around the neck. Their blonde heads looked like a matched set.

"Well, I love you, too, Babygirl," Candy said and hugged her tighter.

Babygirl leaned back and ran her hand over Candy's hair. "Like Mommy...just like Mommy," she said, her voice tiny but filled nevertheless with awe. Her hand shook.

"Your mommy had blonde hair, sweetheart?" Candy asked, her voice gentle.

"Before she did, but then it wasn't anymore." Babygirl's eyes had gone round, almost dazed. She started to slide from Candy's arms, but Candy held her tighter.

"Sami! Help me!" Candy called, alarmed by the girl's relaxing weight.

"I can't help you, Mommy," Babygirl said, her eyelids fluttering alarmingly.

"Babygirl! Sweetheart, what is it?" Candy shook her gently, but Babygirl's eyes began to roll back into her head. Candy lowered her to the deck. "Babygirl? Babygirl?"

"That's not...not my name..." Babygirl said, her eyes closing.

"What is your name? Stay awake, honey, and tell me your name!" All three adults huddled over the little girl. Sami lifted her eyelid to check her pupils, and Maggie felt for her pulse.

Babygirl felt them and didn't feel them, both at the same time. It seemed as though she'd floated up and away from her own body. On the deck, the lying down Babygirl's lips pursed, and she sighed. "Samantha..."

Standing to the side, Samantha looked at herself under the grownups, and then she leaned in, looking at Sami but whispering in Candy's ear...*my mommy calls me Sammy...*

~ ~ ~

"Sammy! It's time to go, sweetheart!"

Samantha appeared at her bedroom doorway and jittered in an excited circle, her party dress ruffling out. "Time to go! Time to go!" she said, singing the words, peeping like a little sparrow.

Her mom laughed. "Come on, Sammy, you don't want to be late, do you?"

"No! No! No!" Samantha sang and hopped foot to foot down the hall.

Her last hop brought her to her mother, and she stopped and looked up, grinning.

"What day is today, Sammy?" her mommy asked, smiling.

"June SEVEN! June SEVEN!" Samantha hopped up each time, raising her arms excitedly.

"Aaaaaand...what happens on June seven, Sammygirl?"

"BIRTHday! BIRTHday! TODAY is my BIRTHday! Yay! Yay! Yay!" Samantha collapsed in a fit of giggles as Mommy reached down to tickle her.

"That's right, my ladybug, my ladyfair...and we are going to party like it's–"

All at once, her mom wasn't tickling her anymore. She looked up. Mommy was leaning against the hallway wall, her hand to her head.

"Mommy!" Sammy cried with alarm, scrambling to her feet. "Are you okay?"

"I'm fine, Sammy, just a headache. I think I'm getting a cold, can you believe it? In the summer? Who *does* that?" She smiled, but a wince stayed in her eyes.

"Silly mommies do that," Sammy said, but her heart wasn't in it. She'd seen the look on Mommy's face, and it had not been a funny face look at all.

"Silly mommies is right, ladybug," she said and took Samantha's hand in hers. "Ready to hit it?"

"Ready, Mommy," Samantha said, and her mom smiled at her. Then she coughed. A lot of coughing. Then she was bent over with it, and still she kept coughing. Samantha patted her mommy on the back, first very gentle and then harder, smacking Mommy's back.

"Ow, Sammy, ow, okay, thank you, but I'm okay now." She grabbed Samantha's hand again. "Oh boy, now we're really late. Daddy will be maddy."

Samantha snorted out a laugh at the nonsense rhyme, following Mommy to the car. Their car was beat the hell up...that's what Daddy said. Mommy said that wasn't nice to say, and they'd have a better car someday. When she was done with school. Samantha thought it was funny that her mommy went to school. Just like a kid. Mommy's school was different, it was to do x-rays and see inside people for cancer or babies.

They drove away, and Samantha waved to the trailer. "Bye-bye, house, see you when I see you. Windows down, Mommy?"

It was hot and humid. Samantha could smell the ocean. Low tide. Daddy said you could always smell low tide.

"Windows down, Sammy," Mommy said and hit the buttons for all the windows except for Samantha's. Sammy liked to do her own button. They drove past their sign–Tuckerton Family Trailer Park–and bumped onto the highway to town.

"Where is everybody, Mommy?"

Normally, there would be a least a few people out on a nice day like today. The Kellermans liked to sit outside and watch birds, and the Lehman sisters were always in their little kitchen garden, puttering around, as they called it. The park seemed empty.

Her mommy was distracted, looking from the road to the little flip cell-phone in her hand. "I don't know, sweets. Eating lunch, I guess. Now, why can't I make a call? I have a signal." She mashed a few more buttons and then tossed the phone into the open purse at Samantha's feet. "Grab that if it rings, Sammy; it'll be your daddy." She glanced at Samantha and smiled. "You excited for your party?"

Samantha smiled and nodded, and she *had* been excited, back at the house she had been…but she wasn't as much, now. Something was wrong and not just Mommy's cold. Something was wrong with the trailer park, the highway, maybe everything. Her tummy was clenching up like it did sometimes right before her parents had a fight, or when Mrs. Rafern came out and yelled at her for no reason (Mommy said Mrs. Rafern had 'old times disease' and that made her 'difficult to deal with', but Samantha just knew she was a terrifying old lady).

They pulled into the parking lot of a strip mall five stores wide. Heads Up Hairstyling, Tuckerton Five and Dime, Tuckerton's Pizza, Dollar (S)Mart, and The Pet Palace. They were meeting Daddy and three friends from her class and their mommies. She was lucky that school was closed for teacher in-service day on her birthday. Otherwise, they would have had to wait until the weekend. Four was too many days to wait.

Samantha flew from the car as soon as it came to a stop. She danced around to her mother's side, excited to get into Tuckerton's Pizza and claim her gifts.

Mommy had leaned forward, her head against the steering wheel. Samantha opened the door. "Mommy?"

"Yep, I'm with you," she said and sat up straight. There were red dots in one of her eyes, and Samantha felt that deep shift of unease, like a big, mean snake just waking up in her stomach.

"Mommy, your eye…what happened to your eye?"

She flipped the visor down and looked at herself in the mirror, frowning. "It's probably from coughing, Sammy. That can happen if you cough too hard. There are these really small blood vessels in your eyes, that–"

"Birthday girl!"

Samantha turned and here came her daddy from the pizza place. "Daddy!" She ran and jumped into his arms, laughing. Then she remembered Mommy's eye. "Mommy coughed blood into her eye." Saying the words made her feel very bad.

Daddy tilted his cap back on his head and looked to the beat the hell up car where Mommy still sat. "You okay, Melissa?" he called across.

Samantha's mommy and daddy had decided to 'just be friends' instead of being married. That's why Daddy didn't live in the trailer with them anymore. He had an apartment in the town. There was no bedroom for Samantha there, so when she slept over, she slept in a tent in the living room, in her sleeping bag. It was so much fun, but she still would rather Daddy had stayed in the trailer with her and Mommy.

"I'm okay. I just have a cold or something." She came across the lot, smiling a small smile. "How are you, Mark?"

"I'm okay. I stayed home from work today, though. Felt like I was getting the flu." He coughed. "You got the keys?"

"I do," she said and dropped them in his open palm with a secretive smile and a small wink. "Come on, Sammy, let's go inside. Daddy has to get something from the trunk."

A twinkle passed between her parents, and Samantha was happy to see it.

"No one showed yet," Mark said over his shoulder, as he headed back to the car.

Melissa frowned. "That's weird. No one called." Then she remembered how she hadn't been able to make a call. Maybe something was up with solar flares or something.

Melissa and Sammy went in to Tuckerton's.

There was one man behind the counter. He told them to be patient because he was on his own today. Everyone else was sick and had called out.

The pizza place was empty, all ten tables bare.

"At least we get our pick of seats, right, Sammy?" Mommy said and threw the pizza man a smile, but he didn't smile back. Mommy shrugged at Sammy and raised her eyebrows, then lead her to a table near the big plate glass window that showed the parking lot.

"Mommy, what about the other girls?" Sammy said. Her dream of a table full of presents was going up in smoke, it seemed, but she was more worried than upset.

"Oh, Sammy, I know it's disappointing," Mommy said and hugged Sammy, "but I bet I can think of something that will cheer you up!"

She grabbed Sammy by the shoulders and turned her to face the window. "Tada!" she said, exclaiming excitedly.

There was a pink Schwinn with a white banana seat and big red bow leaning against Mommy's car. It was the one Sammy had wanted! She couldn't believe how beautiful it was, shining in the early afternoon sun, and it was hers! Everyone was going to be so–

Daddy's feet were on the ground, sticking out from behind the car. Did Daddy fall down? She tried to ask her mommy, but no words came out.

"Mark?" Her mommy's voice was faint, no way could Daddy hear from all the way out there...Mommy wasn't being loud enough. Samantha felt a swell of desperate anger. She banged on the window, hard enough to make it shiver.

"Daddy!" she yelled. "Daddy, get–"

"Hey, now, don't bang on that glass, little girl. Lady, could you keep–"

Behind Samantha, her mommy screamed, making her jump. It was a long scream, not like when Mommy saw a bug...this was like a scream if the bug was as big as a dog, as big as a lion. "Mommy, what?" Samantha said, and then she saw...

A man had her daddy and was dragging him by the leg–was that man helping Daddy?–he dragged and pulled, and it was like Daddy was stuck on something. Then he came loose, and the man toppled over onto his hiney. Sammy saw her daddy, and he looked all wrong. He was all bloody. The man put Daddy's leg in his mouth and bit into Daddy's jeans, but then a woman came from behind the car, and she looked mad, but she looked sick, too, like people in hospitals.

Not sick–dead, she looked dead, but she was moving, and she kneeled down near Samantha's daddy, almost falling, and she...she...

Mommy put her hand over Sammy's eyes and kept screaming.

"Lady, what the fuck?" The man came over the counter, and Melissa stepped back and screamed at him to stay back, stay away from her. Her hand slipped away form Samy's eyes. He held his hands up at his shoulders, palm out. "Okay, geez, lady...I just wanted to see what was wrong. Are you okay?"

She screamed again, dragging Sammy away from the window, away from the counterman. Something had gone wrong. Something was wrong. "Call the police!" she said, her eyes wild with panic. "Call an ambulance!"

"Mommy, what happened? What happened to Daddy? Let me see, let me see!" Sammy struggled, but Mommy held her tight, and then Mommy put a hand over her eyes again.

The pizza man spoke: "Okay, okay, I'm calling the police, okay? What do you want me to tell them? Are you having trouble with an ex or something? Is this a custody thing?"

Sammy pried her mommy's fingers from her eyes in time to see the man as he walked backward and glanced out the front window. He froze. "What the *fuck*..."

"Call them! Call the police!"

He turned back to Sammy's mommy, his eyes wide with shock. "Yeah, yeah, I am. I'm calling them."

Sammy watched his face go from fear to puzzlement as he looked at the phone in his hand. He shook it as if that would make it work. "I can't get a call to go through," he said.

No police, no help, she and Mommy were on their own.

Sammy looked out the window. The dead-looking man and woman had tugged Daddy's body halfway across the lot like a couple of dogs fighting over a ball.

"Do you have a car?" Mommy asked the counterman. He was still messing with the phone and didn't seem to hear her. "Hey? Do you have a car? Could you take us to–"

He was shaking his head. "No, no car. My wife dropped me off today and I can't get through to her. What's going on?"

"I don't know, but I have to get my daughter home," Mommy said. "Do you have a knife?"

"What's going on? Why can't I get anyone on the phone?"

"I don't know. Can I take a knife? I have to get my daughter home."

"Home?" he said as if he'd never heard the word before. Then he turned away from them.

Mommy relaxed a little when he disappeared behind the counter. She glanced out the window again. "We're going to have to run for the car, Sammy, okay?"

"Mommy." Sammy said, scared. They couldn't go out there. They couldn't.

"It's okay, babygirl, I'm gonna get us back home. Daddy left the keys in the trunk lock. I know he did. I'll get the keys and everything will be okay. Don't worry about anything, sweetie." She brought Sammy in front of her, squeezed her head to her stomach, and shuffled toward the kitchen. "Mister?" She got as far as the counter and even though Sammy's face was pressed to Mommy's stomach, she could still see straight through to the back. A door swung in the light breeze.

He'd left.

"Son of a–" Mommy said and gripped Sammy tighter. A large butcher knife was on the counter. Mommy reached for the knife and then squatted down and took Sammy's chin in her free hand. "We have to run, baby, okay? Look straight ahead and run to the car. Don't look at anything else. Just get in the car and close your eyes. Keep them closed. Okay, babygirl? You understand?"

Sammy nodded, but her eyes filled with tears. They would never make it. Those people would get them.

"It's okay. I've got you, babygirl, okay? I've got you."

Sammy nodded again, and Mommy stood and hugged her.

She pulled Sammy to the door. "Don't look at anything. Go when I say three. Ready?"

Sammy nodded, her stomach in such a knot that she didn't know if her legs were going to go or not, but she would try.

"One…two…three…" On three, Mommy opened the door, and Sammy ran. The car wasn't far, but she looked for Daddy, she couldn't help it, she looked, and she saw…

They were eating him. Eating her daddy. As she watched, the dead lady dug the eyeball from Daddy's face and brought it to her mouth. For a split second, Samantha felt she was seeing herself from her daddy's eye…her dress, shoes, and her face all done up in fear. Then the lady bit down hard, and Samantha was seeing from her own eyes again. Everything wavered for a second, and she felt dizzy.

"Samantha, get in the car!" Mommy said, hissing it, her voice mad but scared more than mad, and Sammy trotted around the car and jumped into the passenger seat. She couldn't see her daddy from here unless she turned around, and she wouldn't turn around. She closed her eyes tight and clapped her hands over her ears.

Her mommy cursed, crying, and the car rocked a little as she struggled with something at the back. Then the car tilted as her mommy sat on the driver's seat, and Samantha was relieved. Her mommy was here.

The trunk slammed. Samantha opened her eyes.

Daddy sat next to her, his face gone except for one eye and his upper lip and a half moon of skin on his forehead. Samantha felt all the blood try to slam out of her body, and she was very cold all at once. She couldn't scream because her breath was caught in her lungs. Her daddy's mouth was a red cave, a black cavern coming closer…

Then her daddy was tilting back the other way, being pulled from the car, and she heard mommy screaming. "Get away from her! Get away from her! You bastard! Get away from my baby girl!"

Then Daddy was gone, and Mommy was in the seat. Mommy was crying and jamming the key in the ignition over and over, and it wasn't going in. Then Daddy was at the window, trying to bite Mommy, and the key went in. Mommy screamed again and hit the buttons, and the windows went up, but not fast...not fast enough. Daddy's head was in. Mommy leaned over onto Samantha, she kicked and kicked, and Daddy's head finally fell away from the window.

Then Mommy drove them home.

Home was scary, too. People thumped and bumped at the door, and her mommy told Sammy to be very quiet. Don't make a peep. They'll hear us and then come in. Trailer doors aren't very strong.

So Sammy had kept very quiet, she'd tried to, but when she fell asleep, she saw Daddy all over again. His face was gone, and he was trying to...trying to...

She kept waking up screaming, and then mommy would put a hand over her mouth and whisper to her, "Shhh, babygirl, ssshhhh, s'okay, babygirl, Mommy's here, Mommy has you, babygirl..." and then Sammy would feel better–a little better–and she'd try to sleep again.

There was light in the trailer, and it was morning. Sammy was alone in the bed. Maybe Mommy was making coffee, because she always made coffee in the morning. Then Sammy had a good thought: *what if it had all been a bad dream? Just a bad dream and today was her birthday party day and there would be presents and...*

Mommy was dead in the kitchen.

Dead on the floor with one slipper on and one slipper off.

Dead with throw up in her mouth.

Sammy screamed and something bumped the trailer door as if trying to get to her, to save her, but not to save her, to eat her. Like Daddy got eated up. So she stopped screaming.

She squatted down near her mommy and shook her even though she knew it wasn't going to do any good. Sammy cried, but she did it quietly, the tears falling to her mommy's face.

Samantha whispered, "Mommy, please, please wake up. Mommy…I'm scared, Mommy, what should I do? Mommy? Please, please wake up, please…" Sammy pushed the hair away from her mommy's eyes, her pretty hair yellow and soft just like her own. "Mommy? Please…"

Mommy's eyes were dull, like dirty ice.

Then Mommy blinked. She blinked, and her lips twitched, and Samantha thought she should be glad, but she wasn't glad.

Then Mommy started to sit up.

~ ~ ~

"Samantha? Honey? Wake up now, sweetheart."

Samantha opened her eyes a crack, and everything was too bright and blurry. Her mommy was leaning over her, her pretty hair glowing in the sun. Mommy.

"Mommy," Samantha said and put her arms up. She was so glad to see her mommy. So glad.

Mommy reached for her. "No, honey, I'm not your mommy. I'm Candy, remember? You love Candy, right?"

The lady's face resolved, coming into focus, and that's when Samantha remembered everything. She remembered all of it. Daddy and Mommy and the knife she'd found in Mommy's purse. The big knife from the pizza parlor. She had gotten away from her mommy by using the knife.

It had been…it had been very bad.

Samantha sat up quickly and put her arms around Candy. She buried her face in Candy's neck and cried.

Candy rocked her, running her hand over and over her hair. "It's okay, Sammy, it's okay…I've got you, I've got you now. Let it out, sweetheart, let it all out."

As Candy rocked Samantha, Maggie turned away as her own throat began to tighten. She stumbled to the chair that Steve had occupied only hours before. She felt empty as though she'd just lost something important, something necessary…but what had she lost, really? She was no worse off right now than she'd been ten minutes or even ten days ago.

Nothing had changed, but she cried anyway.

Chapter Eleven

"You're not going to ThreeBees to take a watch?" Carl asked and looked up at the sun. Early afternoon. It would be at least another day and a half until they knew for sure if Jade was infected or not.

Steve shook his head at Carl's question and didn't stop what he was doing. It seemed very important to him to finish what he'd started, so he continued to curl the jumbled lines into neat coils. Whoever was supposed to be doing this was a dickhead. A lazy fucking dickhead. Steve's stomach soured. He couldn't get Maggie's words from this morning out of his mind.

"Do you want me take a watch?" Carl asked.

Steve shrugged his shoulders. "Yeah, why not? Doesn't matter who goes; they don't care, right? Why should they? Right?" Steve's voice had risen as he talked. His features twisted in anger, but Carl saw something else there, too. Bewilderment. Hurt.

He had to decide whether to ask Steve about it or let it go. Was it something that mattered to the well-being of everyone or just to Steve? The guy could just be in a bad mood. Bad moods happened to everyone. It was easy to get down if you stopped what you were doing long enough to think about everything that had been lost.

Steve's frustration seemed fresh, though, and at a guess, Carl would say that it must have something to do with Maggie. He'd felt the chemistry between the two of them…it was hard to miss.

In courtship, even in the best of circumstances, chemistry was hardly the be all and end all to a relationship, and these times were far from the best.

Carl decided to skip over it and let Steve bring it up if he wanted to. There was something else he and Steve needed to discuss.

"I didn't get a chance to talk to John Smith."

Steve looked up, his features softening from angry to curious. "No? What happened? Adam?"

Carl laughed and shook his head. "Not this time, no. He took me to find John, but John wasn't there each time. It was weird, you know? *Flyboy* is big, but it isn't *that* big...we should have been able to catch up with the guy."

"Maybe Adam was being disingenuous. Leading you astray."

Carl looked surprised at Steve's choice of words. "I keep forgetting you were a professor. You must have been a good one."

"I was," Steve said. "You, too, you know? I keep forgetting you aren't a pirate by trade. Yo ho ho."

Carl laughed. "The funny part is this is how I looked before, too. It usually helped with the people I treated the most."

"Who did you treat?"

"Bikers and vets," Carl said, the laughter dying out of his eyes. "The two worst groups to try and help. They just don't want it...it's a pride thing. Like cops."

"I could see that," Steve said, and both men fell silent for a minute, contemplating the past.

"Well, but anyway," Carl said, "do you want me to head over to ThreeBees? I really do think they could use the help...I don't think Brian is holding onto himself very well. Maybe I could do a little double duty–help watch Jade and talk to Brian, too."

Steve nodded, looking down. "Yeah, go," he said, then looked up. "I appreciate it. Tell Maggie...tell her I'll be over later. Okay?"

"Sure, I'll tell her."

The walkie-talkie next to Steve crackled to life.

"Steve, are you there? It's Maggie. Over."

Steve's face was a study in mixed emotions, and Carl felt an answering empathy in himself. Steve looked angry, resentful, hurt...but underneath all the other emotions rode a dawning hope. He grabbed the walkie.

"Yeah, Maggie, I'm here. Everything okay? Over." His tone was neutral, but Carl heard it as a very on-the-fence neutrality.

"Steve, if Carl is back from *Flyboy*..." the line went silent, but didn't click off. Carl and Steve looked at each other, bewildered. "...we could use his help over here. It's Babygirl...I mean, Samantha, her name is Samantha, and–" The line clicked to silence but not before both men heard Maggie's voice break.

"Maggie? Are you still there? Over."

There was a long space of nothing, and Steve turned, alarmed, and headed for the jet ski. Carl was a step behind him. The walkie crackled again.

"Could you come, too, Steve? I...I wish you would..."

Steve turned back, bumping into Carl, grabbing the walkie-talkie.

"We're on our way, Maggie. Over and out."

~ ~ ~

Maggie came out on the deck with a plate and two bottles of water and sat down next to Steve. She put the food on the deck between them and handed him the water. Then she turned to face the shoreline. It was just getting dark, and the sunset filled the sky over the pines. Sunrises here were gorgeous–fresh with hope and promise–because they came over the ocean, but there was something almost sad about the sunsets. It seemed the sun had gone too far away, leaving them behind.

Maggie shivered.

"Do you want a jacket?" Steve asked, even though it was at least eighty degrees on the deck, the breeze light.

"I'm sorry about earlier," Maggie said, without looking at him. "I don't know what I was thinking. I don't have any responsibilities. No one needs me here."

Steve knew that Dr. Rafiq had suggested Jade live on *Flyboy* when they were able to bring her back on board, and Babygirl...Samantha...had not left Candy's side.

He imagined that Maggie must feel very set adrift, but he didn't think she was doing herself any favors by sinking into self pity. If they were going to chance a relationship, he didn't want it to be based on them clinging to each other only because they'd lost everybody else.

It was unfair to both of them.

"Who needed you before?" His tone was light but direct. Not sympathetic in any way.

A small smile crossed her lips. "My husband did, I guess. From time to time, anyway. We needed each other. He was my responsibility."

"Not like this."

"Not like this, no." She lowered her head. "When we all started to get here...to the shore, the boat, everyone was telling their story, you know? Their survival story."

Steve nodded. It was a compulsion, almost, for people to tell each other what had happened to them. It had become the new way of introducing yourself–instead of asking what you did for a living, it was 'how did you survive it?'

"Everyone, almost everyone, had a story that involved a loved one, a friend, someone they *knew* at least, but not mine. I got here on my own. All on my own. I didn't even find Babygirl...Samantha...until I was almost here. I was starting to feel...jealous, in a way, of everyone else. As though fighting to get through as some kind of team–especially if it was a spouse or sibling–that was somehow better. It made me wish I'd been able to do that last part, or that last battle with my husband, with Joe. Even if he didn't make it, as he didn't, we would have at least had that one last thing together." Maggie shook her head lightly, seeming unaware of the tears on her cheeks. "I just felt...gypped, you know? Like I'd been denied something...something really great. Even if it was just closure. Knowing. Knowing exactly what had happened." She sighed and took Steve's hand. She still didn't look at him. "Then Samantha was telling us what she remembered...about her last two days. The things she had to...to see...to go through–" Maggie stopped with the back of her hand to her mouth and sat that way, her chest hitching, until she could get a hold of herself. "And your story, Amelia, and the things you have to remember, to carry with you." She shook her head. "I'm lucky. I'm the lucky one. I just didn't realize it, and I felt so bad, especially for pushing you away."

Steve squeezed her hand. "It's okay."

Maggie shook her head. "I realized that I've been too selfish, ever since the sickness. Not selfish, because that's the wrong word. Too insulated, maybe. Too stingy with myself. I was just so jealous. So angry all the time." She looked at him. "When Dr. Rafiq suggested that Jade might not want to live on this boat after everything we've had to do, I was shaken up. I felt like I'd only been considering my own feelings, my own viewpoint. Then, when Samantha took to Candy so quickly...I was devastated. Even though I've been holding her at arm's length this whole time. What did I expect?" She gave him a brief, unhappy smile. "Then with you, this morning...you were right, they were excuses. It made me mad that you saw it so quickly. I felt so...like everything I had done, keeping myself safe was ridiculous, worthless, and such a waste of time." Tears overran her lower lids. It was nighttime, now, and the ThreeBees rocked gently in the dark. "That's the worst part. The wasted time."

Steve wanted to take Maggie into his arms, and comfort her fully, but he sensed that he should let her decide...let her come to him when she was ready. To try to force her hand now might plunge her further into the emotional abyss she seemed to be trying to climb out of.

He squeezed her hand and said nothing as the silence drew out, becoming companionable rather than awkward. He could see the tension leaving Maggie's body as her posture softened, the careworn lines in her face smoothing out.

After a while, they began to talk again, but of inconsequential things: weather, fishing, grocery shopping, clean laundry...anything that had nothing to do with past or present horrors.

The night was full dark, pitch black. Clouds had moved in, covering even the cold light of the stars. All sounds in the ThreeBees had ceased as people went to bed. Candy and Samantha bunked down in what used to be Mrs. Allen's bed, while Sami spread blankets on the small bit of floor space left over.

Carl slept on Denny's former bed in the salon across from Brian. They'd had a long talk, a good one, mostly about Brian's family who lived in the Carolinas. He thought they might still be okay–they lived near the water. Carl neither encouraged nor dissuaded that train of thought, because no one really knew, did they? Eventually, they would go south themselves, when the weather began to change. Who knew? Someone from his family might be doing this very thing, at this very moment.

Bonnie and Randy slept in the same bed they'd shared since coming aboard.

Maggie drew her chair closer to Steve's and rested her head on his shoulder. They hadn't said much of anything in the last hour. It was too dark to see Jade. They couldn't even see the rowboat.

All light on board the ThreeBees had been extinguished, but on *Flyboy*, a few rooms were lit with weak lamplight, and occasionally they could see someone crossing the deck with a lantern or sometimes a flashlight. If there was noise on *Flyboy*, Steve and Maggie couldn't hear it from where they sat.

The only sound was the water lapping against the sides of ThreeBees and the occasional splash as fish jumped in search of prey, or avoiding being prey themselves.

Maggie turned her head enough to kiss Steve lightly on his jaw, right at the curve under his ear. She felt him shiver. He turned to her, and she caught a quick glimpse of his eyes, searching hers, questioning. She leaned further forward, found his lips, and they kissed.

At the rowboat, where Jade lay in the throes of the last fever she'd ever have, a hand came out of the black water and cut the rope tethering her to ThreeBees.

For a brief moment, Jade floated free, and then the hand emerged again and grabbed the trailing line. The line pulled taut, small beads of water springing away from it as the rowboat turned, creaking gently.

John Smith transferred the rope to his teeth and began to swim for *Flyboy*.

Towing Jade behind.

Chapter Twelve

In his bed, Adam flopped angrily from his back to his side. He leaned up, punched his pillow into shape, and slammed himself back down. Then he turned again, sighing harshly.

He was too aggravated to get comfortable.

Too pissed at Sami.

That fucking ingrate.

It was a douche move, him going to ThreeBees, but Adam was pretty sure that cunt Candy had put him up to it. If those two thought that Adam didn't know they'd been fucking this whole time, then they were dumb as fucking dirt, and they deserved each other.

He sat abruptly, the idea of going down the narrow hall to John's room crossing his mind. John would commiserate. He'd have to, because he was in a nice room at Adam's good graces. Adam was the one who put him there.

He lay back down, instead. He liked John, but he didn't know him that well. Guy might think Adam was queer for him if he showed up in his room in the middle of the night. Adam laughed in the dark. Then he remembered Sami's betrayal, and the laugh died an abrupt death.

He sat up and lit the gas lantern by his bed. Sami was lucky that Adam had kept his secret for this long. Maybe he wouldn't keep it any longer, but even as the thought occurred to him, he dismissed it. Sami thought he'd let the world down, but Adam was reasonably sure that no one else would think so. They might even be interested to learn what Sami–Dr. Rafiq–*thought* had happened–that the much-celebrated AIDS drug, Lazarus, had most likely caused the mass sickness and then the mass resurrections…but certainly by now it was a moot point as far as assigning blame.

No, he wasn't going to reveal Sami's secret. Let Sami do it. Guy was too dumb to realize that people might actually be interested to know his theory. Let that dumb trailer trash he was banging find out…she was probably dumb enough to think knowledge meant culpability. Not that she'd think of it in those terms. Trailer trash didn't think that way.

He doused the lantern and turned onto his side.

Easier in his mind, he slept.

~ ~ ~

John Smith gripped the rope in his teeth and swam toward the random bits of light on *Flyboy*. He was a strong swimmer because he'd been around water his whole life. He knew how to keep his breathing even, his muscles calm, and tendons relaxed.

The water was cool, but the air was warm. Fine for swimming. The rowboat seemed to have no weight at all. His forehead stung where the salt water soaked into the stitched line across his forehead, but even that felt good in its own way. Seawater cleaned a cut. Kept it free from infection. That's what his old man had always said anyway.

Swimming like this reminded him of his dad. They'd fished, swum, and sunned themselves on the flat rocks of the jetty, just like seals. That's what Dad always said to him. "We're just like seals, Mikey, you know that? Just look at us!" He'd turn and dive, his feet breaking the water and splashing Mikey in the face, and then he'd come back up, throwing his head back to clear the shiny black hair from his eyes. He'd grin, his white teeth shining, and

Mikey would stare, blank faced, water running into his eyes. He'd paddle and paddle to stay in place, trying to understand the flash of white teeth. What did it mean? Sometimes he would bare his teeth in imitation. Sometimes Dad laughed when Mikey did this, and sometimes he did not.

~ ~ ~

He had to go past ThreeBees to reach *Flyboy*. He changed to an even breaststroke so that no part of him would break the waterline except his head. The breaststroke was the quietest stroke he knew. It was also the slowest. As he swam, his mind drifted again to a time when he had been little and his name had been Mikey, and they lived on (almost literally) the ocean. Back to when it was always hot and the bad times hadn't started.

~ ~ ~

Fishing. Mikey had felt good when he and Dad fished. Dad praised him because Mikey didn't mind putting the small fish, the bait fish, onto the hook. Mikey had been little–two, or maybe three, but he could recall the memories with perfect clarity, any time he wanted. He looked down, and there was a long, shiny minnow struggling in his little hand. The fish was both cold and deceptively muscular, and Mikey could feel the minute ripples of its scales as they would come apart and come back together, as the fish bent and twisted.

He put the hook through the minnow's mouth, right where Dad had showed him. He liked the hook going in, the breaking of the tough skin, the extra contractions of the little fish. It shined and glittered in the sun. Some of the scales came off in his hand. Mikey bared his teeth at the minnow.

Dad told him the way to catch the bigger fish was with the little fish. That was bait. Three-year-old Mikey had understood the concept with a clarity that his dad would have found astonishing. Mikey hadn't started talking yet, so his dad didn't know anything he was thinking.

When they caught the bigger fish, Mikey would feel a pleasant sizzle of anticipation in his stomach. The knife would come out, and Dad would put the knife right under the bigger fish's head and slice straight down. Mikey could simultaneously feel the knife in his hand, the resistance, and then lack of resistance as it broke into the cold skin, and a tingling feeling in his chest and stomach of the knife going in.

Is that what a knife going in felt like? First a tingle, and then a hot tickle lower down, right above his pee-pee. He'd squirm a little, especially if was a really big fish, especially if it curled tightly under the knife.

"It's okay, Mikey, they don't feel it. Fish don't work like that."

It had been disappointing to hear, but ultimately, he decided that Dad was wrong. Such muscular contractions meant one thing: pain. Good pain. Tingling and exciting.

They would take the fish back to their little house on the beach, and Dad would say, "Mom is gonna be happy with this lot!" and sometimes she was, but sometimes she wasn't. Sometimes, his mom stared at him, and she didn't bare her teeth, and she didn't blink, she just stared. At those times, Mikey would stare back until it seemed his mom's eyes had become like the fish's eyes…blind and flat. Dead. *Bait mom*, he'd say to himself, in the secret confines of his mind. Then he would bare his teeth at her.

His mom never touched him if she could help it, but Dad did, and they played all the time. He told Mikey that Mikey was lucky to have a young dad, a fun dad. When they swam together, his dad would tickle him, grab his ankle, grab him by the waist and throw him up and up. Mikey would splash back down into the water, sometimes fighting for breath, choking on a lungful of water, and Dad would be laughing. Mouth wide, hahaha and weird breath.

Mikey tried it sometimes at night. He was up a lot when his parents slept in their bed. He'd go to the little bathroom downstairs off the kitchen, drag a chair to the sink, and stand at the mirror. He would open his mouth wide and say "haha" and "hahaha" and try to make the weird breath. It didn't sound the same, so he stopped doing it.

Sometimes he stood and watched his parents as they slept. They kept their eyes closed for a very long time. Mikey didn't know how they did that. He tried, but his eyes always wanted to stay open. Mikey didn't have control over his eyes. They would burn with too much air and too little sleep. He would rub his eyes and stand at his mom's bedside. Her mouth would hang open, and he would stare at her cheek and think about the minnow. The hook going in. Sometimes it made a little 'pop' sound when it did.

The cold fish blood.

People blood would not be cold, though. He knew that already, because people were not fish. His dad said.

When he turned four, they put a box on the floor and told him it was his birthday present. The box moved, and he didn't like that. He knew boxes should not move. He kicked at it and Dad said, "Whoa, whoa, hold on there, Mikey, let me show you what's in the box." His dad and mom had exchanged a glance that Mikey could not read. They were always doing things with their eyes...with their eyebrows...that Mikey didn't understand.

Dad opened the box, and a puppy was in it. It had brown wavy fur, brown eyes, and a brown nose. "That's a Chesapeake Bay Retriever, Mikey, and he's yours, son. You can even name him."

Mikey had looked from his dad to his mom. She had her hands put together and pressed under her chin. She was not baring her teeth, but she had stretched lips, and water leaked from her eyes. "Isn't he a cute puppy, Mikey? Isn't he sweet? Everyone loves puppies, Mikey, and you will, too. It will make you...happy. Puppies make people happy, honey."

Mikey had looked at the puppy a little while longer, waiting for happy (whatever that was), and finally Dad took the puppy out of the box. It had come to where Mikey stood. Its tail was moving, and it was jumping. Its pink tongue hung loosely from its brown lips.

Mikey kicked it. Hard.

His mom was yelling as his dad swept him up and carried him down the hall into his room. She yelled after them, "I *told* you! I *told* you there was something wrong with him!" Her voice was weird like she was choking.

His dad had put him on the bed, and then he had paced back and forth, back and forth. He did it so long that Mikey decided to pick up one of his books instead of watching his dad pace. The pacing was boring.

So he'd begun to slide from the bed, his eyes on the book he wanted, when his dad picked him up by the arms and yelled into his face, shaking him roughly. "You can't *hurt* things! That's just a defenseless puppy! What is *wrong* with you, Mikey?"

Mikey saw the anger and fear in his dad's eyes and came to a conclusion. They hurt the fish all the time, hurting fish was okay, but hurting a puppy was not okay, most definitely not.

"You can't hurt puppies, Daddy," Mikey said. Like a foreigner trying to learn a language by ear, repetition would become his Rosetta Stone–though not much repetition was ever needed, and Mikey was very bright.

His dad lowered him back to the bed, mouth agape. "Mikey, you spoke?" It was both a statement and a question, as if he was trying to convince himself of something.

Mikey nodded.

"Cath! Honey, come in here!" Joy and fright were uncomfortable companions in his tone. They would become more comfortable as time wore on–Mikey's actions would demand it.

His mom came to the door, holding the puppy in her arms. Her lips were tight. Puckered.

"Say it again, Mikey, say what you said before."

Mikey looked from his dad to his mom.

"You can't hurt puppies, Daddy," Mikey said. His voice was tiny, but his pronunciation and diction were perfect. It was as though he'd been speaking for years. His parents stared at him in amazement. They'd had him to a doctor once, but the doctor had said he would speak when he chose to. There was nothing physically wrong with him. That advice had cost them fifteen dollars that they didn't have.

Mikey's parents were poor, very poor. Mikey knew this from overhearing them talk together when they thought he was asleep. His mom wanted to go back to a place called California, where she had been a little girl, or to New Jersey, where Daddy had been a little boy…but his dad wanted to stay where they were: Mexico.

They stayed in Mexico.

When he turned five, his dad started to teach him things from books. He said that Mikey would go to school right here at home, right in the kitchen, isn't that cool? Mikey didn't know if it was cool or not, but he knew to nod. He knew by now that certain phrases–certain tones–demanded that answering nod. He was learning to parrot.

Mikey would study at the little round table. When he felt his dad's eyes on him, he would reach over and run his hand over Chief's head. Dad liked that. He liked when Mikey petted Chief.

Chief was big now, with wavy brown fur that felt coarse under Mikey's hand. The muscles of his brown head would jump and squeeze when Chief panted or twitched his ears, and Mikey liked to feel the muscles, although he didn't know yet that was what they were called. Mikey had an intense desire to *see* whatever it was that jumped under his hand and how it made Chief's ears move. How would he get to see?

Chief liked having a hand on his head. Mikey didn't know why–himself, he hated to be touched.

Mom worked at a hotel, helping people by making sure their rooms were nice and clean, but then she lost her job. His mom and dad fought and fought for three weeks, and they ate more and more fish until one night, his dad said, "Fine, we'll go back to Jersey, then you'll see, Cath. We'll be no better off. We'll be *worse* off. *Much* worse."

"Because you'll have to get a *job*? Is that what's killing you? That you'll have to *work* for once?"

"I'm young! I don't want to waste my life doing a job I'll hate! Do you want to be like your parents? Sweating yourself into an early grave? You think that's cool?"

The fight ended the way all the bad ones did: violently. They hit each other, pulled hair, spit, punched, and screamed. Sometimes, Mikey would come out of his room to watch. When they were to this point, they never noticed him.

Often, there was blood. Mom, Dad, or both would have a bloody nose, or sometimes, cuts on their face. They would have bruises, black eyes, occasionally a broken finger or toe. Then they would strip and do something else. Sometimes, it was more violent, more intense than the fighting. They breathed heavily, moaned, and cursed. There was more hair pulling. Mikey didn't know what they were doing, but there was something about it that excited him…especially if there was already blood.

They moved to New Jersey and lived in his dad's parents' house. Mikey's grandmom and granddad.

Mikey didn't understand his grandparents at all. He didn't understand the things he had to do. He didn't know what was expected of him.

Then there was school, church, cold, shopping, clothes, and shoes. Even the food was different. Nothing Mikey had ever had before, things like hot chocolate. Noodles and cheese. Peanut butter and jelly, and the fish was covered in a crunchy crust and shaped like a plank and covered in cold red from a bottle, and it didn't even taste like fish.

Mikey stopped talking again for a little while, but his granddad didn't like that. His grandmom took him to another doctor, in a big building with lots of other people around, other kids. They had looked at him, into him with lights and things on scopes, prodded him, and took his picture…

They told his grandmom that he would talk when he was ready. There was nothing physically wrong with him.

Eventually, he did talk again. He was learning. Learning his new life.

He learned to suss out who was important. He learned that the one who made the decisions was the one you wanted to be near. He never played with Dad anymore because his dad was…weak. Reduced in some way that Mikey couldn't yet articulate, but that had to do with the fact that his dad lived in the basement and rarely came out. He yelled a lot, and Granddad had to go down and make him be quieter. Then sometimes, his dad would cry, but Granddad ignored the crying as though it was beneath him. Not worthy of notice. Mikey liked that. He liked Granddad because Granddad was mostly one way: cold. Mikey appreciated it. It was easy to understand.

Eventually his mom left, and then some time after that, his dad left, too. Sometimes he came back to visit and would ask if Mikey wanted to come live with him? Mikey always said no. Mikey *endured* his dad's visits…nothing more. It was just time passing as far as Mikey was concerned.

Then his dad stopped visiting, too. By that time, Mikey was eleven and in the fifth grade. School, he found, was no different from anything else–it was just a matter of finding a solid spot to stand, and letting everything occur around you.

Mikey got along okay.

Then Chief died.

Chief had stayed with Mikey. His dad had said you shouldn't separate a boy and his dog. Mikey had been bewildered by that, but had filed it with every other bewildering thing that people said and did.

Chief wasn't very old, but he got sick. Cancer, his grandmom told him, cancer that was eating him up inside.

Mikey thought that was so interesting. Something was eating Chief from the *inside*? How would that work, exactly? He started watching Chief with avid interest, sometimes laying his head on Chief's chest when the dog lay sleeping by the couch.

To his grandmom, Mikey looked just the picture of a boy devoted to his oldest, bestest friend. In reality, Mikey was trying to hear the chewing.

Then one morning, Chief had been dead in the kitchen. Mikey was curious about the cancer. Would he be able to see it? Could he catch it in a jar? So he had gotten the big knife from the butcher block where Grandmom kept it, and he had…

They took him to another kind of doctor after that. A doctor who wanted to talk and talk. Mikey learned a lot from this doctor. He learned the difference between himself (abnormal) and everyone else (normal). He learned about feelings and what they meant to other people. He learned about the teeth baring. The eyebrows. The hahaha with the weird breath.

It was more or less an accelerated course in 'fitting in', and Mikey could never have learned so much on his own in the same short time span.

It was very helpful.

He'd learned to hide the things that satisfied him, and to hide them well, because they were atrocious to other people. Years went by, and Mikey fit in better and better, more and more, until he was well-liked and even loved by the people around him. He was valedictorian of his high school. He had a girlfriend. He began college. He had even decided his major: psychiatry, but then everything changed.

Mikey had watched with curiosity when his roommates died, reanimated, and then ate his current girlfriend. He'd pushed her out of his room and into the shared living room where his roommates stumbled in clumsy circles, moaning. He wasn't sure what reanimated humans would do, he wanted to see, and he had seen.

It had been exciting as they tore her apart. It had taken her a long time to die because she had fallen face down, and it was a while before they got to her jugular. The screaming was irritating, but Mikey (now Michael) had merely tuned that part out.

He called up the memory of his parents fighting, the blood and the moaning. That had been powerful…but this…this was even better. He felt as though sparks were jumping and snapping in his brain. He watched as one reanimated roommate gagged and threw up a wad of wet hair. A good portion of his girlfriend's teacup-handle ear lay in the vomit.

It was satisfying in the way gutting fish had been, gutting Chief.

He'd found a good vantage point to view the carnage, and for three days, watched as people died and reanimated, or died and stayed dead, and ate each other indiscriminately. It was the best time.

Then it had stopped. There were no more survivors except himself. No one for the walking corpses to go after.

For the first time in his life, Michael had felt an emotion: depression. Black, smothering, unmanning depression. He couldn't get the carnage out of his mind, the swelling, almost sexual feeling that he got when he saw the killing occur.

He needed it.

Then he fell ill. In his depression, he neglected himself. He didn't eat. He barely drank anything. He lost fifteen pounds in the space of one week. He contracted bronchitis that quickly became pneumonia, and in his run down state, it was nearly fatal.

He was found in the back of a CVS by another survivor. She was ransacking the pharmacy, looking for anything that would come in handy, when she found Michael curled up next to a blood pressure machine.

She shook him, and he came to briefly. She asked his name, and he could only shake his head, made mute by the clogged, drowning feeling in his filled lungs.

"How about John? John Smith?" She'd smiled down at him, and he'd gone away again, the fever carrying him to dreams of bloodied teeth under cracked lips, rich, red organs spilling forth, and over and over he saw the ear vomited up by his roommate.

The woman and two others had come back for Michael, referring to him as John, and transported him to where they had made an encampment in a nearby apartment building. Over the course of the next two weeks, Michael, now John, was nursed back to health.

Once healthy, he repaid their kindness by leading a contingent of the reanimated humans to the apartment complex while the people inside slept. Michael (John) was not afraid of the undead humans...not in the way the other survivors were. To Michael (John) they were simply another *type* of human, a fun and slightly dangerous type. In some ways, they were easier to understand because they were so singular in nature. They only wanted one thing: to kill and eat the living.

It had done more to buoy his spirits than any antibiotic ever could. The depression lifted. John Smith, formerly Mikey and then Michael, decided to keep his new name. It was as though his own last fever had burned his old life away, awakening him to this new purpose, this extraordinary new human he had become.

When he had discovered the survivors on the boats, it had been even better. The last boat he'd been on, the *Open Rhodes*, had been very exciting. There had been six strong people on that one. The carnage had been magnificent and deeply satisfying. He almost hadn't gotten away, so enamored was he by the killing.

Flyboy would be even better. John Smith had never been on a boat as large as *Flyboy*. It would take a long time, maybe a day, maybe even two, for the festivities on such a large boat to be over.

He'd swum out from shore in the first light of dawn, towing his yellow life raft until he was close to the smallest boat, the *Barbra's Bay Breeze*. He knew the little raft would be hard to see in the yellow, morning light. Then he had climbed aboard, cut his forehead, and waited for them to 'find' him. He knew they would eventually, and he also knew that being injured or ill made people accept you quicker.

That was how humans operated.

The undead ones, anyway.

~ ~ ~

John Smith swam past *Big Daddy*.

In the wooden rowboat he towed, Jade's first life burned out.

Then her second began.

~ ~ ~

His slow and even strokes brought him to *Flyboy* in less than fifteen minutes, but getting his prize on board would be tricky. It wasn't late, only somewhere around nine or nine-thirty–pre-sickness, it would have been prime time, but now, with a lack of resources and lack of interest, people tended to be out just after the sun had fully set.

John paddled near the hull of the big boat, heading for the back. There was a low portion–kind of a large step–that would give him access to the other decks. He'd hang back there until the ship was completely quiet. Then he'd haul the rowboat in, get the girl aboard *Flyboy*, and let the fun begin.

He clambered up onto the step and turned to sit. His lungs, still feeling the lingering effects of the pneumonia, were grateful for the break. He could just see into the rowboat, fifteen feet away. The girl was moving sluggishly, writhing in the bottom of the boat. She was very small. A curl of doubt wormed into John's consciousness. She wouldn't be able to overpower anyone. He'd have to give her a helping hand.

At that thought, the literal image floated into his mind of his hand in the girl's mouth, being bitten. Would he feel different if he were one of the cold reanimated? It occurred to him that in some ways, he was already more like them than he was the other, hotter humans.

Maybe like the transition from Mikey to Michael and then to John, becoming a walking corpse was part of his destined path. Maybe the undead John, nameless from then on, was his ultimate form. The idea held a certain power.

Somewhere behind him, in the depths of *Flyboy*, Adam was tossing and turning in his room, thinking about Sami and secrets…thinking about checking on John Smith and deciding against it.

John Smith sat waiting as August tenth became August eleventh. It had been just over two months from the time of the sickness, and John was eagerly, if quietly, anticipating the hell he was about to unleash.

He had waited this long.

He could wait a bit more.

Chapter Thirteen

"Shit, shit, shit…" Brian said, fairly dancing with agitation. It was somewhere around two in the morning, and Brian had taken over the watch from Steve about fifteen minutes earlier.

Steve had pointed out the slack rope and told Brian to keep an eye out, make sure she didn't drift too close. The lack of tension wasn't in itself cause for alarm. The rowboat often drifted enough for the rope to hang limply from the cleat.

So Brian had kept an eye out in the pitch dark of the overcast night. He sat, but an excess of agitation pushed him back to his feet. He looked out over the black water. He strained to hear anything at all that would tell him if Jade was too close or not. What if she had decided to paddle in by hand?

"Shit…shit, shit, shit…" His agitation increased, and he told himself he was just spooking himself–the feeling wouldn't go away, but it also wasn't enough to sound an alarm. Deciding, he bent to take up the slack rope, and he pulled it in, hand over hand. He would see for himself if Jade was still in the boat.

The more he coiled, the more uneasy he became. Finally, the entire line was curled wetly at his feet, and he considered the frayed end of the rope in his hand. Why would Jade cut herself free? Brian shook his head, his stomach tied in a tight, uneasy knot.

"Carl? Yo...Carl! Wake up, dude!" Brian shouted in a whisper back to the salon. He didn't want to wake everyone. Not yet.

After a minute, Carl ambled out, looking like a disoriented bear fresh from hibernation. Then he saw the frayed end of the rope in Brian's hand, and his eyes focused.

"She's gone?" Carl asked, and Brian nodded. Carl turned and hurried back into the boat.

Brian stood dumfounded, wondering what could have happened to Jade, and then Steve and Maggie were on the deck, followed by Carl.

They all stared at the rope in Brian's hand.

"Why would she cut herself free?" Brian asked, and Maggie shook her head. The clouds covering the moon broke apart, and the moon bathed everyone in its blue glow. They all looked pale and ghostly, their eyes deeply shadowed.

"She wouldn't–or couldn't–actually. She didn't have a knife."

Brian was opening his mouth to ask if a fish could have bitten the line apart when they were all startled by a muffled gunshot from *Flyboy*. They turned in unison just in time to see something fall over the rail. Had it been a person? Did someone just go overboard?

Then a low, ululating scream travelled across the water.

"What the *fuck*–" Steve said, and then the gun went off again, making them flinch.

"Jade," Maggie said, her voice flat, almost a question but not quite.

Steve turned to her, confused, his thoughts a racing jumble. He fumbled for the walkie-talkie. "Jade? What are you saying?"

She held up the frayed end of the rope.

Steve shook his head once and then looked back to *Flyboy*.

It made no sense, but he believed it one hundred percent all the same.

Somehow, Jade had gotten onto *Flyboy*.

Shakily, Steve opened the line on the walkie-talkie.

"Adam, what's going on over there? Over."

"Adam, this is Steve, we're concerned about you guys. Over."

"Are you having trouble? Over."

"Adam?"

~ ~ ~

John Smith was having a tough time. He'd nearly lost Jade already.

As he'd sat and contemplated life as an undead, she'd struggled up before he was ready and swayed side to side in the unsteadily rocking boat that still floated fifteen feet from the back of *Flyboy*. Luckily, she did not face his direction, but rather the empty ocean.

She would have stepped out and sunk, had she been aware of him. He'd seen them do it before. They were blinded by their hunger, made stupid with need.

He scanned the area around him and saw a line curled on the deck. He pulled it down and then began to ease the rowboat forward. He pulled slowly so as not to cause her to tip right out of it. He also had to remain very quiet. After a tense minute, the rowboat was almost within his grasp. He leaned out to grip the leading edge, but his foot slipped on the wet step, and his leg went in.

He righted himself, but Jade had already turned toward him at the sound. She took a step. Then another. She clambered clumsily over the seat. A low moan had begun in the back of her throat. Her arms rose. It was the hunger.

John steadied the rowboat and pulled it closer. The tension had drained from his body, and now he was only cold. Only calculating. He gathered the other rope in his free hand. He had to wrangle her quickly, before she fell, but also before she got too close. If he did decide to become an undead, he'd do it on his own terms.

She got to the front of the rowboat and walked right into the V, then stumbled, her ankle turning. She fell toward the water, arms still reaching for John.

He was ready with the rope, and he snaked a looped a section around her neck as she pitched to the side. He kicked her hip, twisting her as she fell, and the line formed a rough noose. Then she hit the water and sank.

Sinkers were heavy. John's arms strained, and he pulled, stepping up and back onto the deck, and finally, she slid from the water, moaning. Immediately, her arms reached for John standing above her. The line had cut into her neck and a blackish gel oozed out and fell in small clumps to the deck. She struggled to her hands and knees and then stood, swaying.

She would have fallen off the back of *Flyboy* if John hadn't jerked her roughly forward, playing out the line as he walked backward. She followed. She walked to the step first and then struggled a foot up onto it. With her next step, she was unbalanced, and she almost tumbled sideways. John yanked again, pulling her forward onto the deck and onto her knees. One of her kneecaps dislocated with a pop.

She reached for him and struggled up again.

John stepped back, playing out more line. His mind was still coldly calculating. He watched as she lurched, nearly falling. This one was so weak, so small…how was she going to unleash hell?

She won't, John thought, *not without help.*

He let her get close, his eyes half lidded and predatory. When she was close enough that John could feel the cold that came off her in waves, he stepped around, kicked her feet out from under her, and pushed her from behind. She toppled to her hands and knees. John grabbed her under both arms, bringing his hands up to either side of her head, effectively locking both her head and arms in place. Then he lifted her from the deck, bringing her back against his chest. She flailed and kicked, and her strength was more than it should have been for such a tiny person, but she was still no match for John.

He knew right where he wanted to go with her: Adam's room. You always start with the leader because the fastest way to kill a snake was to cut off its head. John had been cheated on ThreeBees. The big kid–Danny? Denny?–had swaggered around saying that he was in charge, and so John had killed him, waiting to see the explosion of disorientation when they found their leader dead–but there had been none. So he'd watched and waited, and then he'd been taken to *Flyboy* and found out who was *really* in charge. Adam was IN CHARGE.

Once Adam was a sinker, the rest would react like panicked sheep, and one by one, they'd become sinkers themselves. If they weren't eaten too quickly.

John struggled his skinny sinker through the narrow hallways of *Flyboy*. She fought, but had become slightly more sluggish. The longer the dead were undead, the slower they became. Their bodies deteriorated, but not nearly as quickly as non-reanimated human bodies. Something to do with the lack of heat in them, John surmised. Heat caused accelerated decomposition and the undead were cold, almost supernaturally so.

The boat was quiet, and the loudest sound was the thin moans of the sinker in his arms. Her vocal cords vibrated, and it was almost like the reedy trill of a cricket. Her thin limbs twisted and turned coldly–almost mechanically–and another person might have dropped her through sheer revulsion, but not John.

He made his way to Adam's door, and when he reached it, he realized he had no way to open it, as his hands were locked on either side of the sinker's head. He couldn't put her down, couldn't let her twist her snapping mouth toward him. Using his elbow, he knocked on the door.

No answer.

He knocked again.

"The fuck?" Adam's voice came muzzily from the room, and John knocked again. The sinker's feet trailed against the door, and her toenails made minute scratching sounds, like cats requesting to be let in. "Hold on, hold on, Christ." There was a hiss as a gas lantern was lit within the room.

John braced himself and as the door swung open, revealing Adam's face full of sleepy disgruntlement, John whispered, "For you!" and pushed the former Jade inside.

Adam's eyes were more confused than alarmed at the cold and stumbling figure filling his doorway. His first startled thought was, *there's a chick in my room!* and as Jade fell forward onto him, twining her thin, cold arms around his neck, Adam's second (jubilant) thought was, *a slut!* As Jade's teeth sank into the side of his soft, vulnerable neck, and he stared in astonishment past his assailant and saw John Smith in the doorway, his third thought was, *what the fuck?*

Jade's head snapped back, and she had a large chunk of ragged flesh in her teeth. Adam watched as her face was suddenly bathed in a gout of dark red blood. He felt a simultaneous pulling sensation in his neck, as though someone were hauling rope out of it, jerkily hand over hand. It was an uncomfortable feeling.

His eyes, now beginning to close, went back to the doorway where John still stood. John's face was alight with warm and vivid interest, and he seemed to search Adam's face caressingly, almost lovingly. Adam's last thought of all time was, *dude's gay for me.*

Then he died, as the blood intended for his body gushed out onto the floor.

John stepped forward and once again grabbed Jade under her arms. He didn't want her to do too much damage to Adam's body and the infection from her dirty mouth would already be well at work. He hauled her backward and in one quick move, tumbled her out into the hall. She began to crawl back to the warm corpse, and John put one boot down on her head, pinning her in place as he pulled Adam's door closed.

She struggled under his foot, arms swinging wildly, rejuvenated by the blood and the enticing meal so close by. John could hear people beginning to stir, the gas lanterns being lit and cautious footsteps in the hall. He reached down, grabbed his sinker by her hair, and dragged her to the next door in the hallway: his room. Formerly Sami's.

He opened the door and struggled Jade inside, avoiding her snapping red mouth. Controlling her now was like trying to control a bag of furious spider monkeys. Her limbs acted independently of each other. She vibrated furiously, sounding like a small electric motor: a sewing machine or child's toy. He pushed her face down and tried to step on her head again, but found he couldn't keep his balance. He dropped down, one knee on her neck, the other at the small of her back. Still, she struggled and buzzed.

The footsteps increased, and now John could hear distant voices. He couldn't make out the words, but the tones were only cautious; alarmed, yes, but ready to be assuaged.

He had to make his sinker stop buzzing. He pulled a small folding knife from his pocket and flicked the blade open. He reached down and grabbed her by the hair, shifted his weight and pulled her head back, exposing her neck. He felt her throat with his fingers, sliding them up and down her neck in the dark of the cabin. He sliced down and across to where her knew her voice box to be, severing it. Her sounds ended as though he'd flicked a switch.

With effort, he turned her face directly into the deep pile carpet, then he lay on top of her, his hands controlling the movement of her head and scissoring her legs between his, stilling most of her movement.

Then he listened again.

There were cautious footsteps in the hall outside his door, then three people whispering. "Do you think we should check on Adam?"

"What? Knock on his door? No fucking way, man."

"Yeah, he'll rip you a new asshole."

"I heard *something*…what if he fell? Had a heart attack, seizure, or who knows what?"

There was a long considering silence, and then the whispers began again. "Well, you do what you want, but no way am I gonna."

"Yeah, me neither, fuck that guy."

"You're right, you're right, never mind…I just thought…"

"Yeah, I hear you, but it's *Adam*, dude. He'll be a total dick if we wake him up. Everything is fine; let's just go to bed. Fuck."

They shuffled off, leaving the hallway in silence.

John let out a breath, and Jade struggled groggily beneath him.

In the room next door, Adam's room, something bumped.

In the flickering light of the gas lantern that still glowed on his bedside table, the former Adam opened his eyes.

John Smith sat on the upper deck, the captain's observation deck, and his eyes were alight with strange emotion. He'd waited until he was sure that Adam had reanimated, and then he'd lifted himself from the struggling Jade. He'd left his bedroom door open, opened Adam's door, and then gone fleetly through the hall, popping each door open by a few inches, giving the sinkers access to each room.

Then he'd climbed to the bridge, blocking access behind him, and listened as the fun began.

It had been about an hour, maybe slightly longer since he'd brought Jade on board, and now *Flyboy* was beginning to come alive around him. John felt that the boat was having a rebirth of sorts, a glorious rise from the mediocrity of mere survival to the visceral and literal fighting for its life.

Wasn't it better to be fully alive and fighting than to be half alive and trudging through the day to day of boring human existence? Yes. It must be.

Like a sign, the clouds above cleared, and the moon came into view, shining cold light onto the deck below. A woman ran, fleet footed across the deck, and behind her trudged a man, heavily dragging his limbs as though they were extra baggage. She turned and fired on him, and above, John's eyes lit with admiring surprise. His mouth dropped open, and he panted briefly, adrenalin coursing through his system.

The woman dropped to her knees at the railing, and for a moment John was awash in disappointment—was she giving up so easily? With a scream of mingled rage and fear, she grabbed the approaching man around the knees and rose, lifting him up and over, and he fell, moaning, into the water below.

The woman screamed again, in triumph this time, and turned to stare after the vanished sinker. She pulled the gun from where she'd stashed it at her waistline and shot into the air, her teeth gritted in a way too frightening to be called a smile.

Sitting on the deck above, John patted his hands together in excitement. Then the walkie-talkie by his foot burst into staticky life. "Adam, what's going on over there? Over."

"Adam, this is Steve, we're concerned about you guys. Over."

"Are you having trouble? Over."

"Adam?"

John glanced at the walkie and then away, distracted. The woman had been magnificent! She was very strong, very much a survivor! If she got to a boat or the jet ski, she'd make it out for sure; John had no doubt of it.

He lifted the gun from his side, took careful aim, and shot the woman in the leg, high up in her thigh. It was lucky the moon had finally decided to show itself; otherwise, he might have killed her by accident, and if she weren't a carrier, she'd never rise. *This one deserves to rise again*, John thought.

She screamed and crumpled to her side, holding her leg. Adam appeared at the other side of the deck, swaying and hungry, one side of his body covered in the drying blood that Jade had let, plus a fresh glaze that was not his own. Behind Adam, down the corridor to the rooms, screams were starting up, one by one.

The woman looked up at John on the captain's deck, and he saw that her teeth were still gritted; she was angry! What an extraordinary woman! Her gaze went from the undead Adam, lurching toward her, back to John, and before he knew what was happening, she'd pulled her gun up and had it trained on him.

He ducked sideways, laughing, throwing himself out of the chair just as the gun fired. He heard the glass of the cabin shatter behind him, bits of it bursting outward and peppering his back. He waited, panting and chuckling, but no more shots came.

He peeked with caution over the rail and saw that Adam had found the woman. John felt a welling of disappointment, but it was quickly assuaged as he watched Adam at work. The woman fought hard, and John felt the heat in his stomach once again, the tingly warmth that went to his penis and even to the ring of his anus, tightening it thrillingly.

Unaware that he was doing it, he curled his lip up, exposing his teeth. He looked feral in the moonlight, crazed with bloodlust.

The walkie-talkie crackled again.

"Adam? What the hell is going on over there? Over!"

Now the undead and alive alike were pouring up from the bowels of the ship, almost as though Steve's voice had called them forth. The screams were exquisite, magnificent, music to John's ears. The main deck was pandemonium, hellish in the unconcerned light of the too far distant moon. Blood shone black and ran like water, slicking every inch of the deck. Bones made the acquaintance of their owners in grossly unacceptable ways. Even as they died, most rose up again, their eyes shiny with silver and uncaring death.

Grinning crazily, John lifted the walkie-talkie and opened the line.

Let them listen.

They'd suffer the same fate soon enough.

On ThreeBees, the blood drained from Maggie's face as the screams from *Flyboy* were broadcast to them via the walkie-talkie. In his surprised horror, Steve fumbled it, almost dropped it, and would have if Carl hadn't stepped forward to steady his hand. Of them all, Carl looked the least shocked, the least shaken. He listened carefully, head cocked.

"Jesus Christ," Steve said, choking on the words, "what do you–"

Carl put his hand up in a 'stop' gesture that would have been insulting if Carl's hand hadn't been shaking.

Under the screams and the noise of general panic, Carl could hear breathing, a faint panting. Probably whoever was holding the walkie-talkie. Was it Adam? Trying to let them know what was happening without being able to speak? *Yes, most likely*, Carl thought. He told the huddled group what he was thinking.

With the line held open, they couldn't get a message to him. They could only sit and listen helplessly.

Then the sound cut out.

Steve depressed the send button. "Adam? Is that you? Over."

The line opened again to the sounds of pandemonium, and the voice whispered, "Yes, it's me, Adam. Over."

A cold line painted itself down Steve's back, and he stared with sudden suspicion at the walkie-talkie. His gut churned with acidic bile. Carl gave him an odd look and took the walkie-talkie from his hand.

"Adam, what's your situation? Over."

The line opened again, and the distant screams seemed to go on and on. They all listened intently. Steve opened his mouth to say something, some word of caution, when the voice came again. It seemed to slink out of the walkie's small speaker.

"It's...it's bad over here. The sinkers got on board, somehow, and they're...they're killing everyone. It's terrible."

The walkie cut off again, and they stared at each other. Brian had wandered to the railing facing *Flyboy*.

Steve's stomach clenched at the word 'sinkers', and he had to swallow an obstruction that was trying to block his throat. Beside him, Maggie grabbed his hand and squeezed it. He glanced at her, and her eyes were black with an emotion he couldn't read.

Carl had noticed the speaker's voice break on the word 'terrible.' It was almost as though…as though he'd begun laughing, but that made no sense. It had probably been the beginning of a sob. That was much more likely.

"Adam, we're coming to help. Stay hidden, do what you have to do. Are you somewhere safe now? Over."

"I'm on the bridge deck, the captain's deck. The door is bolted behind me. I can see…I can see…everything." The last word was drawn out, almost breathed across the line to them.

He's exhausted, Carl thought. *He's barely hanging on.*

"Okay, hang in there, Adam. We're on our way. Over and out."

Carl straightened and turned to Steve.

"I'll raise some guys from *Big Daddy*, and we'll–"

"Don't go over there."

The voice was tiny but drilling and coming from the dark salon, it startled them all.

It was Babygirl, Samantha, and she stepped onto the deck. She was in a white nightgown that fell to her ankles, and it rustled prettily in the breeze. Her eyes were open but unseeing, her hands hung limp at her sides.

"You'll die over there," she said.

"Sam? Samantha, honey, where did you go?" Candy's voice floated out of the salon doors, and then Candy was behind Samantha, a relieved smile on her face. "Sammy, baby, don't wander–"

Samantha swooned, and Candy caught her as she fell.

"Sammy!" Candy said, her voice snapping with alarm.

Sammy blinked and looked up. "Hi, Candy," she said.

Candy smiled. "Hi, Babygirl, you okay?"

"I'm okay, why?" Then she seemed to notice where she was, and she looked around, confused but not frightened. "How did I get out here?"

Steve and Carl looked at each other, and Steve shook his head, as though he, too, was just now coming awake.

"Ring up Dave on *Big Daddy*. Tell him bring at least eight guys and every gun they can carry, plus the flares. Everyone who can, bring a two-man ski so we can pick up anyone who goes overboard." He had a recollection of Singer stepping off the dock back when they'd gone ashore to bury Mrs. Allen, but the water was deeper here, there was less chance of a sinker getting a hold of you. "It will be best if we can get *Flyboy* cleared of sinkers. Better than bringing people back here or to *Big Daddy*. We don't want all the boats compromised. I'll tow the rowboat behind my jet and–"

"Don't do it." Maggie's voice was a flat whip crack. "Don't go over there."

"Maggie, we have to. If Adam is okay, then other people will be, too. I don't know how Jade got over there, but it doesn't matter now." He felt an uncomfortable shift, but dismissed it and pressed on anyway. "We can save the people who aren't bit. We *have* to, Maggie. You know that."

She looked into his eyes and shook her head. "I *don't* know it. Let's just pick up and sail further away." Her hands gripped his, her nails digging in. "We can just *go*."

He stared at her, surprised and confused by what looked like cowardice on her part. Maggie wasn't a coward, so what was the problem?

"Steve, listen to me," she said and leaned close, "if they were able, they would have abandoned ship. Anyone who was okay could have jumped to safety, and swum over here...but they haven't! It's a *lost* cause, Steve. *Flyboy* is lost. We need to go and get as far from here as possible. It's all gone bad here. Can't you see that? Can't you *feel* it?"

Steve shook his head and a vision of Amelia flashed into his mind: Amelia lying in the woods, struggling to get up.

Screams came across the water from *Flyboy*, faint and ghostly. "No," he said, "I'm not leaving anyone behind."

She stepped away from him, dropping her hands.

"Maggie? We have to go over there. We have to help them."

She turned away, giving him her back. He felt himself crumbling inside, wanting to give in to her, but he turned instead and addressed Carl.

"Let's get a move on."

~ ~ ~

Randy tied off the line on the medium-sized rowboat, then he tugged it hard, making sure it was secure to Steve's jet ski. He huffed a little and favored one knee as he stood. His shadow was sharp and black in the bright deck lights of ThreeBees.

"That'll hold," he said. "You could get ten, maybe twelve people in here, if you're careful. I don't know if you should take more than that." He massaged his bunched, arthritic fingers and his face wrinkled into lines of concern. "I'll come with you. If you think–"

"Randy!" Bonnie said from the deck. Randy's eyes never left Steve's, but Steve shook his head as the jet bobbed beneath him.

"I want you and Brian here on ThreeBees. I'm going to get two or three guys from *Big Daddy* over here, too. Listen, if we come back," he glanced up at Maggie, but she was at the railing, her back to him. Her posture was tense, but listening. "*When* we come back...everyone who comes back will need to be checked...*everyone*. You can't let anyone with a bite or a new scratch on ThreeBees. Okay?"

Randy nodded and stepped back. "Yes, I hear you."

There was another gunshot from *Flyboy*, and they all flinched.

Distantly, Steve heard a small contingent of jet skis start up near *Big Daddy*. They were going to meet him and Carl at the back of *Flyboy*. Steve looked at Maggie and then turned and keyed his jet ski to rumbling life. Next to him, Carl did the same.

They started away, Steve going slowly to keep the rowboat from jerking on the line. He glanced at Maggie once more and then faced forward and tried to clear his mind. The line to the rowboat played out behind him, loop over loop.

"Maggie! Don't!" Randy shouted, his voice shocked alarm. Steve looked back in time to see as Maggie brushed past Randy and scrambled into the rowboat. Steve released the jet's throttle and the machine died, rocking in Carl's wake.

Maggie stared hard at him, her posture defiant in the harsh lights. Then she smiled. It was unsteady and sad, almost resigned, and she waved for him to go. As she sat she called across: "I'm going with you!"

"You should stay here, Maggie! You're our only nurse!"

"Dr. Rafiq is here, he can do it! I'm going with you and Carl. I might be needed over there more!" Her voice echoed against ThreeBees giving her tone a tremulous, wavering quality. The rowboat rocked beneath her as the ocean sloshed between the two boats. She waved at him, an impatient gesture. "Let's go!"

Steve hesitated. He didn't want Maggie on *Flyboy*; it was too dangerous. "I want you to stay here!"

"Now you know how I feel!" she called and, to his surprise, her voice was tinged with a laugh.

He shook his head but said: "Are you sure?"

Maggie waved for him to go. He gazed at her a moment longer and then throttled up and fell in behind Carl. The lights from ThreeBees didn't carry far and before long he was plunged into darkness. He glanced behind him as the rowboat went from light to shadow, obscuring Maggie. He shivered and faced into the wind.

Flyboy hung in the distance, ghostly and dark.

Chapter Fourteen

Maggie grabbed the sides of the rowboat to steady herself as the light from ThreeBees disappeared. Her insides were quaking, and it wasn't from incipient seasickness. The strong, salty breeze felt good, and she lifted her face to it, taking a deep breath, and let it push the hair back from her eyes.

She felt she was seeing everything very clearly.

She pictured Candy and Samantha and knew that somehow, Candy was meant to be Samantha's protector. Maggie–whose feelings had been ambiguous at best about the added responsibility–had only been a substitute, a temporary guardian, and a poor one at that. Candy was younger and stronger, and she'd be a real mother to Samantha.

Maggie looked at Steve's back. Only two months had gone by since the end of the first life and the beginning of this second, scarier one–but it felt like longer; it felt like years. Could she be forgiven for admitting her love for Steve? Who, now, would do the forgiving? Who was left to judge?

No one. No one at all.

She'd been selfish–she'd already admitted that–and it was time to redeem herself, if only *to* herself. She'd go to *Flyboy* with Steve and do her best to help. It felt right, and it felt better than cowering in the kitchen, ignoring every pounding on the door…pounding that might have been Joe? In the depths of her terror that mroning…had she been too frozen to let her own husband in? She would take that uncertainty to her grave.

Maggie brushed tears from her eyes that might have been caused by the wind and resolved that she wouldn't think about it again. It's done…whatever else might occur, that part of life was gone.

It was time to let the past die.

Steve throttled down as they approached the back of *Flyboy* and then he cut the engine altogether. The other jet skis sat silent in a rough, bobbing semi-circle, the drivers' eyes wide and glittering in the dark. The random screams and thuds continued on the main deck above them, and each burst of noise caused a fresh ripple of unease to pass through the riders.

Steve turned in his seat and pulled the line to the rowboat hand over hand, bringing Maggie right up next to the jet. "I want you to take this jet ski and circle *Flyboy*…in case anyone goes overboard."

She shook her head. "I'm coming with you. Onto *Flyboy*."

"Maggie, listen–"

"I won't," she said, cutting him off, and then she smiled a brief, nervous smile, "I won't listen. I'm coming with you. Please don't waste time arguing." She smiled again, and this time it was warmer, calm.

It took everything in him to quell his protest, and he simply nodded. "Okay. If you're sure." His eyes searched hers, filled with concern, grief, love…love most of all.

She nodded again, and Steve turned, looking at the men in a searching way, and then his eyes landed on the person he was looking for.

"Dave, I want you to take this jet ski and circle. Go slowly. Pick up anyone who is capable of climbing in the rowboat, but *don't* get near them, okay? No matter what, and don't take them to *Big Daddy* or ThreeBees. Keep them in the rowboat until we get *Flyboy* cleared. Got it?"

Dave nodded and maneuvered his two-person jet ski up to the rowboat. Maggie climbed out of the rowboat and onto the jet. Then Dave and Steve changed places, and Steve settled behind Maggie.

"Good luck. See you in a few," Dave said and throttled slowly away into the dark. Steve watched him go. The rowboat bumped along behind Dave's jet making him look melancholy, like a child pulling an empty wagon at the end of a long day.

Steve had the sudden feeling that it was all about to go very, very wrong. Finally he tore his eyes away from Dave and faced the group.

"Okay. Let's roll on up there."

They docked by twos and tied the jet skis to the back of *Flyboy*. There wasn't enough room to tie them all off, so they ended up tying them the jets to each other. Finally, they were all crouched in a line on the platform that ran across the back of the boat that gave onto the back deck.

Steve had given them each instructions on which area to hit along with the explicit reminder to shoot for the heads of the sinkers. He, Maggie, and Carl, would take the bridge and the bridge deck, see if Adam was still up there. He was the only one they knew for sure who was still alive and well. At least, he had been until his walkie-talkie had cut out.

He looked at each face again and was heartened by the resolve he saw there. Maybe it would be okay after all. It's not as though the sinkers were smart or strategic. This small contingent should be able to restore the ship to order in less than fifteen minutes. *Flyboy* was big, but she wasn't the size of a cruise ship, for Christ's sweet sake.

"Okay, let's–" Steve's command was cut off midway as a body lurched off the back deck, landing directly on Kyle, one of the youngest guys from *Big Daddy*. Kyle was forced to his knees from the impact, and quick as lightning, the sinker wrapped its arms around Kyle's mid-section, its mouth yawning wide. Kyle tried to stand, but he was too unbalanced. Then the sinker's teeth found his bare wrist, and they tumbled together into the water. They sank in a boil of furious bubbles before Kyle had even had a chance to scream.

Everyone stared at the water, shocked at the suddenness of the attack. One man began to stand, as if to jump in after Kyle, but another man restrained him. It was too late to help. They'd all seen the thing sink its teeth in the poor kid's wrist. There was no coming back from a bite.

Steve's eyes met Maggie's, and her eyes were round and shocked. He put a hand to her cheek. "You okay?" he said, just loud enough for her to hear, and she nodded. He leaned over and kissed her once then leaned in and kissed her again, longer. When he pulled back, her eyes were closed. "Here we go," he said, still only for her, and her eyes opened.

"Here we go," she said and turned to face the back deck of *Flyboy*.

Steve popped his head up over the edge. From this vantage point, he could survey the whole deck. There was a bundle about halfway across, possibly a person. It was hard to tell in the blue moonlight. There were still muffled screams from below where the rooms and the engine were located, but this deck was quiet.

Steve motioned everybody up, and they scrambled onto the deck and fanned out, headed for the stairs on either side that would take them to the next deck. Steve stood one minute more watching them disappear. He checked for Carl and Maggie, and then they trotted quickly across the deck to the stairs.

They were almost there when Maggie heard a low moan from behind them.

She stopped short, turning, searching for the source of the sound. It could have been one of the undead, or it could be a survivor with an injury–there was no way to tell until she located the source of the moaning. Steve and Carl had stopped, too, and now they stared at her quizzically. She cupped a hand to her ear and tilted her head...*listen*...the low moan came again and this time, she could tell it was coming from behind one of the large, hard plastic boxes that sat on deck and held all sorts of boat equipment. She began to move toward it, and Steve grabbed her hand and mouthed, *wait*.

A wet, dragging noise came from the spot where she'd heard the moan. The hair went up on the back of her neck.

A white, bloodless hand appeared from behind the deck box, waving spasmodically. Then it slapped onto the deck. It seemed to brace itself, straining, fingers working, and then the wet, dragging noise came again. A shock of blond hair appeared from behind the box, and the arm was bent almost double, elbow sticking straight up into the air. Then the arm straightened out again, waved in the air like a bug antennae, and slapped down flat on the deck. The arm braced again and a face began to appear from behind the box as the arm pulled.

Maggie's heart leapt with fear and pity. She put her hands over her mouth to hold back a scream. It was a sinker.

Where its eyes should have been there were two chewed, blackish cavities, and its lips were gone. It grinned like a skull, teeth shining whitely in the moonlight. Between the eyeless cavities and grinning teeth, its nose sat untouched. There was a small diamond in the side of one nostril, and it glittered surreally in the moonlight. The arm performed its complicated maneuver once more, and it dragged itself further out, and now they could all see that it was just an arm and a head attached at one shoulder, trailing muscle and gore and bits of a ringed tube that Maggie identified automatically as its esophagus–the rest of it was gone.

It moaned again, and a small whimper escaped Maggie's throat. The arm changed course mid-air and angled toward the three of them. It knew they were there.

Carl stepped forward, drawing a knife from his belt. In one swift movement, he bent and jammed the knife into the cavity that had once held the eyes and into the brain behind. The knife sunk to the hilt. The arm spasmed sharply, and then collapsed onto the deck, becoming still.

Carl rejoined Steve and Maggie, wiping his knife on his pants. They ascended the stairs to the next deck. This one was smaller and ringed with once-fancy deck chairs. A large glass doorway led to the main salon, dining room and kitchen (*galley*, Maggie reminded herself with distracted unease). A shadow rushed past behind the door. Maggie gasped and took a startled step back, hitting the rail. She pinwheeled her arms, panicked, and Steve grabbed her around the waist and steadied her.

Another shadow flitted past the glass doors, and then another. It was almost like watching fish in a darkened tank, but those weren't fish, Maggie reminded herself.

"Should we go in there, or…" She let her question trail off, and Steve shook his head.

"No, let's get to the bridge. We have to help Adam, if he's still up there."

They ascended one more deck to the bridge. The door was closed but not locked, and Steve turned the handle and opened it slowly, pushing inward. He scanned the dark room. Facing the window, sat a captain's chair and a seat on either side for crew. A curved bank of screens like blind eyes sat above a board of complicated dials and instruments. No sinkers.

"Adam," Steve said, his voice a rough whisper, "you in here?"

No answer.

He moved to the door behind the captain and crew chairs that gave out onto the smallest top deck, the observation deck. This door wasn't locked, either. He pulled it open. "Adam? Are you out here? Adam?"

The area was small and utilitarian compared to the bigger decks below. There was no movement, no sounds of sinkers wandering clumsily. No Adam.

He turned and motioned Carl and Maggie to move past him out onto the observation deck. "This will give us a good vantage point...we can see the lower decks from up here." He followed them, closing the door behind.

They went to the rail and stood looking down. Everything was eerie in the moonlight, deserted looking. Well below them, Steve saw movement out in the water and could hear the rumble of the jet ski's engine...Dave, patrolling.

"Welcome aboard."

The voice came from behind them. It was soft but strong, full of twisted irony, making them all jump. It was followed by a laugh.

John Smith emerged from the heavy shadow at the far corner of deck and boat. He held a gun.

"John?" Steve said, his voice full of inquiring confusion. "Are you okay? Where's Adam?"

Carl didn't say anything, only regarded John with caution.

"Adam's busy." John said and brought the gun up to point it in their direction.

"What the hell are you doing?" Steve said. "Put that gun down. We have to help everyone who–"

"No, that's okay," John said. He smiled and the smile was full of mischievous good humor. He hefted a coil of line he held in his other hand as if considering its weight. "I already helped everyone. I helped them along to their second life." He laughed.

"You're crazy," Maggie said. Her tone was one of amazed realization. She took a step toward him.

"Oh, no...no you don't," he said and pointed the gun at her chest. "None of that, thank you. But, since you're the closest, you get to help!" He tossed the bundle of line to Maggie. Instinctively, she scrabbled to catch it, but it spilled from her hands like a sprung snake.

"Clumsy," John said absently. He motioned for Carl and Steve to sit. "Hands behind you to the rails and the lady can tie you. Good solid knots. I'll be checking, of course."

Maggie tied Carl and then Steve, her shock so great that she almost had no feeling in her hands. She kept dropping the line, fumbling the knots in her cold, nerveless fingers.

"Maggie, will you just *please*..." John's voice was full of an almost parental frustration–a daddy coaxing a reluctant toddler to eat her peas. Maggie felt a sweep of unreality try and wash over her, and she fought it.

"I'm sorry," she whispered, maybe to John, maybe to Steve and Carl as she tightened the knots on their wrists.

"Good, okay, good enough," John said. "Plop right down there, and scoot your back to the rail."

Maggie did as she was told. The hard, horizontal rails seemed to brand three lines of cold across her back from shoulder blades to tailbone. John Smith leaned over her. She pulled back at his intimate heat, and tears slipped down her cheeks.

He tied her wrists, sat back on his heels, and smiled at her. His eyes clouded with puzzlement and he cocked his head.

"You look sad," he said. His tone was consoling, commiserating. And very, very false. "How about this...I'll get you a dog. You can name it and everything. Would that make it better?"

A floating sense of unreality tried to surge over her at his words and she struggled to quell it. She stared hard at him. He had a shallow scratch that began under his ear and dwindled away by the time it hit his collarbone. It was fresh but already beginning to clot, dotted with little pearls of blackish-looking blood. She had a sudden urge to take his pulse...how was his heart? Sluggish? Slowing?

He smiled, and it was the strangest expression she'd ever seen. If you bisected his face at the nose and only saw the smile, it would look like a more or less normal one...possibly just a bit more strained than most. If you looked from the nose up, just at the eyes, you would see a man who was far away, thinking of nothing, shut off, not home. They were the staring eyes of a catatonic.

"John." Carl's voice, calm and authoritative, just shy of questioning, cut through Maggie's reverie.

John turned his dazed stare to Carl, grin widening.

"John, I can help you," Carl said, "but you have to let us help everyone else first. John, there are sinkers on board *Flyboy*."

John's expression morphed slowly from the grinning mask to a look of surprise so exaggerated that it looked like a caricature of surprise: eyebrows raised, eyes wide and frightened, lips pursed in an 'o'. "You *don't* say!" His voice was laden with the heaviest dose of sarcasm Maggie had ever heard...even that was a caricature of what normal sarcasm sounded like. Then his features snapped all at once into the easy lines of a man completely comfortable with his circumstances.

"You're Carl, right?" He stood and laughed. "You're the psychologist. That makes sense. You know, I was going to do that, too. As a career, I mean. I would have been a good psychologist," he said absently, looking over the railing. A scream came distantly from far below. "You brought more people with you?"

"Listen, John, we're in trouble here," Steve said. "I don't know what this was all about, but I don't care right now. We have to get the sinkers off of *Flyboy*. Then we'll get this...whatever you're doing...figured out."

John turned from the rail to regard Steve. "Are you in charge now?"

Steve glanced to Maggie and Carl in confusion. What was this guy talking about? Carl stared at him hard and moved his head by millimeters left and right...'no'. Steve looked at John Smith again. A gunshot rang out somewhere close by in the dark, maybe the next deck down. Steve felt his stomach begin to twist itself into an anxious knot.

"I don't know what you want,' Steve said, "but whatever it is, just take it...whatever you want...take it and go. Okay? Just go, we won't stop you. We only want to help everyone else."

"Help? Help who?" John asked.

"*Everyone*. We want to help everyone!" Steve's voice was rising in frustration, cycling into anger. "We have to get the sinkers off the ship. They're just as much a threat to you as they are to everyone else! Why aren't you getting this? Are you cra–" His mouth snapped shut and he stared into John's emptily glittering eyes.

Yeah, he was crazy all right.

"The sinkers are *dangerous*," Steve said, trying to keep his voice calm. He thought if he went point by point, then even this crazy man could follow his logic. "The sinkers are on *board*. We *have* to get the sinkers off the boat."

"After all the trouble I went to?" John said. He was once again staring into the dark at the decks below, his eyes searching for something.

"Trouble...?" Steve's voice trailed off in confusion.

Heavy footsteps pounded across the deck directly below theirs, and John's face lit with excitement. "Uh oh...that's one of the men you brought over...he's–" There was a gunshot, then two, then a third. Maggie jumped at every one. Turning her head, she could just see the deck below. A man was at the railing, and he was a black silhouette against the blacker water below. "Ricky, watch out!" Steve bellowed from beside her.

The man–Ricky–glanced up and then stood with his arms straight out in front of him. Just as another figure entered Maggie's sightline, Ricky seemed to crumple over onto himself.

"Gun's jammed," Steve said, his voice tight with panic. He began to thrash against his bonds. "Ricky! Ricky! Look out!"

Ricky began to stand upright, but it was too late. The shambling figure was upon him. They struggled together and looked almost like lovers clinched in a passionate embrace, especially as the sinker tilted its head to the side of Ricky's neck.

Steve thrashed harder against the rope at his wrists, banging himself back against the railing, still straining to turn and watch as Ricky and his attacker fell to the ground. Maggie could feel the whole deck shiver each time Steve threw himself back. "Ricky!" Steve said again, his voice full of panic and raw, incredulous anger.

Ricky's scream ended in an abrupt gurgle. Maggie turned away, but she could still hear what went on below. The wet smacking and chewing sounds drifted upwards, filling her with a deep revulsion. She wished she could put her hands over her ears.

Next to her, Steve had slumped forward, head on his knees. He rolled his head side to side in negation, but still the feasting sounds below went on and on.

Through the whole thing, Carl had kept his gaze fixed on John's face, disturbed by what he saw there. A look of pure, happy excitement lit John's features; he looked like a child seeing Disneyland for the first time. Then the look became one of lascivious interest as Carl heard the bodies hit the deck. When Ricky's scream was cut off, John had closed his eyes for a brief second, reverential and satisfied. Satisfied. That was how he looked now. Calm and satisfied—like a man who had just come from a vigorous sex session.

That's when Carl understood everything.

"You did it," Carl said. From the corner of his eye, he could see Steve's head come up. "You brought Jade over here. Turned her loose. You *wanted* to see this happen."

John looked at Carl and shrugged. "Well, not exactly," he said, his voice conveying modesty. "I wasn't able to just turn her loose; she was too weak, too small. I had to give her an advantage, get the ball rolling, so to speak. So I introduced her to Adam first." His gaze drifted off, recalling. "It was a good idea. Once Adam was changed, I turned them both loose. That's when the fun started. You know what sucks, though?" He turned back to Carl. "I thought it would be really cool, being on the boat and all...nowhere for anyone to run, you get me? They'd have to jump ship to get away, but there is a strong aversion to jumping ship...do you think it's because they've lived on *Flyboy* for two months and are loathe to leave it? Because it has been the safe place? Someone could do a very interesting study on it…but anyway…the problem was that I didn't get to see a lot of it. There are six decks on this ship! I got to hear everything, and that part was great…but I didn't get to…"

He shook his head, and now his face was beginning to suffuse with anger. "Once I came up here–to be safer, you know–there was even less to see. The people from up here poured down to help the ones on the lower decks. If it didn't happen on the deck right below me, over this rail, then I didn't get to see it at all!" His laugh was an ugly bark. "I was like, 'Mikey, you fucked this one up!' and I–"

"Who's Mikey?" Carl's voice, though soft, cut easily into John's raving.

John turned to Carl, and all the animation dropped out of his face in an instant. It made Maggie's blood run cold; she felt she was looking at a wax replica that had mysteriously replaced the original man. In that instant, she would have sworn there was nothing going on behind those blank eyes.

"Mikey," John said, and his voice was flat, devoid of the excitement it had held seconds before. His eyes were unfocused, staring at nothing. Steve was reminded of the deer carcasses that were almost a constant on the sides of the roads in Princeton Township at certain times of the year, their huge eyes glassy in death.

"I used to be Mikey," John said, "but he died in a fire, and then here I was." His grin surfaced slowly. It was a shark's grin, his eyes just as black and flat.

Carl felt a lift and drop in his stomach. Here was something he'd not yet encountered in his practice–a pure sociopath. He'd read the case studies and thought he had a good understanding of the type, but now…

He remembered a colleague who'd treated a sociopath. He had told Carl that he'd *suspected* the patient was a sociopath, but that when he'd known for sure, it had shaken him to his bones. He had said to Carl that it was as though the patient had stepped casually from his man suit, revealing the monster that had been there all along. The words had chilled Carl at the time, and he felt the same chill now, only worse.

"John...Mikey...could we talk about this?" Carl said. "I'd like to help you and–"

John Smith cut him off with his barking laugh. "Playing at analyzing me, are you?" John squatted in front of Carl. His smile looked very genuine, very warm. "Are you analyzing me, Carl?"

Carl swallowed, unsure of how to proceed. He felt tremendously inadequate in the face of such entrenched madness. "I'm just trying to help," he finally said.

"Excellent," John said. "You'll go first, then." He stood, turned, and began to pace. Carl gaped at him, feeling stupidly punch-drunk. "Okay, so let me get back to it," John said, resuming his lecturing tone. "The problem. The problem as I see it...well, ha ha! The problem is that I *can't* see it! You understand?" He was cycling up again, this time into giddiness, his voice almost breathy, almost shrieky. "It all went so fast. Before I knew it, it was pretty much over. That's when I thought of you people on the other boats. I was just trying to lure a couple of you over here with my Adam impression, but you brought so many! Fun! It's so much fun!" Spittle flew from between his lips at every word. He stood on tiptoe like an overexcited three-year-old. Then his heels crashed back to the deck.

He turned toward them, completely calm.

Maggie felt her head spinning. She couldn't keep up with this madman's crazy train of thought.

"So I made this..." John turned and fished in the small deck box against the back wall of the bridge. Maggie heard the clinking even as he turned back, a long length of heavy chain in his hands. There was a handcuff at each end. "What I'm going to do is chain you down there, where I can see you, and then we'll wait. It won't be long, I'm sure you can imagine." He knelt in front of Carl, face lit with excitement. "You'll be able to *fight*...really fight, you see?" He held the chain up. "I'll get to see it all!"

Carl felt his stomach trying to drop out of his body as fear coursed through him. He had to get through to this guy, he had to...he opened his mouth, but before he knew what was happening, John had reached forward and snapped the cuff and chain around his neck. Carl pulled back sharply but only managed to bang his head on the rail, hard enough to see brief fireworks. The pain was immense.

"Oops...be careful!" John said and then reached around Carl again. He cut the line at Carl's hands and then sprung up and away. He produced the gun in the same movement.

Carl was sickened by the man's speed and agility.

John shook the chain that tethered Carl. "Up and at 'em." He shook the chain again. It rattled and clanked against the deck boards.

Carl rolled to his hands and knees, dazed by fear and the knock to his head. His eyes rolled to Maggie's, and in his distraught gaze, she saw his doom. She surged forward, forgetting her tied hands.

"Carl!" she said. She heaved against her bonds again and glared up at John Smith. "Leave him alone! You're a monster! Let him go, you bastard! You animal!"

John's eyes on her were heavy-lidded with an almost sleepy-looking excitement. Carl recognized the look, even if Maggie was too distraught to. It was a look of lust.

"Oh, yeah, nice. You've got a lot of fight in you," John said to Maggie. "Good, that's very good. You're next." He yanked Carl's chain. "Hurry up, or I'll just shoot you and move on to her. She's very...exciting...to watch." His eyes slid over Maggie again, and she pushed back as though his gaze were a physical touch, redolent with lascivious intent.

Carl stood, and John motioned him forward with the gun. Carl's eyes rolled back to Maggie again, and she began to cry at the dazed fear she saw in the big man's features. Steve tried to push himself closer to her as John disappeared through the doorway behind Carl.

As soon as John disappeared through the doorway, Steve began working his hands back and forth against each other, trying to loosen the rope. "Can you turn around? Let me know when you can see them below."

Maggie nodded, her eyes huge. "I'm scared."

"Me too. Watch down there." He was sweating, and his twisted shoulders were already getting sore. The heat in his wrists was tremendous. He could feel the skin blistering, beginning to abrade. He redoubled his efforts despite the pain. He was almost past the widest part of his hands. Just a few millimeters of lost skin and a little blood for grease should get me free, he thought.

"He has…John Smith has a scratch on his neck," Maggie said. "I saw it when he was tying me up. It looked pretty fresh."

"Is he changing?"

"Maybe. He looked very pale, and his eyes were…I see them," Maggie said, her voice a harsh breath. Steve's working arms stilled.

"You're okay, his back is to us," she said. "He's attached the other handcuff to the rail. Oh God, Carl is on his knees, he can't seem to…okay, he's up, he's up. Freeze."

Steve froze, keeping his gaze directed at the outside back wall of the bridge, trying to concentrate and keep his heart from speeding him straight into a panic. Maggie's voice came again, a bare whisper in the dark. "Okay…he's out of my sight. Either he's headed back up or he stayed somewhere down there to…to…watch. Carl is…he's looking around, is he looking for a weapon? I think so."

Steve worked his hands back and forth, back and forth, the rope stretching minutely each time, his skin snagging between the rolling lines and tearing open.

"He's testing the strength of the chain, pulling it, but he's trying to do it quietly. He's keeping his back to the rail, but he's looking around again–that's right, Carl, find something to use as a wea–he sees something, oh God, he sees something, Steve we have to help him. I think there's…something is standing at the other side of the deck." Maggie's voice dropped below a whisper. Steve felt as though he was hearing her like thoughts in his own mind. He worked his hands. "Be very still, Carl, don't move, don't let it see you. I think it's…it looks like it's moving away…oh God,…*Carl!*" Her last word was an abrupt scream, and Steve paused, tensing up. Then he heard a bellow from the deck below–Carl. Maggie went on: "God, no! No! Fight it, Carl, fight it!"

The railing vibrated as Maggie threw herself against it, screaming. In her terror, she didn't feel it as the railing split the side of her face, opening a gash on her cheekbone. She drummed her feet and kicked involuntarily. "Carl! Carl! Please, God, please, God! Help him, Steve, we have to help him, please God, oh God, it's eating him! It's eating him! Oh my Jesus, oh my God, no, no, no…" Her screams wound down, dissolving into gulping sobs, and now Steve could hear the wet, tearing sounds below. His stomach clenched.

Then his hand popped free of the rope.

He stared at it in stunned amazement as though he couldn't believe it was free, as if it hadn't seemed really possible. His hand was covered in blood, and the skin at his wrist and the base of his thumb was nearly eaten away, but his hands were free. He turned to Maggie and began to untie her bonds.

She leaned forward over her knees, sobbing.

"Maggie," he said, his voice quiet. "Maggie, we're free…it's okay, it's okay, Maggie. Please be quiet. Please, Maggie. It'll be okay." He found that his fingers didn't want to work; they were nearly frozen with pain and incipient panic. A catch found its way into his voice as he fumbled at her hands. "Please, Maggie, please listen for John."

She quieted, her breath hitching. "Okay…okay, I'm listening."

Steve glanced at the deck below. Carl lay against the rail, his body shaking as a sinker feasted at his chest. The deck was awash in blood that looked like oil in the moonlight, and two more sinkers shuffled onto the deck, intent on the fresh meal so close by. Steve felt his gorge rise in a bitter lump, and he tore his eyes away.

Maggie's hands were free.

He stood, grabbing her elbow and pulling her up with him. They both staggered against the rail and then righted themselves. Steve hugged Maggie to him, briefly. "Okay, it's okay we're going to—"

"What did you think?"

Steve felt Maggie stiffen against him as John's voice came from the dark doorway leading to the bridge. John slid out into the moonlight, grinning his dead shark grin. "Of course, it was very exciting up here, too. The way you fought against the ropes, and when you bashed your face! That part was great, really, really great."

"You're a…a monster. An animal," Maggie said, her voice tired, worn out from screaming. "Hasn't there been enough? Haven't enough people died?"

An honest confusion suffused John's features. "Is that what you think? That I'm trying to *kill* people? Why the heck would I do that?"

"What do you call that?" Maggie's voice rose as she gestured to the deck below. "You *killed* Carl. You caused him to *die*. Don't you *get* that?"

Steve gripped her around the waist, afraid she was on the verge of launching herself at John.

John shook his head. "You're over reacting! He'll be back up in no time. Look there; he's already starting."

Shaking, Maggie turned her head. The sinkers had left Carl's body. They did that as soon as someone began the change in earnest. Sinkers didn't eat sinkers.

Carl's fingers were twitching, then his legs spasmed and his arms. He looked like a big dog caught in a bad dream. His head rolled side to side, causing a chunk of his neck to slide off where the sinker had been chewing on it. Behind it was coagulated black. Carl's blood–what was left of it–had become as thick and sticky as jam.

His eyes opened, and Maggie couldn't see them very well from this height, but she knew they were milky, cataract covered. She'd seen it enough times to know. She sobbed and turned her face into Steve's chest.

John stepped closer. "See there? Told you so. Feel better?"

Steve kept a wary eye on John, on the gun in John's hand. He decided to take a different tack. "She feels better, yeah." He felt Maggie stiffen in his arms, and he squeezed her once, quickly.

"Good. Then we can move along," John said, his tone brisk. "I only had the one chain, unfortunately, but I feel like I didn't really need it, to be honest, because–"

"Because you still didn't get to see, right? Not as much as you wanted to?" Steve's voice was calm, conversational. He squeezed Maggie again.

"Yes, that's just exactly right. I was distracted. Distracted by you two up here and well, I have to keep a watch out, don't I? I don't want one of them to get me. I don't want to be one of the walking dead. Not now that I've found more alive people."

Steve nodded, his lips pursed consideringly, as though he was trying to figure out a tough but ultimately solvable problem. "Yes, I see what you're saying. You need a safe place to watch from, but you also need to be able to see the whole...the whole struggle."

John's gaze was wary and flat. He's gone from shark to Gila monster. "Yes, that's exactly right. The struggle is...it's the good part. It's very exciting. To me, it is."

Steve nodded again and squeezed Maggie one more time, a warning to be ready. "There's something more though, isn't there? More exciting to watch? Something else you want to see?" He felt Maggie buck slightly against him, but not as much as she might have if he hadn't been preparing her.

John Smith licked his lips, and his eyes lit with cautious fire. He looked at the split on Maggie's face, the blood, the bruise already appearing. "Yes, there is something else. Something better." His voice was low, and his eyes were heavy again, almost drugged looking.

Steve's voice dropped, too, becoming raspy. "You want me to hit her." He didn't ask this time, he knew; oh, yes, he knew. "Hit her and then fuck her. You want that...you want to *see* that."

John nodded again, and Steve noted with satisfaction that the gun in John's hand had drooped as John contemplated Maggie with lip-licking fascination.

Keeping his tone even, matching John's, Steve said: "I'll fuck her up, and then I'll fuck her out. Good?"

John came another step closer and then faltered. He saw Steve's eyes go to the gun. He brought it up sharply, aiming directly at Maggie. "Yeah. That's what you're going to do. Fuck her up, and then fuck her out, and then she's taking a trip down one deck to meet some of the other residents."

Steve looked into Maggie's eyes. He still held her around the waist, but now his hands went to her arms, and he pushed her back a pace. He whispered, "I'm sorry," and brought his hand back. He slapped her across the face–not with all his might, but it rocked her head back anyway. Behind them, John gasped. It was almost a pant.

Steve's stomach turned over on itself and his head filled with black, frustrated rage. He wanted to pull Maggie to him. He hated himself.

He gritted his teeth, and brought his arm back again. He slapped her backhand this time, sending her head the opposite direction, splitting her lip. She cried out, and there was an answering yelp from John.

Steve gripped her, danced her backward to the side railing. He pushed her back against it, bending her over. Her dazed eyes widened in fear and he almost yanked her back. He swallowed his grief and bent over her. He kissed her roughly, grabbed her breast through her T-shirt. He bent her further back. "Scream," he whispered in her ear.

She screamed, and the scream was petrified and furious; it tore at his heart. He twisted her breast and put his mouth over hers, and she screamed again, and it was muffled by his mouth and behind him, John was panting in earnest.

Steve fumbled at the snap on her jeans and pushed them down past her thighs.

In one swift movement, Steve knelt, his face level with Maggie's crotch, and he heard John's hissing "yes!" behind him. He pulled her pants the rest of the way down, dragged them off. She screamed, and now the scream was edged with tears. Her shaking hands beat lightly around his head like terrified birds. Her underwear was white cotton dotted with tiny, faded roses. They were torn at the seam on her waist, just under her belly button. He kissed the ragged tear, lightly and with tenderness, feeling both the cotton and her warm skin under his lips. He grabbed her ankles, closed his eyes, prayed.

Then he stood with a yell, bringing her ankles up. She arched like a diver and he tumbled her over the rail and into darkness.

Falling the thirty feet to the water below, Maggie had time to hear John's outraged howl and then, right before she hit the water, a gunshot.

Then she was under.

She struggled, churning in the water, disoriented and panicked and expecting a sinker to grab her arms or legs at any moment. Then her body, full of good oxygen, unhindered by heavy denim, righted itself, and she kicked hard, propelling herself up. She broke through, and the night air was warm, the stars a million, and the moon gentle. She turned in a frantic circle. Everything was quiet.

"Steve!" She looked up, expecting to see him diving after her, but there was no one at the railing. Not even John Smith. "Steve!" Her scream bounced off the uncaring hull of *Flyboy* and rang back to her ears as though the big boat were mocking her grief. Had he jumped while she was under the water? She turned in another circle, hoping that he would pop up somewhere nearby. He didn't. She screamed until she felt as though her throat was alight with fire, and she sank as all the air left her lungs. Seawater filled her nose and mouth, she struggled up again, blowing the water from her lungs, choking, and still she screamed.

She screamed for a nightmarishly long time, and then Dave appeared on the jet ski, still trailing the rowboat behind him. "Maggie!" he said and drew up even with her. He grabbed her hand and hauled her up behind him. "You're okay? Not bit?"

She shook her head no. She was so tired. She'd never been so tired. She leaned against Dave's back. His voice came to her through his ribcage as much as through the air. "Steve and Carl?" he asked her, and she shook her head no, unable to speak but trusting that he would feel the movement, would understand that they were gone. "I didn't find anyone in the water," he said. "Only you."

She nodded in acknowledgment. He cranked the throttle and turned the jet ski away from *Flyboy*. She saw over his shoulder to ThreeBees sitting peacefully on the water. Just like before, she was home free. She'd never even tried to find Joe, to help him if she could have. He would have come for her.

"You have to take me back." Her voice rasped painfully, and she swallowed, tasting salt. It was either seawater or her blood or both. She didn't care. She tried to increase her volume. "Dave. Take me back!"

"You got it, Maggie, we're on our way," he said, shouting over the engine whine.

She shook her head again. "No." She sat up and thumped his back. "Not there, not ThreeBees!"

He throttled down and turned to her. He took in her battered face, her one eye beginning to blacken, her split lip. The long cut on her cheekbone.

"Back to where, then?" he asked, confused.

"Back to *Flyboy*. I'm going aboard."

Chapter Fifteen

He'd fought her on it, of course he had, but not as much as she would have thought. She'd never felt so determined, had never known that it was *this*–this determination–that caused others to stand back and let you do what you wanted to do.

She stood on the back ledge of *Flyboy* where they'd all been less than an hour prior and waved Dave away to continue his search for survivors in the water. Now it was just her, but she wasn't here to clear the boat. She was only here to find Steve, if she could.

She looked at the horizon. The sky was just beginning to lighten, and the deep, inverted bowl was flattening to a uniform gray. She regretted that the last sunrise she suspected she might ever see was not going to be a pretty one. Then she shrugged and turned away from that, too.

The small deck was clear, and she ascended the starboard side stairs to the next deck and paused, scanning. This deck was clear too; just two bodies lying near the far rail–she knew if she looked she'd probably find gunshot wounds to their heads. The sliding glass doors that led into the main salon were closed but a large, spider-webbed crack ran through one from the bottom to the top. One hard push and the whole thing would crack apart. Listening carefully, she heard distant moaning. The belly of the boat must be filled with sinkers by now. If they blundered onto the stairs, then they might come up–but sinkers were too stupid to seek them out.

The first time they'd come aboard, they were completely unprepared, and she saw that now. They'd been like fish in a barrel, especially the guys who'd gone to the lower decks. There were no survivors on the boat by the time they'd gotten here; John Smith had made sure of that. Even a small army might not have stood a chance against a boat of sixty or so sinkers, not without foreknowledge.

Now she knew what to look for, what to expect. She would go directly to the bridge and find Steve. If he was…if he was gone, dead…then she'd come right back down and take one of the jet skis still tethered to the back of *Flyboy* and get back to ThreeBees. At the thought of driving away from the sinker-filled *Flyboy*, a shift of unease tried to work its way into her consciousness, but she stifled it. Whatever problem her brain had seen, she'd examine it later, not right now.

She ascended the next set of stairs, thankful she could get to the bridge without going inside the boat. It would be way too claustrophobic in there, too dark. Too many nooks and crannies where a sinker might be…what? Resting? Did they rest? She shook her head to clear it. This was the deck below the bridge deck, and she was hoping to see Steve on this one with–at worst–a gunshot to the leg, making his way down to safety, resting…waiting for her?

"Steve," she said, spurred on by a sudden flood of anticipation, and peeked over the edge.

Carl swiped at her head, missing by mere millimeters. His fingertips ruffled her hair as she gasped and nearly fell backwards down the stairs. She braced herself and looked up in time to see Carl disappear from view. The chain still holding him to the rail clanked as he stepped out of sight.

Shit. Shit, shit, shit. She hadn't considered that Carl might still be there, but of course he was. After all, where would he have gone?

She went back to the lower deck, scanning the salon doors for movement from inside. She saw none and crossed to the deck box, avoiding the half-sinker that Carl had knifed the first time they'd come through. She lifted the lid and rifled through pillows, a throw, a plastic margarita pitcher, a line of cotton rope... "Come on, come on, there must be *something*," she said, her words an impatient sigh. Then she heard a metallic clank. She pushed aside a canvas with a flamboyantly ugly sunrise painted on it and then, at the very bottom of the box, she found a horseshoe set. The original owners of *Flyboy* must have used it when they went ashore for beach picnics or maybe even lawn parties. Next to it was a badminton net and an old shuttlecock with tattered tail feathers.

Maggie pulled out the two iron posts that in better days would have been hammered into the sand at the beach to catch the flying horseshoes. The ends of each were rusty and sharply pointed. She hefted them. Heavy. She had nowhere to put the extra post so she held one in each hand and, avoiding the half corpse again, went back to the stairs.

She watched and listened. Nothing. Then she heard a faint clink: the chain. She ascended halfway up the stairs. "Carl?" she said, her voice low. There was an immediate, frantic clanking, and Carl appeared near the top of the stairs, the chain pulled tight behind him. He reached for her, straining, but he could go no further. His arms swung in agitation, and then Maggie heard a sound like wind through fall-dead leaves. Carl, trying to talk.

His throat had been eaten away and part of his chest. The links were buried in the blackened meat of his neck, and Maggie wondered briefly how much longer he would be held before the chain just cut right through his spine.

He had the advantage of the higher ground. How she was going to get the spike in his eye before he was able to grab her? He had a much longer reach than she did. She wished she had a gun. She wished she'd taken Steve up on the lessons he'd offered her in firing one.

Well, too late now, she told herself. Figure something out.

Then she had a thought.

She went back down the stairs again, and Carl disappeared. Both times, she'd said something as she came up. Maybe if she kept quiet, he would forget she was here. They forgot things in the blink of an eye.

She crept back up, breath held, iron posts clutched in either hand, staying silent. She peered over the edge, tensed and ready for anything. Carl was on the other side of the deck, the chain pulled taut behind him. A large seagull stood on the railing just out of his reach. As Maggie watched, Carl lunged forward, and the bird lifted itself up on large wings as its head darted forward. It flapped a few feet backward, still on the rail, but now something dangled from its mouth–Carl's eye. The seagull snapped its head up, opening its beak, and the eyeball flipped into its mouth and down its throat. Still Carl fought and struggled toward the bird.

It tilted its head at Carl, watching his waving arms, seeming to gauge them, and it hopped a foot closer. *Probably going in for the other eye*, Maggie thought. Her stomach twisted with grief, outrage, anger and even a dark variety of humor.

She'd had enough. She slid the few feet to the stairs that would take her to the bridge. She'd worry about getting back down when (if) the time came. She ascended to the bridge, slipping distractedly on blood that had puddled on one riser.

The door was pushed in, giving onto the dark bridge. There was no one there. On the far side, the door to the observation deck was closed. She went to that door and peeked out, seeing nothing. She opened the door.

"Steve?" she said, voice barely above a whisper. From where she stood, she could see Carl below, still struggling to grab the seagull. His chain clinked and clanked fretfully as the bird flapped and danced just out of his reach.

"Steve?" She pushed the rest of the way out onto the deck, but it was empty. There was a pool of blood near the far rail where she'd gone over. It was just beginning to dry at the edges, and then she remembered slipping on the stairs coming up. She made her way back through the bridge, this time actively looking for a blood trail, and she found it. Someone had come through here, bleeding pretty heavily. It continued down the stairs.

As she was descending past Carl, she paused, wishing she had a way to relieve him of his torment. The seagull was eating him piece by piece. She shuddered as it nipped in for a go at one of Carl's lips, pulling it out like a fat, elastic worm.

Sorry, Carl, I'm so sorry, she thought and continued down.

The blood trail led into the lounge on the next deck. She hurried through, trying to see everything at once, conscious of being silent. The rising sun was beginning to light the inside of *Flyboy*, but it only served to make the space scarier. In the half-light, distracted by the glittering mirrors and chandeliers, everything seemed animated, moving eerily.

The trail took her through the lounge, past a dining room that had been stripped of its finery, and then into a kitchen.

Steve sat on a stool, slumped over the large butcher-block that dominated the middle of the kitchen. He wasn't moving. Half his face–the half she could see–was covered in blood from a large knot on his forehead. That must be where all the blood had come from. Had he been shot in the head?

She sucked in a breath and then checked herself and went to him, lowering the horseshoe posts to the counter as she went by. She reached out a shaking hand and placed it on the exposed nape of his neck. He was warm. Thank God.

She shook his shoulder and put her mouth to his ear. "Steve," she said, but he didn't move. She slid her hand around to the side of his neck and felt for his pulse…nothing. Her stomach sank. She palpated his neck, moving her fingers slightly and was so surprised by the strong pulse under her fingers that she nearly jumped back.

A flood of relief weakened her knees, and she gripped his shoulder harder than she'd intended.

He came to groggy life, striking out, and she caught his arm, pressing herself against him, her ear to his mouth again. "It's me, Steve, it's Maggie. It's okay. I've come for you."

"Maggie?" He blinked and shook his head. Then he tilted backward, almost toppling from the stool. She righted him, holding him steady.

"You have to be very quiet, okay? Tell me what happened to your head. Were you shot?"

He blinked again, a slow, owly blink. He shook his head and then nodded. "Sorry, I…I did get…after you…God, Maggie, I'm so sorry, are you okay? I didn't…I didn't mean…"

"It's okay, I'm okay, see? You saved me." She smiled, her split lip stinging. "Where did John Smith go? Did he shoot you?"

"Yes, but it's not…it isn't that bad, see here?" He lifted his shirt to reveal a wound at his ribs–the bullet must have only grazed him–then he tilted again, almost falling. "It turned me…spun me around, and I fell…hit my head pretty good." His fingers strayed to the sticky wound on his forehead, and she pulled them gently away. "I don't know where he went. I don't care. My head hurts."

"Yes, you hit it pretty hard. Can you drink this?" She pulled a box of apple juice from the refrigerator, put it to his lips, and squeezed a few swallows into his mouth. The sugar would help to revive him.

Viciously, she hoped that John Smith had turned. She hoped that scratch on his neck meant that being one of the animated dead was his final stop in life. He deserved it, probably more than anyone else on *Flyboy*, probably more than most anyone left in the world.

"Can you stand, Steve? I want to get you out of here. Can you walk?"

He nodded and pushed himself up, groaning. Maggie froze, listening. Far below, the water lapped against the hull, but that was all–no answering moans from the sinkers, but they were so vulnerable. "Hang on; sit back down," she said, and he did so with a groan.

She rummaged in a cabinet and pulled forth a white linen tablecloth. She tore one edge and ripped down, making one long strip. She held onto the strip and dropped the bulk of the tablecloth. Then she fashioned it around her waist, tying it, and slid the horseshoe poles into it, one on each hip like fat, stubby swords.

She turned back to Steve and lifted his arm over her shoulder, and his weight settled on and against her. She took a deep breath.

"Okay. Let's go."

They made their way back through the dining room and salon. The dove-gray light coming in through the windows made the large room ghostly, as though it were stuck in time, its true purpose forgotten. Even the silence was eerie, and Maggie almost felt she could hear the laughter and music of parties from days so long past it seemed they'd never come round again. They were the sounds of deepening despair buried in a place held in gloom, forever more.

Maggie shivered and hurried Steve through. He carried more and more of himself, and his weight on her lessened. He was already doing better, because Maggie had come back for him.

They got to the glass doors leading out just as lightning ripped through the morning sky. A sinker stood just outside the door, and Maggie reared back, blinded and gasping, nearly tumbling Steve to his knees. Thunder clapped right over them, and Maggie cried out, throwing her hands over her ears. She looked wildly back to the door. There was no sinker, just the crack that went bottom to top, fanning out like shoulders, like raised arms. She blew out a pent-up breath of relief.

"Sorry," she said and gathered Steve back to her, but he stood on his own. He put an arm around her shoulders and squeezed. His gaze was steadier now, more concentrated.

"I'm glad you came back," he said.

Maggie shifted from foot to foot under the weight of his arm, and then she acquiesced and leaned against him. Her arms went round his middle, and she hugged him tight.

"Oof...careful of my gunshot," he said, and she could *almost* hear the smile in his voice. She smiled and buried her face in his side, wiping away the tears trying to flow down her cheeks. *Enough*, she thought to herself, *enough crying. Time to go.*

"Come on," she said and led him through the doors.

They made their way to the very back deck and the small lip where the jet skis were still tied up. Maggie selected a long, two-person jet ski, and she pulled it in closer. She turned back to Steve. He was staring at the other jet skis, his face creased into a frown. Lightning struck again, running sideways across the sky. It burnt its tree branch impression onto her retinas, and she blinked a few times, dislodging it.

Rain was imminent. She could see it out over the water. Headed this way.

"Steve!" she said, straddling the jet ski, turning the key. It rumbled beneath her bare, outspread legs.

He looked at her and gestured at the tethered jets. "Who got away? Who left?"

Maggie shook her head. "No one! Dave would have told me if someone else made it! Why?" She had to yell over the approaching storm.

The rain was close, hissing across the ocean, making fog jump before it.

Steve looked back at the jet skis, and then he turned to scan *Flyboy*.

"Steve! Come on!" The rain hit, unexpectedly cold and stinging across her thighs.

He jumped on behind her and kicked them away. He tapped her shoulder, and she twisted in the seat to look at him. His hair was plastered to his head, and the rain was already washing some of the blood away.

"Someone took one of the jet skis!" His voice was a hoarse roar over the pounding rain. Maggie's mouth fell open, and she turned to look for ThreeBees in the dim light.

The rain fell over her like a gray curtain.

~ ~ ~

John Smith had watched with irritation as Steve was spun around from the force of the shot and thrown against the rail. From there, he went down like a sack of bricks. John Smith had considered the pool of blood accumulating under Steve. *Dead for sure*, he'd thought with some annoyance. *Now I have one less person to play with.* He hadn't wanted to shoot Steve; really, he'd done it more in surprise than anger. It had gotten very good, right at the end there; it had been very satisfying, what Steve was doing to Maggie.

The killing was excellent, but the hitting...and the stuff that would come after...that was even better. It had spread warmth through his lower stomach, reminding him nostalgically of being a kid.

Didn't everyone want that? To be a kid again?

He hurried to the rail and looked over, but Maggie hadn't popped up yet. Maybe she was dead, too, but he hoped not. He would get a jet ski and go find her, drag her back on board. Maybe he could try and finish what Steve had started, although he'd never raised his hand to anyone, and certainly, he'd never had sex, but maybe there really *was* a first time for everything.

He turned and made his way through the bridge and then descended the stairs. At the last step, he heard Maggie's screams as she emerged from the water. He turned his head in the direction of her screaming, distracted and entranced.

That's when Carl grabbed him.

John twisted like a snake, dislodging himself from Carl's grip, and threw himself forward, head-first down the stairs. The tips of Carl's fingers grazed his calf. Close one. Close call.

He scrambled to his feet on the next deck and trotted to the last set of stairs. He was stopped by the moans from below. They were such an arresting sound, almost peaceful, like waves on the beach. Between the living dead and the living, all in all, John preferred the living dead. *Certainly, they were more predictable,* he thought, as the sight of Maggie going over the rail came back to him.

Maggie.

He'd go and fish her out right now.

Once on the jet ski, he went cautiously around the far side to the front of *Flyboy.* He heard the other jet ski before he saw it and watched from the shadows as a man pulled Maggie aboard. They conversed and then headed toward ThreeBees, but then stopped and after a moment, reversed direction and were headed for the back of *Flyboy.*

Curious.

What really captured John's attention was the sight of ThreeBees sitting peacefully half a mile away. There were more people aboard her...fresh people. He started to feel another swell of excitement. He could use ThreeBees as a kind of holding tank, bring them over one by one and really enjoy what would happen when he got them here. For that was his biggest regret about *Flyboy*...that everything had happened so quickly and so much of it had been out of his sight.

He could even do the tethering method again, but give them more rope, more opportunity to fight for their lives. Maybe he could supply them with a weapon of some kind, but he'd have to be cautious about that.

He pictured Candy–the woman who'd left *Flyboy* with the Indian doctor. He pictured her ripeness and her strength. She'd be good, very good. Very exciting. It would be best if the doctor and Candy fought first and then did…the other thing…but how could he make them? What would cause them to fight? What did they hold dear, besides each other?

He wasn't sure, but he knew he could find out in a hurry. People were very transparent.

~ ~ ~

As Maggie began her struggle to find Steve and get him off *Flyboy*, John Smith pulled up to the back of ThreeBees.

"Dave? Is that you?" The voice came floating out of the dark, uneasy and edged with concern.

"No, it's John Smith. Steve sent me. Who's that?"

A figure loomed up and shifted nervously from side to side. "John Smith? Oh, the guy from the raft, right? It's me, Brian." He came forward and grabbed the line that John tossed to him. He pulled the jet ski in and tied it off. "How's it going over there? Everybody okay? We kept hearing shots and what not."

John clambered aboard ThreeBees and stood silently, hands on his hips and head down, as though he were deep in thought.

"Is everything okay?" Brian asked, his face drawing down in concern. "Everybody okay over there on *Flyboy*? Like I said, we heard shots, and the guys over on *Big Daddy* keep calling here."

At the mention of *Big Daddy*, John's head came up with a snap. "*Big Daddy*. I forgot all about her," he said and slapped a hand to his forehead. He shook his head, amused.

Brian, just beginning to sense the oddness of the conversation, took a step back. "Yeah, uh…the guys over there are–"

"Brian," John said and brought the gun up into Brian's stomach. "Shut up, okay? Sit down right there." He motioned Brian into a deck chair, and then he scanned the deck. He glanced back at Brian as he crossed to the bench. "Don't move now. Just be a second." He scooped up the walkie-talkie and dropped it over the side where it blooped into the water below.

"Hey, man, listen, what do you–" Brian started, but John cut him off.

"Be quiet, Brian. Who else is here besides you?" Brian shook his head, mouth hanging open. John rolled his eyes. "Well, there's *you*, obviously, then the old man and old lady...Candy and the doctor...who else? Anybody? Anybody I'm missing?"

Brian hesitated, blinking rapidly, and then shook his head. John grimaced and chuckled. "Okay, who am I missing? You're a terrible liar. Not that you should let that get you down, most people are terrible liars. It takes lots and lots of practice to get good at it. So?"

"So..." Brian parroted stupidly.

John stepped toward him, gun coming up. All evidence of good-natured ribbing had left his voice and face, especially his eyes. They were dead flat.

"So...who else is here? Tell me or I will shoot you."

"Babygirl...I mean...Samantha, her name is Samantha, but we just found that out. We've called her Babygirl until now, until Candy..."

John raised his eyebrows, politely inquiring. "Until Candy what, Brian? Until Candy...what?"

Brian's stomach rolled over on itself, and he gripped the wooden arms of the deck chair convulsively. He felt that he'd painted himself into a dangerous corner, but what the hell? How was he supposed to know this guy was some kind of fucking psychopath? He sighed and slumped forward.

"She...Babygirl...had some kind of, I don't know, breakthrough or something. She was calling Candy mommy, saying she loved her and stuff. Then she told Candy everything that had happened to her when Maggie had barely been able to get a peep out of the girl. Not that she tried too hard." Brian rocked his head in his hands, near tears, thinking that he was dooming the girl, but not knowing how it had happened. Or why. "She's in the room with Candy and the Doc. They're like a family already. You can see how happy Babygirl–I mean, Samantha–is with the situation. Man, it just kind of breaks your heart, you know?" Brian glanced up at John, and what he saw turned his stomach even more.

John Smith was grinning, but it was the grin of a small baby with gas: painful and strained looking.

"Where is everyone now? In their rooms sleeping?"

Brian nodded. "Trying to. Because we figured we'd need our sleep in case they brought people back. What happened over there? Did Jade get over there somehow? Are there survivors?"

"Survivors? Depends on what you mean by that," John said and fished in the deck box. He came out with a length of rope and tied Brian to the deck chair. "They've *changed*, but they're there. Kicking up Dickens, you could say."

"Steve and Maggie? Carl?"

John shook his head. "I don't think they made it. I shot Steve, and it looked like Maggie was going back on board. Extremely inadvisable since the whole boat has changed. I'm pretty sure she didn't make it. As for Carl, well, he fought a good fight. Does that make you feel better?" The question seemed an honest one, asked in genuine tones of concern, but by now, Brian's head was swimming.

He would yell out, warn the others. At least they'd have a chance. He hitched in a deep breath and opened his mouth.

John Smith reached forward with alarming speed and shoved a wad of cloth into his mouth. Then he tied it in place with another length of rope. Brian huffed and heaved against the ropes, straining his voice around the tight cloth, but it was partially down his throat and choking him. He couldn't breathe. He was smothering; he was dying. He struggled harder.

"If you calm yourself, you will see that you can breathe quite easily through your nose, but you can't keep trying to scream...you'll lose too much air that way. Calm down, Brian. Better...that's better. Feel the difference? Feel the air going in? Don't puke, whatever you do. Puking will kill you for sure."

Brian took another deep whistling breath through his nose and nodded, his head spinning. His eyes had filled with tears, and now John Smith was a soft and blurry blob.

"I don't want to kill you, Brian, believe me. It's the last thing I want. You're young and strong, and I bet you'll fight for your life, won't you? I mean really *fight*!" John raised a fist to chest level, as if cheering on an athlete. "I'll take you over last; how's that?"

Brian shook his head in confusion and raised his shoulders.

"I'll take Candy and the doctor and the little girl first, then the old man and old woman–because between you and me, I don't think they'll do well at all–and then finish it up with you! You'll be like the headliner, you see? The main event!" John did not think Brian would be the main event, Candy and the new little family were the main event, but it didn't hurt to try and make the boy feel better. Flattery just made people feel better. John had noticed that.

Thunder rumbled distantly. The sky had begun to lighten, but it was a gray light, the morning sky full of tumultuous storm clouds. It was going to rain soon.

A crack of lightning made John blink, and Brian cried out around the cloth and turned his head into his shoulder. John put a hand on Brian's neck and squeezed. It was what his dad had always done for him, when he was little Mikey. He would say "Don't be scared, son, it's just lightning." Although Mikey hadn't been scared. What was there to be scared of?

He squeezed Brian's neck again. "Don't be scared, son," he said, and Brian jerked under his hand. "It's only lightning."

Brian didn't *look* comforted, he was trying to pull away from John's hand...but it was hard to tell, sometimes. Well, he'd done the boy a good turn. *That was nice of me*, he thought.

"Stay nice and quiet now so I don't have to kill you or anyone else. Okay? Then we'll get you a dog, okay? You want a dog, son?"

John stood and strode off, not waiting for an answer, as though it was not a question that required one. To John, it wasn't.

He rounded up the sleepy and disoriented Randy and Bonnie first and herded them up on deck with the gun. He tied them to each other, sitting back-to-back, their legs straight out in front of them, tied at the ankles. They'd never be able to get up; they were too old and too fat.

Bonnie's varicose veins stood out distinctly in the gray light. She'd lost a slipper on the way out. She was crying, trying to wipe her face on the shoulder of her robe.

Everything had happened so quickly that Randy felt as though he was just beginning to wake up *to* a nightmare instead of *from* one. Bonnie's crying twisted him in two with anger. Her tears did that to him.

The gag end tickling his throat was making him nauseous as his sour morning breath was backing up into his nostrils. Bonnie shook and sobbed against him, then she made an odd yurking sound, and the ropes tightened as she heaved. She yurked and heaved again. She was vomiting into the rag tied at her mouth.

He felt it as she began to choke.

Her feet drummed on the deck as she tried to draw a breath, but the vomit packed her throat. She slammed against him and slammed against him again. Panic bloomed in his brain like squid ink, darkening his thoughts. She was going to choke to death.

He looked at John Smith and pleaded with his eyes, his voice straining against the rag. He was shrieking, but it still wasn't as loud as Bonnie's struggles. Suddenly, she was over on her side, kicking like a landed fish, and he was pulled over, too, landing hard on his shoulder. He could just see her from the corner of his eye...her face red, mucous plugging her nostrils, her eyes bugging out of her head. Her neck was red and swollen and blue veins stood out sharply.

In his extremity, Randy was able to push the cloth out of his mouth with his tongue, past the length of rope. It hung at his lips like a wadded up bib. He began to plead for Bonnie's life. "Please, she's choking. Help her, just...please, just take the goddamn rag out of her mouth! Please! Can't you see she's dying? Can't you see that? Take that rag out of her mouth and–"

John Smith knelt next to them with a look of deep concern on his features. He pulled the ropes that tied them back-to-back, and with a grunt, yanked them upright to a seated posture. Randy heaved a sigh of relief. "Thank you, tha–"

John shoved the rag back into Randy's mouth and tied the rope tighter. Then he brought the gun up and shot Bonnie in the head.

Randy tried to pull in a breath, and he nearly aspirated the cloth that was already halfway down his throat. He'd *felt* it; he'd *felt* Bonnie jump as the bullet entered her brain. Her head had bumped his, but not hard; it was almost a companionable knock, a friendly, billy-goat head butt. Now her dead weight sagged against Randy's back, pulling him over again. He could feel the rush of hot blood that flowed between them. He looked at John Smith, his eyes wide in shock, all the color drained from his tired and puffy face.

"I'm sorry, but that was just too…that was just gross," John said. "With the mucous and the…she peed her pants, are you aware of that?" John's face had a look of mildly disgusted incredulity. He shook his head at Randy and then looked at Brian who sat, stunned and shaking, in the deck chair. He shrugged his shoulders. "I'm sorry, but it was gross. It was just gross, and anyway…" He turned toward the salon doors, head tilted, listening. "Oh ho…we have company coming."

Lightning flashed again, reflecting in the blood that pooled around Bonnie and Randy. Thunder clapped like a judgment, and Randy felt a corresponding burst in his chest that shot down his arm, numbing it. He couldn't pull a breath. He greeted the pain with gratitude and closed his eyes. *At least we won't rise again, thank God. Thank God for that at least*, he thought. Then: *Wait Bonnie; wait for me, honey bunny, I'm right behind you.* His body jerked in spasm. He smiled around the rag in his mouth.

His heart stopped for good.

Rain rolled over ThreeBees, cold and stinging. It sizzled across the teak deck boards and washed the blood under Bonnie and Randy to a light pink.

Dr. Rafiq stood at the salon doorway, his face a frozen mask of horror as he took in the confusion of the scene before him. Candy, however, standing behind Dr. Rafiq with Samantha at her side, had her eyes trained on John Smith. The rain hit the deck and bounced back up to where she stood, splashing against her ankles and shins, making it feel uncannily as though someone were pricking her skin with small pins.

She reached to push Samantha behind her. She had assessed the situation in an instant, remembering John from *Flyboy*, understanding fully and without hesitation what he was. She wanted only to get Samantha away from him.

John smiled, seemingly oblivious to the rain that ran in rivulets down his face. "Hello, Candy! Dr. Rafiq!" He had to yell to be heard over the drumming. His eyes had developed a crazy spin that only Candy could see. "I have a proposition for you both."

Sami started to step out onto the deck, and Candy stayed him with a hand on his bicep. She looked up into his deep, mournful brown eyes. She loved him so much. He was the kindest, most thoughtful person she'd ever met. "Save Samantha," she said and stepped past him and onto the deck, pulling the sliding glass door closed behind her.

She didn't look back.

She walked the few feet to John Smith without acknowledging Brian, never glancing at the sad hump of Bonnie and Randy. She stood before John, arms crossed over her chest. The rain plastered her blonde hair flat to her skull, and another flash of lightning lighted the delicate, white contours of her face. Mascara and eye shadow combined in a blue-black slide under her eyes. She looked bruised. Damaged.

Her eyes twirled as busily as his.

"What's your proposition?" she asked.

John took a small step back. "Don't come any closer, or I'll shoot you." Even though she was tiny, he felt crowded by her...almost...intimidated? She intimidated him? How was that possible? *Why* was that possible?

He licked his lips. "I want you and that doctor to...I'm taking you over to *Flyboy*, and you have to fight...fight each other, I mean. Then I want you to...after you fight, you have to..."

She stared at him, and then her eyes slitted, catlike. "I think I know...what you want to see..." She reached into her rain-soaked nightgown and lifted a breast into the deep V opening. She pinched her dark pink areola, and it reddened instantly, rain slipping over and down her inflamed nipple. She stepped closer to him. "This?" she said and twisted again. "And this?" She slapped herself across the face. Hard.

John felt the warmth start across the area just under his bellybutton. When she slapped herself again, he felt an excited lift and fall, like being on a roller coaster.

Within seconds, she was up against him, her breast still out and painfully red, a bruise beginning on her cheekbone. Still the mascara seemed to have no end as it flowed down her cheeks like tears of blackest sin. She looked up into his eyes. She smiled emptily.

He flushed a deep red. He'd never felt flustered before, never felt anything even approaching…shame? Was this shame? Or was this lust? He wasn't sure. Her eyes were so flat, so unflinching, unfeeling. It was like talking to a life-size doll or…then he realized. He realized why she was both familiar and uncomfortable.

He leaned closer, squinting, staring intently into her flat but somehow twirling eyes. He was amazed in his own limited way.

"You're like me," he said, his voice full of quiet awe.

"Not exactly," Candy whispered. She brought her knee up sharply into his engorged dick.

He lifted the gun even as he doubled over. He caught Candy under her chin, splitting it and flinging her head back. She stumbled and toppled over onto her back, hitting her head. John Smith groaned, gasping, and brought the gun up again, straining against the pain in his groin.

The sliding glass door trundled back on its track, and Sami stepped out, yelling. "No! Don't shoot her!"

John smiled, grimacing, struggling to stand straighter. The rain and sweat mixed and ran down into his eyes, making him blink. He brought the gun up higher, shaking, but trained on Dr. Rafiq.

John gasped out, "How about…I shoot you…instead?" His finger tightened on the trigger. Lightning flashed again.

"How about: no?" Maggie said from behind him and drove the iron horseshoe stake into his shoulder. He reared back, reaching for it, his eyes rolling to Maggie, bringing the gun around. Sami kicked him in the chest, toppling him backward over the rail.

~ ~ ~

They couldn't find him. They'd looked, but then the storm had gone beyond a hindrance to dangerous. Then it had gotten even worse. It had rocked *Barbra's Bay Breeze* fiercely at her anchor.

They huddled in the salon to watch the fury being flung down from above, not wanting to separate into the staterooms. They looked like survivors of a war. Maggie ran her fingers lightly over the cut on her forehead. Her lip was swollen, too. She put her head in her hands and breathed deeply, trying to chase the remains of the poisoned adrenalin from her system.

When she and Steve had gotten close enough to ThreeBees to see that John Smith was aboard, Maggie had pulled the jet ski around to the side of the boat. Under cover of the storm, she had swum to the back to see what she could do. The only weapons she had were the ones she'd carried from *Flyboy*–the horseshoe posts.

After it was done, and Dr. Rafiq was seeing to Candy and Brian, Maggie had gone to the side and given Steve the all clear, and he'd come around. Then he and Maggie had driven the perimeter of ThreeBees. They hadn't seen a single sign of John Smith.

"I think he sank. I think he'd been on the verge of changing anyway and..." She shook her head and pulled her sweater tighter around her. She'd never been so happy to have dry clothes. The skin on her hands and feet was still puckered from the overexposure to water.

"You think he was infected?" Candy asked from the short loveseat. She, too, was in dry clothes–a skin-tight, pink track-suit–with Samantha sleeping curled in her lap. Candy ran her hands over and over Samantha's soft blond hair. Sami sat with his arm around Candy; he seemed unable to take his eyes from her. Brian sat nearby in a club chair. He stared out the window, his arms crossed over his chest. He hadn't said anything since they'd gathered together.

"I think so, but I don't know for sure. Not really." Maggie rearranged the ice on Steve's forehead, and he smiled up at her from the long couch he lay on, then he closed his eyes again.

Dave had radioed from *Big Daddy*, saying he'd found no survivors and had finally packed it in because the storm was just too violent. He was glad to hear that Maggie and Steve had both made it back to ThreeBees, but even that good news was tempered by the losses they'd had today. They'd lost twelve people from ThreeBees and *BigDaddy*. It seemed certain now that they'd lost everyone on *Flyboy*.

Maggie stood at the salon door and looked out at the bodies of Bonnie and Randy although it hurt her to do so. They were like lost children, huddled together, afraid of the storm. At least all the blood had washed away.

Then she glanced out the window at the vague, gray shape of *Flyboy* in the distance. All those sinkers, just wandering around over there…it made her sad and sick at the same time.

She shivered and turned away.

Chapter Sixteen

September 16, 2011

Dr. Rafiq looked at the board on the bridge, and then he glanced back at Steve. "We are ready to leave at any time. As soon as you and Maggie get back, we can go."

Steve nodded and ruffled Samantha's hair and then dropped a captain's hat onto her head. She sat in a crew seat next to Dr. Rafiq, and the hat was miles too big for her. It kept tilting over, covering one eye.

"You look more like a pirate than a captain, Sammy-girl! Where's your parrot?" Steve asked her, and she giggled, bringing her hands to her mouth. She was still much too thin, waifish even, and her nightmares were terrifying to everyone aboard ThreeBees, but Candy was changing all that. Samantha was better now than she'd been before; that much was obvious. Candy was just the person for the job of bringing a child through this new world, too. She had the strength, the resources. Steve knew that Sami was in awe of Candy, and truth be told, Steve was a little in awe of her too, even though she also put him on edge. There was just something about her. Something off.

He wondered: once they got south, Florida or maybe even further…would he and Maggie split away from Candy and Dr.

Rafiq and Samantha? Or would they wait until next season? When the time came to trek north again, maybe he and Maggie would have found their own ThreeBees by then. Or would everything change once they ran across other people? Steve didn't know, and he was tired of thinking about it.

He looked out at the shore. It was deserted. They hadn't seen any other survivors for the past month and had decided to pull stakes now, in September, to give them time to beat the weather by getting to a warmer clime.

He smiled at Dr. Rafiq. "Feeling pretty confident, huh? Those lessons paying off?"

Dr. Rafiq laughed and nodded. "Yes, we can sail this boat anywhere, now! Just please, providence, spare us any major storms until we are very good at it!"

Everyone had learned the fundamentals of driving the yacht; even Samantha was included in the lessons, and Steve had begun daily training in firearms. Also for everyone, although Steve kept a very careful watch on Samantha. He had been against teaching the little girl, but Candy had insisted in her implacable manner, and Steve had relented. It still bothered him to watch Samantha shoot...but he guessed it might save her life one day.

Candy was also teaching Samantha how to fight, and Dr. Rafiq was trying to temper the nightmares by teaching the girl how to meditate. Together, they made extraordinary parents. Samantha would become an exceptional woman.

Steve shivered, and his arms rashed out in superstitious goose bumps. It was as though a part of his brain was telling him that imagining a future would cause it not to be. He shook his head and smiled at Dr. Rafiq, but it was perfunctory. Now that the goose had walked over his grave, the day seemed a little darker.

He wanted to find Maggie.

Maggie and Candy stood together on the deck of ThreeBees, pulling in the last of the laundry. They had been very lucky so far with the weather, breezy and warm and very few storms...nothing as bad as the one they'd had the night *Flyboy* fell to the sinkers.

Candy saw Steve before Maggie did. "Samantha okay?"

"Yep, she's with the Doc, she's fine." He smiled at her concern. She surveyed him levelly and then bent back to the sheet she'd been folding. The new white scar on her chin barely showed.

He caught Maggie's glance. He knew that her train of thought was similar to what his own had been up on the bridge: there was no one more fitted to keeping Samantha safe than Candy.

"Want help carrying them below?" Maggie asked as Candy tucked everything into the basket.

"No, I've got it. Besides, I guess you and Steve better get going. There are only a few things left to see to over here, and I can take care of them. Then we can head south." She put her hand on her hip. "I guess that raft is long gone."

"Brian and I couldn't find a trace of it anywhere," Steve said, slightly irritated. He didn't know why Candy couldn't get off the topic of the raft. It's not as though they'd need it, they still had the rowboat if there was trouble. "Storm took it away would be my guess. It was pretty light, you know, just a rubber life raft."

"How is Brian doing?" Maggie asked, remembering that Steve had talked to him earlier today.

"He's good; he likes being on *Big Daddy*. Although he did say he hopes we run across some girls his age at some point."

"I think he'll get his wish as we move south. We've seen a few boats heading that direction."

Steve nodded. "Yeah, he'll find a girlfriend. Get a boat of his own, someday." He was staring moodily at *Flyboy*, and Maggie wondered if a goose had run over his grave. He seemed a little down all of a sudden.

She also wondered at 'a boat of his own, someday'. Is that the way it was going to be? Had it become a seafaring world? What about food? Crops? Things like that? Canned goods wouldn't last forever, and forays onto land would only get more dangerous as they cleared the shorelines and had to travel further in.

She shook her head. She wouldn't think about it, now. Wouldn't worry about it. She sloshed a gas can, listening to the contents. It was wasteful, what they were about to do, but it needed to be done.

It was the only decent thing to do.

Just like when they'd wrapped Bonnie and Randy in clean white sheets before sliding them into the water of the bay from the big rowboat. Steve had said a few words, officiating because Maggie had been too close to tears. Candy and Dr. Rafiq had not come along, electing instead to stay on ThreeBees. They hadn't known Bonnie and Randy, really.

Maggie followed Steve's gaze to *Flyboy*. Even though the day was clear and bright, a pall seemed to hang over the formerly beautiful super yacht. She knew it was a figment of her own mind brought on by knowing the contents of the boat, but still...she couldn't shake the feeling that it was haunted.

Maybe it is though, in a way, she thought. The ghosts on *Flyboy* are just slightly more substantial than the accepted definition of a spirit...in body, anyway. In mind, the sinkers are even *less* substantial than their ethereal counterparts. The walking dead seemed to have very little thinking brain and possibly nothing left in the way of souls. Maybe that soulessness contributed to the sinking.

Maggie hated the idea of someone coming across *Flyboy*, maybe at night when she was shrouded in fog, beckoning with her long, elegant white body. They would go aboard and step into a nightmare.

But it was the thought of Carl that hurt her most of all. He must still be tethered on that deck, being slowly picked apart by seagulls, straining against his chain as he struggled to catch one of the coldly intelligent birds. His pirate's beard falling out bit by bit, growing thinner as time wore on.

Fire. Fire would put an end to all of it: the enticement to go aboard, and all the sinkers...Jade, Carl, even Adam...no one deserved that soulless life of hungry shuffling. No one deserved that as his or her ongoing epitaph.

There were only two jet skis tied up at the back of ThreeBees now that they were getting ready to move. They were the big ones, though. Candy was also teaching Samantha how to drive one.

Steve and Maggie got on one together.

"Big waste of diesel. We might end up regretting it," Steve said, and Maggie grabbed him around the middle and rested her face on his back.

"We'll get a boat with sails, how's that sound to you?" she said and squeezed again.

He marveled that she was still one step ahead of him. Then her embrace derailed his thoughts. It felt so good to be hugged by someone so warm.

He turned in the seat, and she sat up, looking at him expectantly. She was smiling, but it was tinged with sadness for what they were about to do. He planted a kiss on her forehead and one on her nose.

"Ready?" he asked, and she nodded.

He keyed the jet ski to life, and they drove toward *Flyboy*, gas cans tied to either side of the jet. It was enough to get the boat started.

Then she'd burn.

All on her own.

Epilogue

A beautiful sailboat called *SillySally* sat idly at anchor, four people playing cards on her deck as twilight set in. They were on their way south from Maine and had been going slowly, trying as much as possible to enjoy the trip.

The days before had been hard ones, for everyone. Now they were trying to heal as much as they could.

Adelaide Wilds put down her cards with a sigh. "I fold. You guys are too sharp for me." She smiled. She was pretty with long brown hair and dark brown eyes to match. She had a wholesome, girl-next-door look and a down-to-earth personality to go with it.

"It's not your turn. Can't you just wait till your turn?" her sister, Camille, said with irritation. At twenty four, Camille was older than Adelaide by three years.

Adelaide stuck her tongue out at Camille, and Camille rolled her eyes.

"Ladies," Tuck said mildly, looking over his bifocals. At sixty-seven, he was the patriarch of their group. He enjoyed the sisters' shenanigans more than he let on. They reminded him of his own sprawling clan of six kids. All of whom he missed every second of every day.

"Tuck, can I quit, too? This game is so *boring*." Johnny rolled his eyes and slumped his shoulders as though the game were, quite literally, killing him. The cards had magically become grubby in his twelve-year-old hands. Tuck took a second to marvel at a male child's ability to soil anything he touched.

Tuck sighed heavily and shook his head. "No. You'll have to see it through. You have to finish what you start."

Johnny rolled his eyes again, but settled more solidly in his chair. He loved Tuck, would do anything Tuck said to do. Being around him helped him feel like he didn't miss his parents as bad. Although he still dreamt about them, sometimes it seemed like every night. A lot of the dreams were good, but even the good ones were still bad to wake up from...because it was like he had to remember over and over that they were...that they'd been...

He shook his head and sat straighter, focusing on the cards in his hand. He sniffed, trying to do it quietly. Adelaide gave his shin a light kick under the table, and he looked up, smiling. She winked. He liked Adelaide a lot, too. She was really pretty. She was too old to be his girlfriend, he'd decided a month ago, but he did still really like her, anyway.

Adelaide went to the rail to look at the sunset. She thought she could see a big ship, south of them, way down the coast, but it looked odd, almost skeletal. She shivered. Maybe she'd go below and grab a sweater. Tonight, you could almost feel that September was already more than half over. She turned, going to the deck stairs that would take her below when movement caught the corner of her eye. She turned to look.

A yellow life raft floated peacefully, a hundred feet or so from the back of *SillySally*. In the fading light, she saw that a man lay in it.

His leg moved.

"Oh my gosh!" she said, her hands flying up in alarm. She turned back to the card players. "You guys! There's someone out there!"

~ ~ ~

Lying on his back in the bottom of the life raft, John Smith heard the girl's alarmed cry. He opened his eyes.

The End

I hope you enjoyed *The Boat* and if you did, please take a second to leave me a review on Amazon. I'd greatly appreciate it.
Very Best Regards – Chris Dougherty

 SEVERED**PRESS**

facebook.com/severedpress
twitter.com/severedpress

CHECK OUT OTHER GREAT ZOMBIE NOVELS

VACCINATION
by Phillip Tomasso

What if the H7N9 vaccination wasn't just a preventative measure against swine flu?

It seemed like the flu came out of nowhere and yet, in no time at all the government manufactured a vaccination. Were lab workers diligent, or could the virus itself have been man-made? Chase McKinney works as a dispatcher at 9-1-1. Taking emergency calls, it becomes immediately obvious that the entire city is infected with the walking dead. His first goal is to reach and save his two children.

Could the walls built by the U.S.A. to keep out illegal aliens, and the fact the Mexican government could not afford to vaccinate their citizens against the flu, make the southern border the only plausible destination for safety?

ZOMBIE, INC
by Chris Dougherty

"WELCOME! To Zombie, Inc. The United Five State Republic's leading manufacturer of zombie defense systems! In business since 2027, Zombie, Inc. puts YOU first. YOUR safety is our MAIN GOAL! Our many home defense options - from Ze Fence® to Ze Popper® to Ze Shed® - fit every need and every budget. Use Scan Code "TELL ME MORE!" for your FREE, in-home*, no obligation consultation! *Schedule your appointment with the confidence that you will NEVER HAVE TO LEAVE YOUR HOME! It isn't safe out there and we know it better than most! Our sales staff is FULLY TRAINED to handle any and all adversarial encounters with the living and the undead". Twenty-five years after the deadly plague, the United Five State Republic's most successful company, Zombie, Inc., is in trouble. Will a simple case of dwindling supply and lessening demand be the end of them or will Zombie, Inc. find a way, however unpalatable, to survive?

SEVEREDPRESS

f facebook.com/severedpress
y twitter.com/severedpress

CHECK OUT OTHER GREAT ZOMBIE NOVELS

900 MILES
by S. Johnathan Davis

John is a killer, but that wasn't his day job before the Apocalypse.

In a harrowing 900 mile race against time to get to his wife just as the dead begin to rise, John, a business man trapped in New York, soon learns that the zombies are the least of his worries, as he sees first-hand the horror of what man is capable of with no rules, no consequences and death at every turn.

Teaming up with an ex-army pilot named Kyle, they escape New York only to stumble across a man who says that he has the key to a rumored underground stronghold called Avalon..... Will they find safety? Will they make it to Johns wife before it's too late?

Get ready to follow John and Kyle in this fast paced thriller that mixes zombie horror with gladiator style arena action!

WHITE FLAG OF THE DEAD
by Joseph Talluto

Millions died when the Enillo Virus swept the earth. Millions more were lost when the victims of the plague refused to stay dead, instead rising to slaughter and feed on those left alive. For survivors like John Talon and his son Jake, they are faced with a choice: Do they submit to the dead, raising the white flag of surrender? Or do they find the will to fight, to try and hang on to the last shreds or humanity?

SEVERED**PRESS**

 facebook.com/severedpress
 twitter.com/severedpress

CHECK OUT OTHER GREAT ZOMBIE NOVELS

Z BURBIA
by Jake Bible

Whispering Pines is a classic, quiet, private American subdivision on the edge of Asheville, NC, set in the pristine Blue Ridge Mountains. Which is good since the zombie apocalypse has come to Western North Carolina and really put suburban living to the test!

Surrounded by a sea of the undead, the residents of Whispering Pines have adapted their bucolic life of block parties to scavenging parties, common area groundskeeping to immediate area warfare, neighborhood beautification to neighborhood fortification.

But, even in the best of times, suburban living has its ups and downs what with nosy neighbors, a strict Home Owners' Association, and a property management company that believes the words "strict interpretation" are holy words when applied to the HOA covenants. Now with the zombie apocalypse upon them even those innocuous, daily irritations quickly become dramatic struggles for personal identity, family security, and straight up survival.

ZOMBIE RULES
by David Achord

Zach Gunderson's life sucked and then the zombie apocalypse began.

Rick, an aging Vietnam veteran, alcoholic, and prepper, convinces Zach that the apocalypse is on the horizon. The two of them take refuge at a remote farm. As the zombie plague rages, they face a terrifying fight for survival.

They soon learn however that the walking dead are not the only monsters.

www.ingramcontent.com/pod-product-compliance
Lightning Source LLC
Chambersburg PA
CBHW051503170626
46811CB00002B/626